WOMEN AND THINGS

"THAT IS ONE OF THE NEW GERMAN KINDERGARTEN
APPLIANCES"

WOMEN AND THINGS

AMERICA'S BEST
FUNNY STORIES

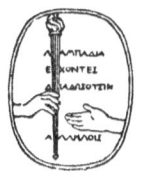

WILDSIDE PRESS

www.wildsidebooks.com

CONTRIBUTORS

CONTENTS

CONTENTS

ILLUSTRATIONS

THE ESQUIMAU MAIDEN'S ROMANCE

BY MARK TWAIN

"YES, I will tell you anything about my life
that you would like to know, Mr. Twain," she
said, in her soft voice, and letting her honest eyes
rest placidly upon my face, "for it is kind and
good of you to like me and care to know about
me."

She had been absently scraping blubber-grease
from her cheeks with a small bone-knife and
transferring it to her fur sleeve, while she watched the Aurora Borealis swing its flaming stream-
ers out of the sky and wash the lonely snow-plain
and the templed icebergs with the rich hues of
the prism, a spectacle of almost intolerable splen-
dor and beauty; but now she shook off her reverie
and prepared to give me the humble little history
I had asked for. She settled herself comfortably
on the block of ice which we were using as a sofa,
and I made ready to listen.

She was a beautiful creature. I speak from
the Esquimaux point of view. Others would
have thought her a trifle over-plump. She was
just twenty years old, and was held to be by far

the most bewitching girl in her tribe. Even now, in the open air, with her cumbersome and shapeless fur coat and trousers and boots and vast hood, the beauty of her face was at least apparent; but her figure had to be taken on trust. Among all the guests who came and went, I had seen no girl at her father's hospitable trough who could be called her equal. Yet she was not spoiled. She was sweet and natural and sincere, and if she was aware that she was a belle, there was nothing about her ways to show that she possessed that knowledge.

She had been my daily comrade for a week now, and the better I knew her the better I liked her. She had been tenderly and carefully brought up, in an atmosphere of singularly rare refinement for the polar regions, for her father was the most important man of his tribe and ranked at the top of Esquimau cultivation. I made long dog-sledge trips across the mighty ice-floes with Lasca—that was her name—and found her company always pleasant and her conversation agreeable. I went fishing with her, but not in her perilous boat: I merely followed along on the ice and watched her strike her game with her fatally accurate spear. We went sealing together; several times I stood by while she and the family dug blubber from a stranded whale, and once I went part of the way when she was hunting a bear, but turned back before the finish, because at bottom I am afraid of bears.

However, she was ready to begin her story,
now, and this is what she said:

"Our tribe had always been used to wander
about from place to place over the frozen seas,
like the other tribes, but my father got tired of
that, two years ago, and built this great mansion
of frozen snow-blocks—look at it; it is seven feet
high and three or four times as long as any of
the others—and here we have stayed ever since.
He was very proud of his house, and that was
reasonable, for if you have examined it with care
you must have noticed how much finer and com-
pleter it is than houses usually are.   But if you
have not, you must, for you will find it has luxurious appointments that are quite beyond the
common.   For instance, in that end of it which
you have called the 'parlor,' the raised platform
for the accommodation of guests and the family
at meals is the largest you have ever seen in any
house—is it not so?"

"Yes, you are quite right, Lasca; it is the
largest; we have nothing resembling it in even
the finest houses in the United States."   This admission made her eyes sparkle with pride and
pleasure.   I noted that, and took my cue.

"I thought it must have surprised you," she
said.   "And another thing: it is bedded far
deeper in furs than is usual; all kinds of furs—
seal, sea-otter, silver-gray fox, bear, marten, sable
—every kind of fur in profusion; and the same
with the ice-block sleeping-benches along the

walls, which you call 'beds.' Are your platforms
and sleeping-benches better provided at home?"

"Indeed, they are not, Lasca—they do not begin to be." That pleased her again. All she
was thinking of was the *number* of furs her æs-
thetic father took the trouble to keep on hand,
not their value. I could have told her that those
masses of rich furs constituted wealth—or would
in my country—but she would not have understood that; those were not the kind of things
that ranked as riches with her people. I could
have told her that the clothes she had on, or the
every-day clothes of the commonest person about
her, were worth twelve or fifteen hundred dollars,
and that I was not acquainted with anybody at
home who wore twelve-hundred-dollar toilets to
go fishing in; but she would not have understood
it, so I said nothing. She resumed:

"And then the slop-tubs. We have two in the
parlor, and two in the rest of the house. It is
very seldom that one has two in the parlor. Have
you two in the parlor at home?"

The memory of those tubs made me gasp, but I
recovered myself before she noticed, and said with
effusion:

"Why, Lasca, it is a shame of me to expose my
country, and you must not let it go further, for I
am speaking to you in confidence; but I give you
my word of honor that not even the richest man
in the city of New York has two slop-tubs in his
drawing-room."

She clapped her fur-clad hands in innocent delight, and exclaimed:

"Oh, but you cannot mean it, you cannot *mean* it!"

"Indeed, I am in earnest, dear. There is Vanderbilt. Vanderbilt is almost the richest man in the whole world. Now, if I were on my dying bed, I could say to you that not even he has two in his drawing-room. Why, he hasn't even *one*—I wish I may die in my tracks if it isn't true."

Her lovely eyes stood wide with amazement, and she said, slowly, and with a sort of awe in her voice:

"How strange—how incredible—one is not able to realize it. Is he penurious?"

"No—it isn't that. It isn't the expense he minds, but—er—well, you know, it would look like showing off. Yes, that is it, that is the idea; he is a plain man in his way, and shrinks from display."

"Why, that humility is right enough," said Lasca, "if one does not carry it too far—but what does the place *look* like?"

"Well, necessarily it looks pretty barren and unfinished, but—"

"I should think so! I never heard anything like it. Is it a fine house—that is, otherwise?"

"Pretty fine, yes. It is very well thought of."

The girl was silent awhile, and sat dreamily gnawing a candle-end, apparently trying to think the thing out. At last she gave her head a little toss and spoke out her opinion with decision:

"Well, to my mind there's a breed of humility which is *itself* a species of showing-off, when you get down to the marrow of it; and when a man is able to afford two slop-tubs in his parlor, and don't do it, it *may* be that he is truly humble-minded, but it's a hundred times more likely that he is just trying to strike the public eye. In my judgment, your Mr. Vanderbilt knows what he is about."

I tried to modify this verdict, feeling that a double-slop-tub standard was not a fair one to try everybody by, although a sound enough one in its own habitat; but the girl's head was set, and she was not to be persuaded. Presently she said:

"Do the rich people, with you, have as good sleeping-benches as ours, and made out of as nice broad ice-blocks?"

"Well, they are pretty good—good enough—but they are not made of ice-blocks."

"I want to know! *Why* aren't they made of ice-blocks?"

I explained the difficulties in the way, and the expensiveness of ice in a country where you have to keep a sharp eye on your ice-man or your ice-bill will weigh more than your ice. Then she cried out:

"Dear me, do you *buy* your ice?"

"We most surely do, dear."

She burst into a gale of guileless laughter, and said:

"Oh, I *never* heard of anything ·so silly! My, there's plenty of it — it isn't worth anything. Why, there is a hundred miles of it in sight, right now. I wouldn't give a fish-bladder for the whole of it."

"Well, it's because you don't know how to value it, you little provincial muggins. If you had it in New York in midsummer, you could buy all the whales in the market with it."

She looked at me doubtfully, and said:

"Are you speaking true?"

"Absolutely. I take my oath to it."

This made her thoughtful. Presently she said, with a little sigh:

"I wish *I* could live there."

I had merely meant to furnish her a standard of values which she could understand; but my purpose had miscarried. I had only given her the impression that whales were cheap and plenty in New York, and set her mouth to watering for them. It seemed best to try to mitigate the evil which I had done, so I said:

"But you wouldn't care for whale-meat if you lived there. Nobody does."

"What!"

"Indeed they don't."

"*Why* don't they?"

"Wel-l-l, I hardly know. It's prejudice, I think. Yes, that is it—just prejudice. I reckon

somebody that hadn't anything better to do started a prejudice against it, some time or other, and
once you get a caprice like that fairly going, you
know, it will last no end of time."

"That is true—*perfectly* true," said the girl, reflectively. "Like our prejudice against soap,
here—our tribes had a prejudice against soap at
first, you know."

I glanced at her to see if she was in earnest.
Evidently she was. I hesitated, then said, cautiously:

"But pardon me. They *had* a prejudice
against soap? Had?"—with falling inflection.

"Yes—but that was only at first; nobody
would eat it."

"Oh—I understand. I didn't get your idea
before."

She resumed:

"It was just a prejudice. The first time soap
came here from the foreigners, nobody liked it;
but as soon as it got to be fashionable, everybody liked it, and now everybody has it that can
afford it. Are you fond of it?"

"Yes, indeed; I should die if I couldn't have it
—especially here. Do you like it?"

"I just *adore* it! Do you like candles?"

"I regard them as an absolute necessity. Are
you fond of them?"

Her eyes fairly danced, and she exclaimed:

"Oh! Don't mention it! Candles!—and
soap—!"

"And fish-interiors—!"

"And train-oil—!"

"And slush—!"

"And whale-blubber—!"

"And carrion! and sour-krout! and beeswax! and tar! and turpentine! and molasses! and—"

"Don't — oh, don't — I shall expire with ecstasy—!"

"And then serve it all up in a slush-bucket, and invite the neighbors and sail in!"

But this vision of an ideal feast was too much for her, and she swooned away, poor thing. I rubbed snow in her face and brought her to, and after a while got her excitement cooled down. By-and-by she drifted into her story again:

"So we began to live here, in the fine house. But I was not happy. The reason was this: I was born for love; for me there could be no true happiness without it. I wanted to be loved for myself alone. I wanted an idol, and I wanted to be my idol's idol; nothing less than mutual idolatry would satisfy my fervent nature. I had suitors in plenty—in over-plenty, indeed—but in each and every case they had a fatal defect; sooner or later I discovered that defect—not one of them failed to betray it—it was not me they wanted, but my wealth."

"Your wealth?"

"Yes; for my father is much the richest man in this tribe—or in any tribe in these regions."

I wondered what her father's wealth consisted

of. It couldn't be the house—anybody could
build its mate. It couldn't be the furs—they
were not valued. It couldn't be the sledge, the
dogs, the harpoons, the boat, the bone fish-hooks
and needles, and such things—no, these were not
wealth. Then what could it be that made this
man so rich and brought this swarm of sordid
suitors to his house? It seemed to me, finally,
that the best way to find out would be to ask.
So I did it. The girl was so manifestly gratified
by the question that I saw she had been aching
to have me ask it. She was suffering fully as
much to tell as I was to know. She snuggled
confidentially up to me and said:

"Guess how much he is worth—you never
can!"

I pretended to consider the matter deeply, she
watching my anxious and laboring countenance
with a devouring and delighted interest; and
when, at last, I gave it up and begged her to appease my longing by telling me herself how much
this polar Vanderbilt was worth, she put her
mouth close to my ear and whispered, impressively:

"*Twenty-two fish-hooks*—not bone, but foreign
—*made out of real iron!*"

Then she sprang back dramatically, to observe
the effect. I did my level best not to disappoint
her. I turned pale and murmured:

"Great Scott!"

"It's as true as you live, Mr. Twain!"

"Lasca, you are deceiving me—you cannot mean it."

She was frightened and troubled. She exclaimed:

"Mr. Twain, every word of it is true—every word. You believe me—you *do* believe me, now *don't* you? *Say* you believe me—*do* say you believe me!"

"I—well, yes, I do—I am *trying* to. But it was all so *sudden*. So sudden and prostrating. You shouldn't do such a thing in that sudden way. It—"

"Oh, I'm *so* sorry! If I had only thought—"

"Well, it's all right, and I don't blame you any more, for you are young and thoughtless, and of course you couldn't foresee what an effect—"

"But oh, dear, I ought certainly to have *known* better. Why—"

"You see, Lasca, if you had said five or six hooks, to start with, and then gradually—"

"Oh, I see, I see—then gradually added one, and then two, and then—ah, why couldn't I have thought of that!"

"Never mind, child, it's all right—I am better now—I shall be over it in a little while. *But*—to spring the whole twenty-two on a person unprepared and not very strong anyway—"

"Oh, it *was* a crime! But you forgive me—say you forgive me. Do!"

After harvesting a good deal of very pleasant coaxing and petting and persuading, I forgave her and she was happy again, and by-and-by she got under way with her narrative once more. I presently discovered that the family treasury contained still another feature—a jewel of some sort, apparently—and that she was trying to get around speaking squarely about it, lest I get paralyzed again. But I wanted to know about that thing, too, and urged her to tell me what it was. She was afraid. But I insisted, and said I would brace myself this time and be prepared, then the shock would not hurt me. She was full of misgivings, but the temptation to reveal that marvel to me and enjoy my astonishment and admiration was too strong for her, and she confessed that she had it on her person, and said that if I was *sure* I was prepared—and so on and so on—and with that she reached into her bosom and brought out a battered square of brass, watching my eye anxiously the while. I fell over against her in a quite well-acted faint, which delighted her heart and nearly frightened it out of her, too, at the same time. When I came to and got calm, she was eager to know what I thought of her jewel.

"What do I think of it? I think it is the most exquisite thing I ever saw."

"Do you really? How nice of you to say that! But it *is* a love, now isn't it?"

"Well, I should say so! I'd rather own it than the equator."

"I thought you would admire it," she said.

"I think it is *so* lovely.   And there isn't another one in all these latitudes.   People have come all the way from the Open Polar Sea to look at it. Did you ever see one before?"

I said no, this was the first one I had ever seen. It cost me a pang to tell that generous lie, for I had seen a million of them in my time, this humble jewel of hers being nothing but a battered old New York Central baggage-check.

"Land!" said I, "you don't go about with it on your person this way, alone and with no protection, not even a dog?"

"Ssh! not so loud," she said.   "Nobody knows I carry it with me.   They think it is in papa's treasury.   That is where it generally is."

"Where is the treasury?"

It was a blunt question, and for a moment she looked startled and a little suspicious, but I said:

"Oh, come, don't you be afraid about me.   At home we have seventy millions of people, and although I say it myself that shouldn't, there is not one person among them all but would trust me with untold fish-hooks."

This reassured her, and she told me where the hooks were hidden in the house.   Then she wandered from her course to brag a little about the size of the sheets of transparent ice that formed the windows of the mansion, and asked me if I had ever seen their like at home, and I came right out frankly and confessed that I hadn't, which pleased her more than she could find words to dress her gratification in. It was so easy to please her, and such a pleasure to do it, that I went on and said:

"Ah, Lasca, you *are* a fortunate girl!—this beautiful house, this dainty jewel, that rich treasure, all this elegant snow, and sumptuous icebergs and limitless sterility, and public bears and walruses, and noble freedom and largeness, and everybody's admiring eyes upon you, and everybody's homage and respect at your command without the asking; young, rich, beautiful, sought, courted, envied, not a requirement unsatisfied, not a desire ungratified, nothing to wish for that you cannot have—it is immeasurable good-fortune! I have seen myriads of girls, but none of whom these extraordinary things could be truthfully said but you alone. And you are worthy—worthy of it all, Lasca—I believe it in my heart."

It made her infinitely proud and happy to hear me say this, and she thanked me over and over again for that closing remark, and her voice and eyes showed that she was touched. Presently she said:

"Still, it is not all sunshine—there is a cloudy side. The burden of wealth is a heavy one to bear. Sometimes I have doubted if it were not better to be poor—at least not inordinately rich. It pains me to see neighboring tribesmen stare as they pass by, and overhear them say, reverently, one to another, 'There—that is she—the million-

aire's daughter!' And sometimes they say sor-
rowfully, 'She is rolling in fish-hooks, and I—I
have nothing.' It breaks my heart. When I
was a child and we were poor, we slept with the
door open, if we chose, but now—now we have
to have a night-watchman. In those days my
father was gentle and courteous to all; but now
he is austere and haughty, and cannot abide
familiarity. Once his family were his sole
thought, but now he goes about thinking of his
fish-hooks all the time. And his wealth makes
everybody cringing and obsequious to him. Formerly nobody laughed at his jokes, they being
always stale and far-fetched and poor, and desti-
tute of the one element that can really justify a
joke—the element of humor; but now everybody
laughs and cackles at those dismal things, and if
any fails to do it my father is deeply displeased,
and shows it. Formerly his opinion was not
sought upon any matter and was not valuable
when he volunteered it; it has that infirmity yet,
but, nevertheless, it is sought by all and applauded by all—and he helps do the applauding
himself, having no true delicacy and a plentiful
want of tact. He has lowered the tone of all our
tribe. Once they were a frank and manly race,
now they are measly hypocrites, and sodden with
servility. In my heart of hearts I hate all the
ways of millionaires! Our tribe was once plain,
simple folk, and content with the bone fish-hooks
of their fathers; now they are eaten up with

avarice and would sacrifice every sentiment of
honor and honesty to possess themselves of the
debasing iron fish-hooks of the foreigner. However, I must not dwell on these sad things. As I
have said, it was my dream to be loved for myself alone.

"At last, this dream seemed about to be ful-
filled. A stranger came by, one day, who said
his name was Kalula. I told him my name, and
he said he loved me. My heart gave a great
bound of gratitude and pleasure, for I had loved
him at sight, and now I said so. He took me to
his breast and said he would not wish to be happier than he was now. We went strolling together far over the ice-floes, telling all about each
other, and planning, oh, the loveliest future!
When we were tired at last we sat down and ate,
for he had soap and candles and I had brought
along some blubber. We were hungry, and
nothing was ever so good.

"He belonged to a tribe whose haunts were far
to the north, and I found that he had never
heard of my father, which rejoiced me exceed-
ingly. I mean he had heard of the millionaire,
but had never heard his name—so, you see, he
could not know that I was the heiress. You
may be sure that I did not tell him. I was
loved for myself at last, and was satisfied.
I was so happy — oh, happier than you can
think!

"By-and-by it was toward supper-time, and I

led him home. As we approached our house he was amazed, and cried out:

"'How splendid! Is *that* your father's?'

"It gave me a pang to hear that tone and see that admiring light in his eye, but the feeling quickly passed away, for I loved him so, and he looked so handsome and noble. All my family of aunts and uncles and cousins were pleased with him, and many guests were called in, and the house was shut up tight and the rag lamps lighted, and, when everything was hot and comfortable and suffocating, we began a joyous feast in celebration of my betrothal.

"When the feast was over, my father's vanity overcame him, and he could not resist the temptation to show off his riches and let Kalula see what grand good-fortune he had stumbled into—and mainly, of course, he wanted to enjoy the poor man's amazement. I could have cried—but it would have done no good to try to dissuade my father, so I said nothing, but merely sat there and suffered.

"My father went straight to the hiding-place, in full sight of everybody, and got out the fish-hooks and brought them and flung them scatteringly over my head, so that they fell in glittering confusion on the platform at my lover's knee.

"Of course, the astounding spectacle took the poor lad's breath away. He could only stare in stupid astonishment, and wonder how a single individual could possess such incredible riches.

Then presently he glanced brilliantly up, and exclaimed:

"'Ah, it is *you* who are the renowned millionaire!'

"My father and all the rest burst into shouts of happy laughter, and when my father gathered the treasure carelessly up as if it might be mere rubbish and of no consequence, and carried it back to its place, poor Kalula's surprise was a study.   He said:

"'Is it possible that you put such things away without counting them?'

"My father delivered a vainglorious horse-laugh, and said:

"'Well, truly, a body may know *you* have never been rich, since a mere matter of a fish-hook or two is such a mighty matter in your eyes.'

"Kalula was confused, and hung his head, but said:

"'Ah, indeed, sir, I was never worth the value of the barb of one of those precious things, and I have never seen any man before who was so rich in them as to render the counting of his hoard worth while, since the wealthiest man I have ever known, till now, was possessed of but three.'

"My foolish father roared again with jejune delight, and allowed the impression to remain that he was not accustomed to count his hooks and keep sharp watch over them.   He was showing off, you see.   Count them?   Why, he counted them every day!

"I had met and got acquainted with my darling just at dawn; I had brought him home just
at dark, three hours afterwards — for the days
were shortening toward the six-months night at
that time. We kept up the festivities many
hours; then, at last, the guests departed and the
rest of us distributed ourselves along the walls on
sleeping-benches, and soon all were steeped in
dreams but me. I was too happy, too excited,
to sleep. After I had lain quiet a long, long
time, a dim form passed by me and was swallowed up in the gloom that pervaded the farther
end of the house. I could not make out who it
was, or whether it was man or woman. Presently that figure or another one passed me going
the other way. I wondered what it all meant,
but wondering did no good; and while I was still
wondering I fell asleep.

"I do not know how long I slept, but at last I
came suddenly broad awake and heard my father
say in a terrible voice: 'By the great Snow God,
there's a fish-hook gone!' Something told me
that that meant sorrow for me, and the blood in
my veins turned cold. The presentiment was
confirmed in the same instant: my father shouted, 'Up, everybody, and seize the stranger!'
Then there was an outburst of cries and curses
from all sides, and a wild rush of dim forms
through the obscurity. I flew to my beloved's
help, but what could I do but wait and wring my
hands?—he was already fenced away from me by

a living wall, he was being bound hand and foot.
Not until he was secured would they let me get
to him. I flung myself upon his poor insulted
form and cried my grief out upon his breast
while my father and all my family scoffed at me
and heaped threats and shameful epithets upon
him. He bore his ill usage with a tranquil dignity which endeared him to me more than ever
and made me proud and happy to suffer with
him and for him. I heard my father order that
the elders of the tribe be called together to try
my Kalula for his life.

"'What?' I said, 'before any search has been
made for the lost hook?'

"'Lost hook!' they all shouted, in derision; and
my father added, mockingly: 'Stand back, everybody, and be properly serious—she is going to
hunt up that *lost* hook; oh, without doubt she
will find it!' Whereat they all laughed again.

"I was not disturbed—I had no fears, no
doubts. I said:

"'It is for you to laugh now; it is your turn.
But ours is coming; wait and see.'

"I got a rag-lamp. I thought I should find
that miserable thing in one little moment; and I
set about the matter with such confidence that
those people grew grave, beginning to suspect
that perhaps they had been too hasty. But,
alas and alas!—oh, the bitterness of that search!
There was deep silence while one might count his
fingers ten or twelve times, then my heart began

to sink, and around me the mockings began again, and grew steadily louder and more assured, until at last, when I gave up, they burst into volley after volley of cruel laughter.

"None will ever know what I suffered then. But my love was my support and my strength, and I took my rightful place at my Kalula's side, and put my arm about his neck, and whispered in his ear, saying:

"'You are innocent, my own—that I know; but say it to me yourself, for my comfort, then I can bear whatever is in store for us.'

"He answered:

"'As surely as I stand upon the brink of death at this moment, I am innocent. Be comforted, then, O bruised heart; be at peace, O thou breath of my nostrils, life of my life!'

"'Now, then, let the elders come!'—and as I said the words there was a gathering sound of crunching snow outside, and then a vision of stooping forms filing in at the door—the elders.

"My father formally accused the prisoner, and detailed the happenings of the night. He said that the watchman was outside the door, and that in the house were none but the family and the stranger. 'Would the family steal their own property?' He paused. The elders sat silent many minutes; at last, one after another said to his neighbor, 'This looks bad for the stranger'— sorrowful words for me to hear. Then my father sat down. O miserable, miserable me! at that very moment I could have proved my darling innocent, but I did not know it!

"The chief of the court asked:

"'Is there any here to defend the prisoner?'

"I rose and said:

"'Why should *he* steal that hook, or any or all of them? In another day he would have been heir to the whole!'

"I stood waiting. There was a long silence, the steam from the many breaths rising about me like a fog. At last one elder after another nodded his head slowly several times, and muttered, 'There is force in what the child has said.' Oh, the heart-lift that was in those words!—so transient, but, oh, so precious! I sat down.

"'If any would say further, let him speak now, or after hold his peace,' said the chief of the court.

"My father rose and said:

"'In the night a form passed by me in the gloom, going towards the treasury, and presently returned. I think, now, it was the stranger.'

"Oh, I was like to swoon! I had supposed that that was my secret; not the grip of the great Ice God himself could have dragged it out of my heart. The chief of the court said sternly to my poor Kalula:

"'Speak!'

"Kalula hesitated, then answered:

"'It was I. I could not sleep for thinking of the beautiful hooks. I went there and kissed them and fondled them, to appease my spirit and drown it in a harmless joy, then I put them back. I may have dropped one, but I stole none.'

"Oh, a fatal admission to make in such a place! There was an awful hush. I knew he had pronounced his own doom, and that all was over. On every face you could see the words hieroglyphed: 'It is a confession!—and paltry, lame, and thin.'

"I sat drawing in my breath in faint gasps— and waiting. Presently, I heard the solemn words I knew were coming; and each word, as it came, was a knife in my heart:

"'It is the command of the court that the accused be subjected to the *trial by water*.'

"Oh, curses be upon the head of him who brought 'trial by water' to our land! It came, generations ago, from some far country that lies none knows where. Before that, our fathers used augury and other unsure methods of trial, and doubtless some poor, guilty creatures escaped with their lives sometimes; but it is not so with trial by water, which is an invention by wiser men than we poor, ignorant savages are. By it the innocent are proved innocent, without doubt or question, for they drown; and the guilty are proven guilty with the same certainty, for they do not drown. My heart was breaking in my bosom, for I said: 'He is innocent, and he will go down under the waves and I shall never see him more.'
3

"I never left his side after that. I mourned in his arms all the precious hours, and he poured out the deep stream of his love upon me, and oh, I was so miserable and so happy! At last they tore him from me, and I followed sobbing after them, and saw them fling him into the sea—then I covered my face with my hands. Agony? Oh, I know the deepest deeps of that word!

"The next moment the people burst into a shout of malicious joy, and I took away my hands, startled. Oh, bitter sight—he was *swimming!* My heart turned instantly to stone, to ice. I said, 'He was guilty, and he lied to me!' I turned my back in scorn, and went my way homeward.

"They took him far out to sea and set him on an iceberg that was drifting southward in the great waters. Then my family came home, and my father said to me:

"'Your thief sent his dying message to you, saying, "Tell her I am innocent, and that all the days and all the hours and all the minutes while I starve and perish I shall love her and think of her and bless the day that gave me sight of her sweet face." Quite pretty, even poetical!'

"I said, 'He is dirt—let me never hear mention of him again.' And oh, to think—he *was* innocent all the time!

"Nine months—nine dull, sad months—went by, and at last came the day of the Great Annual Sacrifice, when all the maidens of the tribe wash

their faces and comb their hair. With the first
sweep of my comb, out came the fatal fish-hook
from where it had been all those months nestling,
and I fell fainting into the arms of my remorseful
father! Groaning, he said: 'We murdered him,
and I shall never smile again!' He has kept his
word. Listen: from that day to this not a month
goes by that I do not comb my hair. But oh,
where is the good of it all now!"

So ended the poor maid's humble little tale—
whereby we learn that since a hundred million
dollars in New York and twenty-two fish-hooks
on the border of the Arctic Circle represent the
same financial supremacy, a man in straitened
circumstances is a fool to stay in New York when
he can buy ten cents' worth of fish-hooks and
emigrate.

MR. SIMPKINS'S DOWNFALL

BY WILLIAM LIVINGSTONE ALDEN

MAN is the only animal that wears short socks. This is not only a more accurate definition than any hitherto devised by scientific persons, but it shows the inferiority of man to all other animals, and ought to have even more effect in humbling our wicked pride than has the famous story of the little girl who was excessively proud of her silk dress until she was told that it was spun, woven, cut out, made up, and trimmed by a loathsome worm.

The great trouble with the short sock is, that it will not keep its place. There being nothing whatever to hold it, the force of gravitation necessarily drags it down about the ankle. This causes an amount of misery which is appalling. There is no man who can feel any confidence in his socks. Whether he is walking or sitting, he knows that his socks are slowly but surely slipping down. Garters being out of the question, since the shortness of the sock does not permit a garter to be placed in a position where it will not slip, there is absolutely no remedy for what we

may fairly call the giant evil of the age.   Pins
and mucilage have both been tried by desperate
men, but they have proved useless, and have
merely added to the misery of the user.   In these
circumstances there is nothing left for man to do
except to bear the sock in silence, or to boldly
cast it aside and adopt the full-grown stocking.

The latter alternative was recently chosen by
that eloquent but unfortunate clergyman, Rev.
Charles Simpkins, of Westbridge, Pennsylvania.
Previous to the catastrophe which lately overtook
him, the Church did not possess a more popular
and promising young clergyman.   He could repeat
the opening exhortation all the way from " Dearly
beloved " to " forgiveness for the same," without
once pausing for breath; and it has been asserted
that he could monotone the entire Apostles'
Creed while breathing only three times.   As he
was unmarried, and not yet twenty-seven years
old, he was regarded with peculiar reverence by
the unmarried ladies of his parish, and he received more annual slippers than any other
clergyman in the United States.

Neatness was one of the distinguishing charac-
teristics of Mr. Simpkins, and there are probably
few men who have suffered more keenly from
short socks.   When walking through the village
he was in continual dread lest his socks should
descend into public view, and even while preaching his most eloquent sermons the perspiration
would gather on his brow as he felt that one of

his socks was gradually slipping down. This
wore upon him to that extent that his massive
intellect threatened to totter, and on the morning of the eighty-first Sunday after Trinity he
deliberately paused, after remarking "here end-
eth" — and stooped down to repair damages.
That night he resolved that vigorous measures
must be taken, and he accordingly wrote a confidential letter to his sister's husband, who re-
sided in this city, and enclosed the necessary
measurements. Shortly afterwards he received,
ostensibly from the husband, but really from the
affectionate sister, two dozen pair of Balbriggan
hose, together with a pair of scarlet elastics an
inch in width and of precisely the right size.

As soon as Mr. Simpkins had learned, by repeated experiment, how to wear the scarlet appliances, his spirits began to rise. He was no
longer a prey to doubt and despair. His stockings firmly kept their place, and he felt that he
could even attend a church picnic and climb over
a fence without fear of consequences. Accordingly, for the first time during his residence at
Westbridge, he consented to attend the Sunday-
school picnic of the 21st of October last, and
thereby filled with unutterable delight the souls
of all the unmarried teachers of the church.

Mr. Simpkins, being free from care, entered into
the sports of the picnic with great zest, and the
children insisted that he, together with their
teachers, should take part in a game of blind-

man's-buff. The request was acceded to, and
the usual running, laughing, and shrieking followed. It was while Mr. Simpkins was fleeing,
in company with six excited teachers, from the
pursuit of a blindfolded small boy, that he suddenly noticed that one of his elastics had become
unclasped, and had fallen to the ground. At the
same moment it was perceived by the prettiest
of the teachers, who made a frantic effort to
seize it, but was anticipated by the unhappy
clergyman. It was bad enough for him to
know that the teacher had discovered his mis-
fortune; but what was his horror and amazement when, with every appearance of anger, she
demanded that he should "hand her that" instantly. He was so astonished at her evident
desire to make sport of him that he did not
deign to answer her, but put the disputed article
in his pocket and walked away. Whereupon the
teacher burst into tears, and informed her confidential friends that Mr. Simpkins had had the
inconceivable audacity to steal one of her—in
fact, her private property.

The scandal spread rapidly and widely, and
grew as rapidly as it spread. At the end of half
an hour every lady at the picnic had cut the
clergyman in the most marked manner. Burning
with shame and indignation, he forgot to repair
the deficiencies of his toilet, and went home feeling rather more crestfallen than did the prophet
Daniel when he found that the lions would not

recognize his existence. It was not until he was on the point of seeking a sleepless pillow that he discovered that both his scarlet elastics were in their proper place, while the one which he had picked up at the picnic lay on his table. The full horror of his situation flashed upon him. The teacher had really dropped a scarlet elastic, and he had seized it under the impression that it was his own.

The utter hopelessness of ever making any satisfactory explanation of the affair was only too apparent. Early the next morning Mr. Simpkins fled from Westbridge a ruined man. The fatal articles which had caused his downfall he left behind him, and they teach with mute but powerful eloquence the lesson that we should bear the socks we have, and never dream of flying to stockings, of which we know nothing except by hearsay.

HE SAW THAT IT WAS NOT HIS GARTER

A SLEEPING-CAR EXPERIENCE

BY BRET HARTE

It was in a Pullman sleeping-car on a Western road. After that first plunge into unconsciousness which the weary traveller takes on getting into his berth, I awakened to the dreadful revelation that I had been asleep only two hours. The greater part of a long winter night was before me to face with staring eyes.

Finding it impossible to sleep, I lay there wondering a number of things: why, for instance, the Pullman sleeping-car blankets were unlike other blankets; why they were like squares cut out of cold buckwheat-cakes, and why they clung to you when you turned over, and lay heavy on you without warmth; why the curtains before you could not have been made opaque, without being so thick and suffocating; why it would not be as well to sit up all night half asleep in an ordinary passenger-car as to lie awake all night in a Pullman. But the snoring of my fellow-passengers answered this question in the negative.

With the recollection of last night's dinner weighing on me as heavily and coldly as the blankets, I began wondering why, over the whole extent of the continent, there was no local dish; why the bill of fare at restaurant and hotel was invariably only a weak reflex of the metropolitan hostelries; why the *entrées* were always the same, only more or less badly cooked; why the travelling American always was supposed to demand turkey and cold cranberry sauce; why the pretty waiter-girl apparently shuffled your plates behind your back, and then dealt them over your shoulder in a semicircle, as if they were a hand at cards, and not always a good one. Why, having done this, she instantly retired to the nearest wall, and gazed at you scornfully, as one who would say: "Fair sir, though lowly, I am proud; if thou dost imagine that I would permit undue familiarity of speech, beware!"

Lying broad awake, I could not help making some observations which I think are not noticed by the day traveller. First, that the speed of a train is not equal or continuous. That at certain times the engine apparently starts up, and says to the baggage-train behind it: "Come, come, this won't do! Why, it's nearly half-past two; how in h—ll shall we get through! Don't you talk to *me*. Pooh, pooh!" delivered in that rhythmical fashion which all meditation assumes on a railway train. *Exempli gratia:* One night, having raised my window-curtain to look over a moonlit snowy landscape, as I pulled it down the lines of a popular comic song flashed across me.

Fatal error! The train instantly took it up, and
during the rest of the night I was haunted by
this awful refrain: "Pull down the bel-lind, pull
down the bel-lind; somebody's klink klink, O
don't be shoo-shoo!" Naturally this differs on
the different railways. On the New York Central, where the road-bed is quite perfect and the
steel rails continuous, I have heard this irreverent
train give the words of a certain popular revival
hymn after this fashion: "Hold the fort, for I am
Sankey; Moody slingers still. Wave the swish
swash back from klinky, klinky klanky kill."
On the New York & New Haven, where there
are many switches, and the engine whistles at
every cross-road, I have often heard: "Tommy,
make room for your whoopy! that's a little clang;
bumpity, bumpity, booby, clikitty, clikitty clang."
Poetry, I fear, fared little better. One starlit
night, coming from Quebec, as we slipped by a
virgin forest, the opening lines of "Evangeline"
flashed upon me. But all I could make of them
was this: "This is the forest primeval-eval; the
groves of the pines and the hemlocks-locks-locks-
locks - loooock!" The train was only "slowing"
or "braking" up at a station. Hence the jar in
the metre.

I had noticed a peculiar Æolian-harp-like cry
that ran through the whole train as we settled to
rest at last after a long run—an almost sigh of
infinite relief, a musical sigh that began in C and
ran gradually up to F natural, which I think

most observant travellers have noticed day and
night. No railway official has ever given me a
satisfactory explanation of it. As the car, in a
rapid run, is always slightly projected forward of
its trucks, a practical friend once suggested to
me that it was the gradual settling back of the
car body to a state of inertia, which, of course,
every poetical traveller would reject. Four o'clock
—the sound of boot-blacking by the porter faintly
apparent from the toilet-room. Why not talk to
him? But, fortunately, I remembered that any
attempt at extended conversation with conductor
or porter was always resented by them as implied
disloyalty to the company they represented. I
recalled that once I had endeavored to impress
upon a conductor the absolute folly of a midnight
inspection of tickets, and had been treated by
him as an escaped lunatic. No, there was no
relief from this suffocating and insupportable
loneliness to be gained then. I raised the win-
dow-blind and looked out. We were passing a
farm-house. A light, evidently the lantern of a
farm-hand, was swung beside a barn. Yes, the
faintest tinge of rose in the far horizon. Morning, surely, at last!

We had stopped at a station. Two men had
got into the car, and had taken seats in the one
vacant section, yawning occasionally and con-
versing in a languid, perfunctory sort of way.
They sat opposite each other, occasionally looking out of the window, but always giving the

strong impression that they were tired of each other's company. As I looked out of my curtains at them the One Man said, with a feebly concealed yawn:

"Yes, well, I reckon he was at one time as pop'lar an ondertaker ez I knew."

The Other Man (inventing a question rather than giving an answer, out of some languid, social impulse): "But was he—this yer ondertaker—a Christian—hed he jined the church?"

The One Man (reflectively): "Well, I don't know ez you might call him a purfessin' Christian; but he hed—yes, he hed conviction. I think Dr. Wylie hed him under conviction. Et least, that was the way I got it from *him*."

A long, dreary pause. The Other Man (feeling it was incumbent upon him to say something): "But why was he pop'lar ez an ondertaker?"

The One Man (lazily): "Well, he was kinder pop'lar with widders and widderers — sorter soothen 'em a kinder keerless way; slung 'em suthin' here and there, sometimes outer the Book, sometimes outer hisself, ez a man of experience as hed hed sorror. Hed, they say (*very cautiously*), lost three wives hisself, and five children by this yer new disease—dipthery—out in Wisconsin. I don't know the facts, but that's what's got round."

The Other Man: "But how did he lose his pop'larity?"

The One Man: "Well, that's the question.

You see, he interduced some things into onder-
taking that waz new. He hed, for instance, a
way, as he called it, of manniperlating the features of the deceased."

The Other Man (quietly): "How manniperlating?"

The One Man (struck with a bright and aggressive thought): "Look yer; did ye ever notiss
how, generally speakin', onhandsome a corpse is?"

The Other Man had noticed this fact.

The One Man (returning to his fact): "Why,
there **was** Mary Peebles, ez was daughter of my
wife's bosom friend—a mighty pooty girl and a
professing Christian—died of scarlet-fever. Well,
that gal—I was one of the mourners, being my
wife's friend—well, that gal, though I hedn't,
perhaps, oughter say — lying in that casket,
fetched all the way from some A1 establishment
in Chicago, filled with flowers and furbelows—
didn't really seem to be of much account. Well,
although my wife's friend, and me a mourner—
well, now, I was—disappointed and discouraged."

The Other Man (in palpably affected sympathy): "Sho, now!"

"Yes, *sir!* Well, you see, this yer ondertaker,
this Wilkins, hed a way of correctin' all thet.
And just by manniperlation. He worked over
the face of the deceased ontil he perduced what
the survivin' relatives called a look of resignation
—you know, a sort of smile, like. When he
wanted to put in any extrys, he perduced what

he called—hevin' reg'lar charges for this kind of work—a Christian's hope.''

The Other Man: "I want to know!''

"Yes. Well, I admit, at times it was a little startlin'. And I've allers said (a little confidentially) that I had my doubts of its being Scriptooral or sacred, we being, ez you know, worms of the yearth; and I relieved my mind to our pastor, but he didn't feel like interferin', ez long ez it was confined to church membership. But the other day, when Cy Dunham died—you disremember Cy Dunham?''

A long interval of silence. The Other Man was looking out of the window, and had apparently forgotten his companion completely. But as I stretched my head out of the curtain I saw four other heads as eagerly reached out from other berths to hear the conclusion of the story. One head, a female one, instantly disappeared on my looking around, but a certain tremulousness of her window-curtain showed an unabated interest. The only two utterly disinterested men were the One Man and the Other Man.

The Other Man (detaching himself languidly from the window): "Cy Dunham?''

"Yes; Cy never hed hed either convictions or purfessions. Uster get drunk and go round with permiscous women. Sorter like the prodigal son, only a little more so, ez fur ez I kin judge from the facks ez stated to me. Well, Cy one day petered out down at Little Rock, and was sent up yer for interment. The fammerly, being proud-like, of course didn't spare no money on that funeral, and it waz—now between you and me—about ez shapely and first-class and prime-mess affair ez I ever saw. Wilkins hed put in his extrys. He hed put onto that prodigal's face the A1 touch—hed him fixed up with a 'Christian's hope.' Well, it waz about the turning-point, for thar waz some of the members and the pastor hisself thought that the line oughter be drawn somewhere, and thar waz some talk at Deacon Tibbett's about a reg'lar conference meet-in' regardin' it. But it wazn't thet which made him onpop'lar."

Another silence; no expression nor reflection from the face of the Other Man of the least de-sire to know what ultimately settled the unpopu-larity of the undertaker. But from the curtains of the various berths several eager, and one or two even wrathful, faces, anxious for the result.

The Other Man (lazily recurring to the fading topic): "Well, what made him onpop'lar?"

The One Man (quietly): "Extrys, I think— that is, I suppose, not knowin' (cautiously) all the facts. When Mrs. Widdecombe lost her hus-band, 'bout two months àgo, though she'd been through the valley of the shadder of death twice —this bein' her third marriage, hevin' been John Barker's widder—"

The Other Man (with an intense expression of interest): "No; you're foolin' me!"

The One Man (solemnly): "Ef I was to appear before my Maker to-morrow, yes! she was the widder of Barker."

The Other Man: "Well, I swow!"

The One Man: "Well, this Widder Widde-combe, she put up a big funeral for the deceased. She hed Wilkins, and thet ondertaker just laid hisself out. Just spread hisself. Onfort'nately —perhaps fort'nately in the ways of Providence —one of Widdecombe's old friends, a doctor up thar in Chicago, comes down to the funeral. He goes up with the friends to look at the deceased, smilin' a peaceful sort o' heavinly smile, and everybody sayin' he's gone to meet his reward, and this yer friend turns round, short and sudden on the widder settin' in her pew, and kinder en-joyin', as wimen will, all the compliments paid the corpse, and he says, says he:

"'What did you say your husband died of, marm?'

"'Consumption,' she says, wiping her eyes, poor critter. 'Consumption—gallopin' consumption.'

"'Consumption be d——d,' sez he, bein' a pro-fane kind of Chicago doctor, and not bein' ever under conviction. 'Thet man died of strychnine. Look at thet face. Look at thet contortion of them fashal muscles. Thet's strychnine. Thet's *risers Sardonikus*' (thet's what he said; he was always sorter profane).

"'Why, doctor,' says the widder, 'thet—thet is his last smile. It's a Christian's resignation.'

4

"'Thet be blowed; don't tell me,' sez he. 'Hell is full of thet kind of resignation. It's pizon. And I'll'—why, dern my skin, yes, we are; yes, it's Joliet. Wall, now, who'd hev thought we'd been nigh onto an hour."

Two or three anxious passengers from their berths: "Say; look yer, stranger! Old Man! What became of—?"

But the One Man and the Other Man had vanished.

A WOMAN IN A SHOE-SHOP

BY MAY ISABEL FISK

She enters the shoe-shop

SHOES. . . . High or low? Why, I haven't decided—this is very sudden. . . . Oh, you want to
know to show me where to sit? . . . Here for ties
and there for boots? . . . Isn't this a new idea? . . .
No? I don't seem to remember at all. I suppose I've forgotten. . . . Well, I haven't made up
my mind yet which I want. Let's see. . . . Of
course, it is really spring now—and yet it seems
as though winter had scarcely gone—and I am
always taking cold in my ankles. . . . I think boo—
Still, the weather does get so warm so quickly
when it does start in. . . . No, I—no, I. . . . Well,
I will look at your ties first, though I think in
the end I shall take the boots.

Now you must get some one to wait on me
right away—I am in the greatest hurry. . . . No,
if you please, I don't intend to divide a salesman
with any one! I want one to wait on me alone.

Yes, ties. . . . Two and a half, A. . . . Well, I
can't help what is marked in the shoes—that's

what I wear. Probably they have made a mistake in marking the size—I presume they are careless.

Now, I'll tell you exactly what I want. . . . Now, I don't want anything too fancy to wear in the street—and for rainy days; and yet it must be suitable for evening dress—yes, and for golf—oh yes, and to wear on the steamer. I think of going abroad this summer. . . . I could have gone last year just as well as not if I'd said the word. . . .

Well, I like that. [*To near-by salesman.*] Will you kindly bring back that man who was waiting on me? . . . Why did you go off that way in such a rush? I wanted to tell you to hurry—I am in the greatest haste.

[*To salesman waiting on woman neighbor.*] Would you mind lending me your pencil—and a piece of paper? . . . You haven't any paper? Then get some, please. . . . I am sure you won't mind, madam; it won't take him but a moment. . . . Get the paper. . . . You see, I just met a friend who told me how to make that fidget— no, that isn't it—that chocolate stuff—oh, fudge —and if I don't write it down at once I'll forget. . . . Thank you. [*Writes.*]

Oh, take them away—I wouldn't wear those things if you gave them to me. . . . Flat heels and great big soles! Do I look like a woman with a big sole? . . . I should think not. Take them away. [*To neighbor.*] Do you know how long you boil the chocolate—or do you boil it at all? . . . You don't know? How annoying!

Patent leather? I didn't tell you to get patent leather. I don't believe I like it—it's so cold in hot weather and so hot in cold weather—well, whichever way you put it, it's disagreeable. Besides, I think it makes the feet look large—not that *I* have to worry about that. And the heels are too high. You know, you don't seem to understand what I want. . . . Well, bring me something like this—this person next to me is trying on.

Is that it? I don't like that at all— Oh no, that's horrible—perfectly awful! They look so big—and there's no arch at all. You see, I have such a high instep. . . . All right, you can try it on, but I know by looking at it it's miles too large. . . . Oh no, it's not too small—wait till I step on it. . . . It's *not* too small—there. . . . Oh yes, perfectly comfortable, but take it off quick! . . . Well, I couldn't wear a larger size! Get something else. Besides, I don't care for that medium heel—I don't want anything exaggerated, but I must have one thing or the other! It is the strangest thing, you have all manner of pretty shoes in the window, and when you come inside you can't find anything fit to be seen. . . .

Floor-walker, that is such a stupid man waiting on me—he doesn't seem to have an idea what I want. Can't you get some one else to wait on me? . . . All right.

Two and a half A—and never mind what's
marked in the shoe! . . . Yes, something in ties,
and I don't care what you bring me as long as
it is just what I want. [*To returning salesman.*]
No, this ma—gentleman is waiting on me—you
didn't seem to know what I wanted. . . .

What is that shoe over there in the case? . . .
You haven't my size? Well, if that isn't too ex-
asperating! That is the only decent shoe I've
seen here, and there you have gone and not got
my size. . . . I never knew it to fail.

No, I don't care for that—I don't like all that
fancy business around there. . . . Very youthful-
looking? Try it on. . . . Very good fit—they
look much better now they are on. . . . What
size are they? . . . Four B? Take it right off!
. . . I don't care whether they fit or not—I never
wore a four B in all my life, and I'm not going
to begin now! . . . No, you needn't bring any
other size in that style—I am all out of the idea
of it now.

. . . Floor-walker! Floor-walker! will you
kindly have some one put on my shoe? I can't
wait like this—my husband is home very ill, and
I've got to rush right back. . . . Well, then, make
him hurry.

[*Discovers woman friend.*] Ahem — a — hem!
Man, will you please attract the attention of that
lady over there in the boots? . . . No, not that
one—the one in the badly fitting jacket—I want
to speak to her.

How do you do? What on earth are you doing here? . . . Buying boots? I suppose so.
Miserable shop, isn't it? And such stupid, dis-
obliging salesmen. . . . I don't care if they do
hear it—it may do them good. . . . Will? Oh,
he's home sick. And cross! . . . You know how
they are. Get the least little pain we wouldn't
notice, and they think they are going to die right
off! But this time Will is awfully sick—I told
him it was about time he found out what real
suffering was. If he had been through what I
have. . . . To-day is his worst day, so I just
started out first thing this morning, and I am
not going back till dinner-time, and then only to
get dressed to go to the theatre. . . . No, no—of
course not—Will can't go. But it seemed such a
shame to lose the tickets—so I am going—with a
sort of a brother-in-law of my sister—who lives
up in the northern—part of Canada. . . . No, you
have never seen *her*. . . . No, you have never seen
him. . . . Tell me, how is your husband? . . . Indeed, I am so glad—

No, I don't care for that at all. Well, I can't
tell you what I don't like about it—I just know
it doesn't suit me. . . . Don't you keep the Ozone
shoes? . . . Never heard of them? Why, that's
very funny. I have a friend who lives out in
Spokane—I think it is in Delaware—anyway, I
know it is one of those Western States, and I
should think if they kept them in a little bit of a
place like that, you would have them in a great

city like this! . . . Well, I suppose I'll have to take these things—they are perfectly horrid—

Say, isn't it great about Marion Gray making such a hit on the stage? . . . Has she? Well, I should think so. She's famous. She's had a new kind of health food named after her! . . . Of course you know Margaret is engaged? . . . Yes, "at last," that's what I said, too. . . . I should think it was about time. Funny you didn't hear about it, though; she isn't making any secret of it; she could hardly contain herself till she told me. She's simply tickled to death. . . . Good-bye—I suppose I will see you at the Brownes' tea to-morrow? . . . Yes, they are always awful, but I shall go, I think. If you don't, people think you haven't been invited. Good-bye.

I'll take these—I want them charged—Mr. Faulkner knows me. . . . Yes, Mr. Faulkner. . . . What? This isn't Faulkner's store? Well, I thought it looked strange when I came in. I would just like to know why that floor-walker didn't tell me this wasn't Faulkner's when I first entered! I never get my shoes anywhere else. . . . No, I wouldn't take them now. And here you have wasted all my time—under—under—false pretences—while my poor husband is lying ill at home! I consider you have taken great advantage of me. . . . Good-afternoon!

SANTA FÉ CHARLEY'S KINDERGARTEN

BY THOMAS A. JANVIER

WHEN Bill Hart, who was a good fellow and kept the principal store in Palomitas, got word his aunt in Vermont was coming out to pay him a visit—it being too late to stop her, and he knowing he'd have to worry the thing through somehow till he could start her back East again —he was the worst broke-up man you ever saw. He had a right to be. It was that year when the end of the track was stuck at Palomitas, and when it seemed as if about all that was toughest in the Territory was stuck there too. Just thinking how his aunt would feel, getting tangled up with a crowd like that, was enough to—and it did—give him the worst jolt he'd ever had.

"Great Scott! Sam," Hart said, when he was telling Cherry about it, "Palomitas ain't no sort of a town to bring aunts to; and it's about the last town I know of where Aunt Maria 'll fit in. She's the old-fashioned kind, right up to the limit, Aunt Maria is. Sewing societies and Sunday-schools are the hands she holds flushes in; and she has the preacher once a week to supper; and

when it comes to kindergartens "—Hart was so
worked up he talked careless—"she's simply h—ll!
What's a woman like that going to do, I want to
know, in a place like this—that's mainly made up
of saloons and dance-halls and faro-banks, and
most of the men usually drunk, and shooting-
scrapes going on all the time? It just makes me
sick to think about it." And Hart groaned.

Cherry swore for a while, sort of friendly and
sociable—he was a sympathetic man, Cherry was,
and always did what he could to help—and as
Hart was too far gone to swear for himself, in a
way that amounted to anything, hearing what
Cherry had to say seemed to do him good.

"I'd stop her, if there was any stop to her," he
went on in a minute or two, speaking hopeless
and miserable; "but there ain't. She says she's
starting the day after she writes — having a
chance to come sudden with friends—and that
means she's 'most here now. And there's no
heading her off—because she says the friends
she's hooked fast to may be coming to Pueblo
and may be coming to Santa Fé. But it don't
make any difference, she says, as she's told she
can get down easy by the railroad from Pueblo,
or she can slide across to Palomitas by a short
and pleasant coach-ride—that's what she calls it
—from Santa Fé.

"That's all she tells about her coming. The
rest of what's in her letter is about how glad
she'll be to see me, and about how glad she knows

I'll be to see her—being lonely so far from my folks, and likely needing my clothes mended, and pleased to be eating some of her home-made pies. It's just like Aunt Maria to put in things like that. You see, she brought me up—and she's never got out of her head I'm more'n about nine years old. What I feel like doing is going out in the sage-brush and blowing the top of my fool head off, and letting the coyotes eat what's left of me and get me out of the way!"

Hart really did look as if he meant it, Cherry said, afterwards. He was the miserablest-looking man, he said, he'd ever seen alive.

Cherry said he begun to have a notion, though, while Hart was talking, how the thing might be worked so there wouldn't be no real trouble if it could be fixed so Hart's aunt wouldn't stay in Palomitas more'n about a day; and he come right on down to the Forest Queen to see if he could get the boys to help him put it through. He left Hart clearing out the room he kept flour and meal in—being the cleanest—trying to rig up for his aunt some sort of a bunking-place. He was going to give her his own cot and mattress, he said; and he could fit her out with a looking-glass and a basin and pitcher all right because he kept them sort of things to sell; and he said he'd make the place extra tidy by putting a new horse-blanket on the floor. Seeing his way to getting a grip on that much of the contract, Cherry said, seemed to make him feel a little less bad.

Cherry waited till the deal was over, when he got to the Forest Queen; and then he asked Santa Fé Charley—Charley was the dealer at the Forest Queen—if he'd let him speak to the boys for a minute before the game went on.   He was always polite and obliging, Santa Fé was, and he said of course he might; and he rapped on the table with his derringer for order, and said Mr. Cherry had the floor.   Charley was old-fashioned in his ways of fighting.   He always had a six-shooter in his belt, same as other folks; but he said he kept it mainly for show.   Derringers, he said, was better and surer—because you could work 'em around in your pocket, while the other fellow was getting his gun out, and before he was ready for business you could shoot him right through your pants. Later on, it was that very way Santa Fé shot Hart.   But he was always friendly with Hart, till he did shoot him; and it was more his backing than anything else—especially when it come to the kindergarten—that made Cherry's plan for helping Hart out go through.

When the game was stopped, and the boys was all listening, Cherry told about the hole Hart was in and allowed it was a deep one; and he said it was only fair—Hart having done good turns for most everybody, one time and another — his friends should be willing to take some trouble to get him out of it.   Hart's aunt, he said, come from a quiet part of Vermont, and likely would be jolted bad when she struck Palomitas if things

was going the ordinary way—she being elderly,
and like enough a little set in her ways, and not
used much to crazy drunks, and shooting-matches,
and such kinds of lively carryings-on.   But she'd
only stay one day, or at most a day and a half—
Hart having agreed to take her right back East
himself, if she couldn't be got rid of no other way
—and that gave 'em a chance to fix things so her
feelings wouldn't be hurt, though doing it was going to be hard on all hands.   And then, having
got the boys worked up wondering what he was
driving at, Cherry went ahead and said he wanted
'em to agree—just for the little while Hart's aunt
was going to stay there—to run Palomitas like it
was a regular back East Sunday-school town.
He knew he was asking a good deal, he said; but
he did ask it—and he appealed to the better class
of citizens assembled around that faro-table to do
that much to get Bill Hart out of his hole.   Then
Cherry said he wasn't nobody's orator, but he
guessed he'd made clear what he wanted to lay
before the meeting; and he said he was much
obliged, and had pleasure in setting up drinks for
the crowd.

As was to be expected of 'em, all the boys—
knowing Hart for a square-acting man, and liking
him—tumbled right off to Cherry's plan.   Santa
Fé said—this was after they'd had their drinks—
he s'posed he was chairman of the meeting, and
he guessed he spoke the sense of the meeting
when he allowed Mr. Cherry's scheme was about

the only way out for their esteemed fellow-citizen Mr. Hart, and it ought to go through. But as it was a matter that seriously affected the comfort and convenience of everybody in Palomitas, he said, it was only square to take a vote on it—and so he'd ask all in favor of Mr. Cherry's motion to say "Aye." And everybody in the room—except the few that was asleep, or too drunk to say anything — said "Aye" as loud as they knew how.

"Mr. Cherry's motion is carried, gentlemen," Santa Fé said; "and I will now appoint a committee to draft a notice to be posted at the deepo, and to call around at the other banks and saloons in the town and notify verbally our fellow-citizens of the action we have taken."

The Sage-brush Hen, along with some of the other girls, had come in from the back room—where the dancing was — to find out what the circus was about; and when they caught on to what Palomitas was going to be like when Hart's aunt struck it they all just yelled.

"You've come out well as the Baptist minister, once, Charley," the Hen said, shaking all over; "and I reckon you can do it again—only it won't be so easy showing off the new church and the parsonage by daylight as it was in the dark."

Cherry was more pleased than a little the way things had gone—and he said so to the boys, and set up drinks all round again. Then he and Abe Simons—they was the committee to do it—wrote

out a notice that was tacked up on the deepo
door and read this way:

TO THE CITIZENS OF PALOMITAS.

Mr. William J. Hart's aunt is coming to pay him a
visit, and will strike this town either by the Denver train
to-morrow morning or the Santa Fé coach to-morrow
afternoon.

She is a perfect lady, and it is ordered that during her
stay in Palomitas this town has got to behave itself so
her feelings won't be hurt. She is to be took care of and
given a pleasant impression. All fights and drunks must
be put off till she's gone. Persons neglecting to do so
will be taken out into the sage-brush by members of the
committee, and are likely to get hurt.

Mr. Hart regrets this occurrence as much as anybody,
and agrees his aunt's visit sha'n't last beyond one day if
she comes down from Denver, or a day and a half if she
comes in from Santa Fé.

(Signed)   THE COMMITTEE.

When Cherry got a-hold of Hart and told him
what the town had agreed to do for him he was
that grateful—being all worked up, anyway—he
pretty near cried.

As it turned out, Hart's aunt come in on Hill's
coach from Santa Fé—her friends having gone
down that way by the Atchison—and as Hill had
been at the meeting at the Forest Queen he was
able to give things a good start. Hill always was
a friendly sort of a fellow, and—except he used
terrible bad language, which he said come of his

having to drive mules—he was a real first-class ladies' man.

Hill said he knew Hart's aunt the minute he set his eyes on her waiting for the coach at the Fonda, there not being likely to be more'n one in the Territory of that kind. She was a trig little old lady, dressed up in black clothes as neat as wax, he said, with a little black bonnet setting close to her head; and she wore gold specs and had a longish nose. But she'd a real friendly look about her, he said; and while she spoke a little precise and particular she wasn't a bit stuck up, and seemed to be taking things about as they happened to come along. When he asked her if she wouldn't set up on the box with him, so she could see the country, she said that was just what would suit her; and up she come, he said, as spry as a queer little bird. Then he whipped up his mules—being careful not to use any language— and got the coach started; and begun right off to be agreeable by telling her he guessed he had the pleasure of knowing her nephew, and asking her if she wasn't the aunt of Mr. William J. Hart.

Well, of course, that set things to going pleasant between 'em; and when she'd allowed she was Hart's aunt, and said she was glad to meet a friend of his, she started in asking all the questions about Bill and about Palomitas she knew how to ask.

Hill said he guessed that day they had to lay off the regular recording angel and put a hired

first-class stenographer on his job—seeing how no
plain angel, not writing shorthand, could 'a' kept
up with all the lies he felt it his duty to tell if he
was going to bring Bill through in good shape
and keep up the reputation of the town.   It
wasn't square to charge them lies up to him, anyway, Hill said, seeing he only was playing Cherry's
hand for him; and he said he hoped they was put
in Cherry's bill.   By the time he'd got through
with his fairy tales, he said, he'd given Hart such
a character he didn't know him himself; and he'd
touched up Palomitas till he'd got it so it might
'a' been a town just outside Boston—only he allowed they was sometimes troubled with hard
cases passing through; and he told her of course
she'd find things kind of half-baked and noisy
out there on the frontier.   And she must remember, he told her, that all the folks in the town was
young—young men who'd brought their young
wives with 'em, come to hustle in a new country
—and she mustn't mind if things went livelier 'n
the way she was used to back East.

Hill said she said she wasn't expecting to find
things like they was at home, and she guessed
she'd manage all right—seeing she always got on
well with young people, and wasn't a bit set in
her own ways.   And she said she was as pleased
as she was surprised to find out the kind of a
town Palomitas was—because her nephew William's letters had led her to think it had a good
many bad characters in it; and he'd not men-

5

tioned any church but the Catholic one where the
natives went; and as to the Bible Class and the
Friendly Aid Society and the Sunshine Club he'd
never said a word about 'em at all. She went on
talking so cheerful and pleasant, Hill said, it give
him creeps in his back; and he got so rattled the
last half of the run—coming on from Pojuaque,
where they'd had lunch at old man Bouquet's—
he hardly knew what he'd told and what he
hadn't, and whether he was standing on his head
or his heels.

Being that way, he made the only break that
gave trouble afterwards. She asked him if there
was a school in Palomitas; and he told her there
wasn't, because all the folks in town was so young
—except the natives, who hadn't no use for
schools—they hadn't any children big enough to
go to one. And then she said sudden, and as it
seemed to him changing the subject: "Isn't there
a kindergarten?" Hill said he'd never heard tell
of such a concern; but he sized it up to be some
sort of a fancy German garden—like the one
Becker 'd fixed up for himself, over to Santa Cruz
—and he said he allowed, from the way she asked
about it, it was what Palomitas ought to have.
So he told her there was, and it was the best one
in the Territory—and let it go at that. He said
she said she was glad to hear it, as she took a
special interest in kindergartens, and she'd go
and see it the first thing.

Hill said he knew he'd put his foot in it some-

how; but as he didn't know how he'd put his foot
in it, he just switched her off by telling her about
the Dorcas Society. He had the cards for that,
he said, because his mother 'd helped run a Dorcas
Society back East and he knew what he was talking about. The Palomitas one met Thursdays,
he told her, at the Forest Queen. That was the
principal hotel, he told her, and was kept by Mrs.
Major Rogers, who was an officer's widow, and
had started the society to make clothes for some
of the Mexican poor folks—and he said it was a
first-rate charity and worked well. It tickled
him so, he said, thinking of any such doings at
the Forest Queen—with Tenderfoot Sal, who
kept it, bossing the job—he had to work off the
laugh he had inside of him by taking to licking
his mules.

But it went all right with the little old lady;
and she was that interested he had to strain himself, he said, making up more stories about it—
till by good luck she took to telling him about
the Dorcas Society she belonged to herself, back
home in Vermont; and was so full of it she kept
things going easy for him till they'd crossed the
bridge over the Rio Grande and was coming up
the slope into the town at a walk.

Up at the top of the slope Santa Fé Charley
was standing waiting for 'em—dressed in black,
like he always was, with a long frock-coat and a
white tie. As the coach come along he sung out,
pleasant and friendly: "Good day, Brother Hill.

I missed you at the Bible Class last evening. No
doubt you were detained unavoidably, and it's all
right. But be sure to come Friday. We don't
get along well without you, Brother Hill." And
Santa Fé took off his black felt hat and made the
old lady the best sort of a bow.

Hill caught on quick and played right up to
Santa Fé's lead. "That's our minister, Mr.
Charles, ma'am. The one I've been telling you
about," he said. "He's just friendly and sociable like that all the time. He looks after the
folks in this town closer 'n any preacher I ever
saw." A part of that, Hill said, was dead certain truth—seeing as Santa Fé had his eyes out
straight along for everybody about the place who
had a dollar in his pocket, and wasn't satisfied till
he'd scooped in that dollar over his table at the
Forest Queen.

"There's the new church we're building," Hill
went on, as they got to the top of the slope and
headed for the deepo. "It ain't much to look at
yet, the spire not being put on; and even when it
gets the spire on it won't show up well with
churches East. But we're going to be satisfied
with it—seeing it's the best we can do. You'll
be interested to know, ma'am, your nephew give
the land."

"William hasn't let on anything about it,"
Hart's aunt said, looking pleased all over. "But
what in the world is a church doing with a railroad track running into it, Mr. Hill?"

Hill said he'd forgot about the track when he settled to use the new freight-house for church purposes; but he said he pulled himself together quick and told her the track was temp'r'y—put in so building material could unload right on the ground. And then he took to talking about how obliging the railroad folks had been helping 'em —and kept a-talking that way till he got the coach to the deepo, and didn't need to hustle making things up any more. He said he never was so thankful in his life as he was when his stunt was done. He was just tired out, he said, lying straight ahead all day over thirty miles of bad road and not being able once to speak natural to his mules.

Hart was waiting at the deepo, on the chance his aunt would come in on the coach; and when she saw him she give a little squeal, she was so pleased, and hopped down in no time off the box —she was as brisk as a bee in her doings—and took to hugging him and half-crying over him just like he was a little boy.

"Oh, William," she said, "I am *so* happy getting to you! And I'm happier 'n I expected to be, finding out how quiet and respectable Palomitas is—not a bit what your letters made me think it was—and such real good people living in it, and everything but the queer country and the queer mud-houses just like it is at home. Mr. Hill has been telling me all about it, coming over; and

about this new church you're building that you
gave the lot for. To think you've never told me!
Oh, William, I am so glad and so thankful that
out here in this wild region you've kept serious-
minded and are turning out such a good man!"

Hart looked so mixed up over the way his aunt
was talking, and so sort of hopeless, that Hill cut
in quick and give him a lift. "He's not much
at blowing about himself, your nephew ain't,
ma'am," Hill said. "Why, he not only give
the land for the church over there"—and Hill
pointed at the freight-house, so Hart could ketch
on—"but it was him got the company to lay
them temp'r'y tracks, so the building stuff could
be took right in. He's going to give the organ,
too."

"Dear William!" Hart's aunt said. "It re-
joices my heart you're doing all these good deeds
—and all the others Mr. Hill's been telling me
about. I must kiss you again."

"Oh, what I've done ain't nothing," Hart said,
pulling himself together while she was kissing
him. "Land's cheap, cheap as it can be, out
here; and I give the company such a lot of freight
they're more'n willing to oblige me, and as to the
organ—"

Hart sort of gagged when he got to the organ,
and Santa Fé Charley—who'd come up while they
all was talking away together—reached across
the table and played his hand. "As to the organ,
Mr. Hart," Santa Fé put in, "you said that being

in business you could get it at a discount off.
But that does not appreciably lessen your generosity, Mr. Hart; and your aunt"—Santa Fé
took off his hat and bowed handsome—"is justified in taking pride in your good deeds. I am
glad to tell her that in her nephew our struggling
church has its stanchest pillar and its strongest
stay."

"Yes, that's the way it is about the organ,
Aunt Maria," Hart said, kind of weak and mournful. "Being in business, I get organs at such a
discount off that giving 'em away ain't nothing
to me at all. And now I guess we'd better be
getting along home. It's a mighty mean home
to take you to, Aunt Maria; but there's one comfort—as you'll find out when I get the chance to
talk to you—you won't have to stay in it long."

There was a lot of the boys standing round on
the deepo platform watching the show, and they
all took their hats off respectful—following the
lead Santa Fé give 'em—as Hart started away up
the track, to where his store was, with his Aunt
Maria on his arm. The town looked like some
place East keeping Sunday: the Committee having talked strong as to what they'd do if things
wasn't quiet, and having rounded up—and cor-
ralled in a back room Denver Jones lent the use
of—the few who'd got drunk as usual before they
had to, and so had to be took care of that way.
It was a June evening, and the sun about setting;
and somehow it all was so sort of peaceful and

uncommon—with everybody in sight sober, and
no fighting anywhere, and that little old lady going along believing Palomitas was like that always, instead of the hell on earth it was—some
of us more 'n half believed we'd gone to sleep and
got stuck in a dream.

Things was made dreamier by the looks and
doings of the Sage-brush Hen. As Hart and his
aunt went off together along the track, she
showed up coming down it; and she was dressed
that pretty and quiet—in the plainest sort of a
white frock, and wearing a white sunbonnet—
and was looking so demure, like she could when
she'd a mind to, nobody knew at first who it was.

"Being the minister's wife, I've been taking
the liberty, Mr. Hart," she said, smiling pleasant, when the three of 'em come together on the
track, "of looking around a little up at your
place to see that everything has been fixed for
your company the way it should be." (She
hadn't been nowheres near Hart's place, it turned
out—but gospel truth wasn't just what there was
most of that day in Palomitas.) She went right
on down the track without stopping; passing on
Hart's side, and saying to him: "My husband ex-
pects you as usual at the Friendly Aid meeting
to-morrow evening, Mr. Hart. We never seem
half to get along, you know, when you're not
there."

Hart's aunt give a little jump, and said: "Why,
William, that must be Mrs. Charles, the minister's

wife. What a pleasant-spoken lady she is. We met her husband just as we were driving into town."

Hart said he come pretty near saying back to her: "The h—ll you did!"—Hart talked that careless way, sometimes—but he said he pulled up before it was out; and all he did say was: "Oh."

"She must be at the head of the Dorcas Society and the Sunshine Club that Mr. Hill was telling me about," Hart's aunt went on; "and like enough she manages the kindergarten, too. I suppose, William, it's not surprising you haven't said anything in your letters about the Dorcas Society—for all you were so liberal in helping it; but you might have mentioned that nice Sunshine Club, and I do think you ought to have told me about the kindergarten—knowing what a hobby of mine kindergartens are. I want to go and see it to-morrow morning, the first thing."

"It's—it's not in running order just now," Hart said. "Most of the children was took sick with the influenza last week, and there's whooping-cough and measles about, and so the school committee closed it down. And they had to stop, anyway, because they're going to put a new roof on. I guess it won't blow in again for about a month—or maybe more. In fact, I don't know —you see, it wasn't managed well, and got real down unpopular — if it 'll blow in again at all. I'm sorry you won't be able to get to it, Aunt

Maria. Maybe it 'll be running if you happen to come out again next year."

"Why, how queer that is, William!" Hart's aunt said. "Mr. Hill told me it was the best kindergarten in New Mexico. But of course you know. Anyhow, I can see the school-room and the school-fixtures, and Mrs. Charles can tell me about it when I go to the Dorcas Society—and that 'll do 'most as well. Of course, I must go to the Dorcas Society. Mrs. Charles will take me, I'm sure. It meets, Mr. Hill says, every Thursday afternoon."

"Did he say where it was meeting now?" Hart asked. He was getting about desperate, he told Cherry afterwards; and what he wanted most was a chance to mash Hill's fool head for putting him in such a lot of holes.

"Of course he did, William," said Hart's aunt; "and I'm surprised you have to ask—seeing what an interest you take in the society, and how you've helped it along. It was just lovely of you to give them all those goods out of your store to make up into clothes."

"That—that wasn't anything to do," Hart said. "What's in the store comes with a big discount—same as organs. Sometimes I feel as if I was saving money giving things away."

"You can talk about your generosity just as you please, William," she went on. "*I* think it's noble of you. And Mr. Hill said that Mrs. Major Rogers—who keeps the Forest Queen Hotel, he

said, and lets the society have a room to meet in
for nothing—said it was noble of you, too. I
want to get to know Mrs. Major Rogers right off.
She must be a very fine woman. She's an officer's
widow, Mr. Hill says; and a real lady, for all she
makes her living keeping a hotel out here on the
frontier. If she's a bit like that sweet-looking
Mrs. Charles, I know we'll get along. I'm surprised, William, you've never told me what pleasant ladies live here. It must make all the difference in the world. Don't you think it would do
for me not to be formal, but just to go to Mrs.
Major Rogers's hotel to-morrow and call?"

"I guess—well, I guess you hadn't better go
right off the first thing in the morning, Aunt
Maria," Hill said. Thinking of his aunt going
calling at the Forest Queen and running up
against Tenderfoot Sal, he said, gave him the
regular cold shakes. "And come to think of it,"
he said, "it's no use your going to-morrow at all.
Mrs.—Mrs. Major Rogers, as I happen to know,
went up to Denver yesterday; and she won't be
back, she told me, before some time on in the end
of next week—likely as not, she said, she wouldn't
come then."

By that time they'd got along to Hart's store,
and Hart said: "Here's where I live, Aunt Maria.
You see what sort of a place it is. But I've done
my best to fix things for you as well as I know
how. Come right along in—and when we've had
supper we've got to have a talk."

Along about ten o'clock that night Hart come down to the Forest Queen pale and haggard, and he was that broke up he had to get three drinks in him before he could say a word. Everybody was so interested, wanting to hear what he had to tell 'em, he didn't need to ask to have the game stopped—it just stopped of its own accord.

When he'd had his third drink, and was beginning to feel better, he said he couldn't thank everybody enough for the way they'd behaved; and that his aunt had gone to bed tired out; and he'd been talking with her steady for two hours getting things settled; and she'd ended by agreeing she'd start back East with him the next night —he having made out he'd smash in his business if he waited a minute longer—and they were going by the Denver train. And he'd got her fixed, he said, so she'd keep quiet through the morning —as she was going right at mending all his clothes and darning his stockings the first thing when she got up; and after that she was full of getting to work with canned peaches and making him a pie.

"But what's going to happen in the afternoon," he said, "the Lord only knows! That blasted fool of a Joe Hill"—Hart spoke just that bitter way about it—"hasn't had no more sense 'n to go and tell her this town's full of kindergartens; and she's so worked up there's no holding her, as kindergartens happens to be the fullest hand she holds. I've allowed we have one—

things being as they was, I had to—but I've told
her it's out of order, and the children laid up
with whooping-cough, and the teacher sick abed,
and the outfit damaged by a fire we had, and—
and the Lord knows what lies I haven't told her
about the d—n thing." (Hart was that nervous
he couldn't help speaking that way.) "But all
I've said hasn't made no difference. She's just
dead-set on getting to what's left of that kindergarten, and I can't budge her. See it she will,
she says; and I guess the upshot of Hill's chuckle-
headed talk 'll be to waste all the trouble we've
took by landing us in the biggest give-away that
ever was!" And Hart called for another drink,
and had to set down to take it — looking
pale.

All the boys felt terrible bad about the hole
Hart was in; and they felt worse because most of
'em hadn't no notion what a kindergarten did—
when it did anything—and that made 'em more
ashamed Palomitas hadn't one to show. Only
Becker—Becker 'd happened to come over from
Santa Cruz that night—sized it up right; and
Becker shook his head sort of dismal and said
there wasn't no use even thinking about it—and
that looked like a settler, because Becker seemed
to know. Nobody didn't say anything for a
minute or two; and then Ike Williams spoke up
—he was the boss carpenter on the freight-house
job, Ike was—and said if what was wanted could
be made out of boards, and made in a hurry, he'd

lay off the freight - house gang the next morning and engage to have one ready by afternoon.

Santa Fé Charley 'd been setting still thinking,
not saying a word. He let out a big cuss—and
Charley wasn't given to cussing—when Ike made
his offer; and then he banged his hand down on
the table so hard he set the chips to flying, and
he said: "Mr. Hart, don't you worry—we're going
to put this job through!"

Everybody jumped up at that—some of 'em
scrambling for the dropped chips—asking Santa
Fé what he meant to do. But Charley wouldn't
answer 'em. "Just you trust to Ike and me,
Bill," he said. "We'll fix your kindergarten all
right—only you tell your aunt it ain't a good one,
and go ahead telling her how most of it got
burned in the fire. It's luck you let on to her
there'd been a fire—that makes it as easy as rolling off a log. All you've got to do is to bring her
down here at four o'clock to-morrow afternoon—
you'd better till then keep her in the house,
mending you up and making you all the pies she
has a mind to—and when she gets here the
kindergarten 'll be here, too!"

"Bring her here—to the Forest Queen?" Hart
said, speaking doubtful.

"Bring her here—right here to the Forest
Queen," Santa Fé said back to him. "You
know pretty well I do things when I say I'll do
'em—and this thing 'll be done! Come to think

of it," he said, "maybe it 'll be better if I go to
your place and fetch her along myself.   It 'll help
if I do a little talking to her on the way down.
Yes, we'll fix it that way.   You and she be ready
at four o'clock, and I'll come for you.   That 'll
give her an hour here, and an hour to go home
and eat her supper—and that 'll get us to train-
time, and then the circus 'll close down.   Now
you go home and go to bed, Bill.   You're all beat
out.   Just you leave things to Ike and me, and
go right along home."

Charley wouldn't say another word—so Hart
had one more drink, for luck, and then he went
home.   He looked real relieved.

When Santa Fé went to Hart's place, next
afternoon, he had on his best black clothes, with
a clean shirt and a fresh white tie; and he was
that serious-looking you'd have sized him up for
a sure - enough fire - escape anywhere on sight.
Hart hadn't no trouble, it turned out, keeping
his aunt to home—she'd been working double
tides ever since she got up, making him things to
eat and fussing over his clothes.   They was all
ready when Santa Fé come along, and the three
of 'em stepped off down the track together—Hart
having his aunt on his arm, and Santa Fé walking
on ahead over the ties.   Most of the boys was
standing about watching the procession; but the
girls—the Hen, likely, having told 'em to—was
keeping on keeping quiet, and got what they

could of it peeping through the chinks in the windows and doors.

"Why, where *are* all the ladies, Mr. Charles?" Hart's aunt asked. "Except that sweet young wife of yours, it's just the mortal truth I haven't seen a single lady since I came into this town!"

"They usually keep in-doors at this time of day, madam," Charley said. "They're attending to their domestic duties and—and most of them, about now, are wont to be enjoying the tenderest happiness of motherhood in nursing their little babes."

"It's very creditable they're such good house-wives, I'm sure," said Hart's aunt; "only I do wish I could have met some of 'em and had a good dish of talk. But we'll be finding your wife at the kindergarten, I s'pose; and I'll have the pleasure of a talk with her. I've been looking forward all day to meeting her, Mr. Charles. She has one of the very sweetest faces I ever saw."

"I deeply regret to tell you, madam," said Santa Fé, "that my wife was called away suddenly last evening by a telegram. She had no choice in the matter. Her call was to minister to a sick relative in Denver, and of course she left immediately on the night train. Her disappointment at not meeting you was great. She had set her heart on showing you over our poor half-ruined kindergarten—the fire did fearful damage—but her duty was too manifest to be

ignored, and she had to leave that pleasant task
to me."

"Now that is just too bad!" said Hart's aunt.
"At least, Mr. Charles, I don't mean that exactly. It's very kind of you to take her place,
and I'm delighted to have you. But I did so like
your wife's looks, and I've been hoping she and
I really 'd have a chance to get to be friends."

That brought 'em to the Forest Queen, and
Charley was more'n glad he was let out from
making more excuses why his wife had shook her
kindergarten job so sudden. "Here we are," he
said. "But I must warn you again, madam,
that our little kindergarten is only the ghost of
what it was before the fire. We are hoping to
get a new outfit shortly. On the very morning
of the disaster a subscription was started—your
nephew, as always, leading in the good work—
and that afternoon we telegraphed East our order
for fresh supplies. By the time that the epidemic
of whooping-cough has abated—I am glad to say
that all the children are doing well—we trust that
our flock of little ones again can troop gladly to
receive the elementary instruction that they delight in, and that my wife delights to impart."

"Why," said Hart's aunt, "the kindergarten's
in Mrs. Major Roger's hotel—the Forest Queen!"

"After the fire, Mrs. Major Roger most kindly
gave us the free use of one of her largest rooms,"
Santa Fé said; "and we are installed here until
6

our own building can be repaired. I have spared you the sight, madam, of that melancholy ruin. I confess that when I look at it the tears come into my eyes."

"I don't wonder, I'm sure," said Hart's aunt. "I think I'd cry over it myself. But what a real down good woman Mrs. Major Rogers must be! Mr. Hart told me she gives the Dorcas Society the use of a room too."

"She is a noble, high-toned lady, madam," Santa Fé said. "Since her cruel bereavement she has devoted to good works all the time that she can spare from the arduous duties by which she wins her livelihood. Words fail me to say enough in her praise! Come right in, madam—but be prepared for a sad surprise!"

Hart said he didn't know how much surprised his aunt was—but he said when he got inside the Forest Queen, into the bar-room where Charley's faro lay-out usually was, he was so surprised himself he felt as if he'd been kicked by a mule!

There was the little tables for drinks, right enough; and out of the way in a corner with a cloth over it, same as usual, was the wheel. (It was used so little, the wheel was—nobody but Mexicans, now and then, caring for it—Santa Fé owned up afterwards he'd forgot it clean!) That much of the place was just as it always was; and the big table, taking up half the room, looked so natural—with the chairs up to it, and lay-outs of chips at all the places—that Hart was beginning

to think Santa Fé was setting up a rig on him;
till he saw what a lot of queer things besides chips
there was on the table—and knew they wasn't
any game lay-out, and so sized 'em up to be what
Charley 'd scrambled together when he set out
to play his kindergarten hand. And when he
noticed the bar was curtained off by sheets he
said he stopped worrying—feeling dead certain
Charley 'd dealt himself all the aces he needed to
take him through.

"You don't need to be told, madam, being such
an authority on kindergartens," Santa Fé said,
"how inadequate is our little outfit for education-
al purposes. But you must remember that the
fire destroyed almost everything, and that we
have merely improvised what will serve our purposes until the new supply arrives. We succeeded
in saving from the conflagration our large table,
and our chairs, and most of the small tables—
used by individual children having backward in-
tellects and needing especial care. But nearly all
of the other appliances of the school were lost to
us, and damage was done to much of what we
saved. Here, you see, is a little table with only
three legs left, the fourth having been burned."
And, sure enough, Hart said, Santa Fé turned up
one of the little tables for drinks and one of its
legs *was* burned off! "All of our slates," he
went ahead, "similarly were destroyed—and how
much depends on slates in a kindergarten you
know, madam, better than I do. Here is all that

is left of one of them"—and he showed Hart's
aunt a bit of burned wood that looked like it had
been part of a slate-frame afore it got afire.

"Dear me! Dear me!" said Hart's aunt.
"It's just pitiful, Mr. Charles! I wonder how
you can get along at all."

"It is not easy getting along, madam," Santa
Fé said. "But we have managed to supply ourselves with a lay-out—I—that is—I mean we have
provided ourselves with some of the simpler articles of most importance; and with these, for the
time being, we keep our little pupil's hands and
minds not unprofitably employed. For instance,
the ivory disks of various colors—which you see
arranged upon the table as the pupils have left
them—serve very successfully to elucidate the
arithmetical processes of numeration, addition,
and subtraction; and the more intelligent children
are taught to observe that the disks of varying
colors are varyingly numbered—white, 1; red, 5;
and blue, 10—and so are encouraged to identify
a concrete arbitrary figure with an abstract
thought."

"That's something new in kindergartening,
Mr. Charles," said Hart's aunt; "and it's as good
as it can be. I mean to put it right into use in
our kindergarten at home. Do you get the disks
at the places where they sell kindergarten supplies?"

"Really, madam, I cannot tell you," Santa Fé
said. "You see, we ordered what would be need-

ed through an agent East, and these came along.
I must warn you, however, that they are expensive."

Hart said, remembering what them chips had
cost him, one time and another, he allowed to
himself Charley was right and they was about as
expensive as they could be!

"Our other little appliances, madam," Santa
Fé went on, "are just our own makeshift imita-
tions of what you are familiar with—building-
blocks, and alphabet blocks, and dissected pictures, and that sort of thing. Our local carpenter
made the blocks for us, and we put on the letter-
ing ourselves—as, indeed, its poor quality shows.
The dissected pictures I am rather proud of, because Mrs. Charles may be said to have invented
them." (It really was the Hen who'd made
them, it turned out.) "The method is simple
enough when you have thought of it, of course—
and no doubt I value my wife's work unduly because I take so much pride in all that she does.
You see, she just pasted pictures from the illustrated papers on boards; and then Mr. Williams—
our carpenter, you know—sawed the boards into
little pieces. And there you are!"

"Now that *was* bright of her!" said Hart's
aunt. "If you don't mind, I'll put one of the
pictures together myself right now. I want to
see how it looks, made that home-fashioned
way."

"I fear that our time is getting a little short,

madam," said Santa Fé in a hurry. "I've got
my sermon to finish this afternoon, and I must
be going in a few minutes now." The fact of the
matter was he had to call her off quick. It seems
the Hen hadn't had anything but sporting papers
to work on—and while the bits looked all right
jumbled up, being put together they wouldn't
have suited nohow at all.

"Of course I mustn't keep you," said Hart's
aunt. "You've been more than kind, Mr. Charles,
to give me so much of your valuable time as it is.
I'm just like a child myself, wanting to play with
dissected pictures that way! But I must say
that her making them is a thing for your wife to
be proud of—and I hope you'll tell her so from
me."

"I guess we'd better be going now, Aunt Maria,"
Hart said. "Mr. Charles has his sermon to
write, you know; and I want you to have time to
eat your supper comfortable, before we start down
to the train."

"I do suppose we must go," said Hart's aunt.
"But I hate to, William, and that's a fact! Just
because it's so make-shifty, this is the most interesting kindergarten I've ever been in. When
I get home I shall really and truly enjoy telling
the folks about it. And I know how pleased
they'll be, the same as I am, by finding what
earnest-working men and women can do—out
here in this rough country—with so little to go
on but their wits and their own good hearts!"

And then she faced round sudden on Santa Fé
and said: "I see you have your table covered with
green, Mr. Charles. What's that for? You have
so many good notions about kindergartens that
I'd like to know."

"Well, you see, madam, that green cover is a
—it's a sort of—" Charley went slow for a minute, and then he picked himself up and went
ahead easy: "That is an invention of my good
wife's, too. Out here, where the sun's so violent,
she said we must have a green cover on the table
or the glare would be ruining all our dear little
innocent children's eyes. And it has worked,
madam, to a charm! Some of the children who
had bad eyes to start with actually have got well!"

"Well, I do declare!" said Hart's aunt. "That
wife of yours thinks so sensible she just beats all!"

Santa Fé give Hart a look, as much as to say
he'd got to get his aunt away somehow—seeing
she was liable to break out a'most anywhere, and
he'd stood about all he could stand. Hart allowed what Charley wanted was reasonable, and
he just grabbed her by the arm and began to lug
her to the door. But she managed to give Santa
Fé one more jolt, and a bad one, before she was
gone.

"I haven't seen what this is," she said; and
she broke off from Hart and went to where the
wheel was standing covered up in the corner. "I
s'pose I may look at it, Mr. Charles?" she said—
and before either of 'em could get a-hold of her

to stop her she had off the cloth. "For the land's sake!" she said. "Whatever part of a kindergarten have you got here?"

Hart said afterwards his heart went down into his boots, being sure they'd got to a give-away of the worst sort. Santa Fé said he felt that way for a minute himself; then he said he ciphered on it that Hart's aunt likely wouldn't know what she'd struck—and he braced up and went ahead on that chance.

"Ah," he said—speaking just as cool as if he was calling the deal right among friends at his own table—"that is one of the new German kindergarten appliances that even you, madam, may not have seen. We received it as a present from a rich German merchant in Pueblo who was grieved by our pitiable plight, and wanted to do what he could to help us after the fire."

"But what in the name of common-sense," said Hart's aunt, "do you do with it—with all those numbers around in circles on black and red streaks, and that little ball?"

Charley had himself in good shape by that time, and he put down his words as sure as if they was aces—with more, if needed, up his sleeve. "It is used by our most advanced class in arithmetic, madam," he said. "The mechanism, you will observe, is arranged to revolve"—he set it a-going—"in such a way that the small sphere also is put in motion. And as the motion ceases"—it was slowing down to a stop—"the

sphere comes to rest on one of the numbers
painted legibly on either a black or a red ground.
The children, seated around the table, are provided with the numerating disks to which I have
already called your attention; and—with a varying rapidity, regulated by their individual intelligence—they severally, as promptly as possible, arrange their disks in piles corresponding
with the number indicated by the purely for-
tuitous resting-place of the sphere.   The purpose
of this ingenious contrivance, as I scarcely need
to point out to you, is to combine the amusement
of a species of game with the mental stimulus
that the rapid computation of figures imparts.   I
may add that we arouse a desirable spirit of emu-
lation among our little ones by providing that the
child who first correctly arranges his disks to
represent the indicated figure is given—until the
game is concluded—the disks of the children
whose calculation has been slow, or at fault."

"Well, of all things in the world, Mr. Charles,"
said Hart's aunt, "to think of my finding such a
good thing as this, out here in New Mexico—
when I've time and again been over the best kin-
dergarten-supply places in Boston, and have been
reading all I could lay my hands on about kindergartens for twenty years!"

"Oh, we do try not to be too primitive out
here, madam," said Santa Fé—taking a long
breath over having got through all right; "and I
am even vain enough to think that perhaps we

manage to keep pretty well up with the times. But I must say that it is a pleasant surprise to me to find that I have been able to give more than one point to a lady like you, who knows every card—I should say, to whom kindergarten processes are so exceptionally well known.

"And now I must really beg your permission to leave you, that I may return to my sermon. I give much time to my sermons; and I am cheered by the conviction—you must not think me boastful — that it is time well employed. When I look around me and perceive the lawless, and even outrageous, conditions which obtain in so many other towns in the Territory, and contrast them with the orderly rectitude of Palomitas, I rejoice that my humble toil in the vineyard has brought so rich a reward. I deeply regret, madam, that your present stay with us must be so short; and with an equal earnestness I hope that it may be my privilege soon again to welcome you to our happy little town."

Hart's aunt—she was just pleased all over— was beginning to make a speech back to him; but Santa Fé looked so wore out Hart didn't give her the chance to go on. He just grabbed her, and got her away in a hurry—and Charley went to fussing with the cover of the wheel, putting it on again, so she wasn't able to shake hands with him for good-bye. When she'd fairly lit out, and he was quit of her, Charley felt that weak, he said, he sung out for Mike—Mike was the barkeep at

the Forest Queen—to come and get the sheets
down quick from in front of the bar and give
him his own bottle of Bourbon and a tumbler.
And he said he'd never took so many drinks, one
right on top of another, since he was born!

There was more'n the usual crowd down at the
deepo that night when the Denver train pulled
out—with Hart's aunt in the Pullman, and Hart
standing on the Pullman platform telling the boys
up to the last minute how much he was obliged.

Things went that same Sunday-school way
right on to the end of the game; and Hart said
his aunt told him—as they was coming along
down to the deepo—she never would 'a' believed
there could be such a town as Palomitas was, out
in that wild frontier country, if she hadn't seen it
with her own eyes. As to the ladies of the town,
he said she told him they certainly was the most
domestic she'd ever known!

Hart was so grateful—and he had a right to be
—he left a hundred dollars with Tenderfoot Sal
and told her to blow off the town for him by running a free bar that night at the Forest Queen.
She did it, right enough—and it turned out to be
about the hottest night Palomitas ever had. All
hands allowed, afterwards, that even if there
hadn't been no free bar, things likely would 'a'
been about the same—seeing the town felt the
need of getting back to being natural, and was
all strung up and had to work itself off.

A FINANCIAL GENIUS

BY HENRY EDWARD ROOD

HIRAM BISWEL was his name; Hiram Y. Biswel
—the Y. standing for Yupsilon, he said, which
some thought was a hero of ancient Greece, and
others a new kind of breakfast-food. Anyway,
that was his name, so far as any of us in the village ever found out, which, after all, is the main
thing. For while a rose may smell as sweet if
you call it a German pancake, yet it jars on the
nerves, which is bad physiologically.

Well, Hiram came to town one day last au-
tumn and opened a general store, where he sold
everything in the grocery and drygoods line; also
such innocuous medicinal comforts as porous-
plasters and witch-hazel and rat poison and bad
cigars—vicious these last were, positively wicked.
And he laid in a stock of toys and picture-books,
and fancy Bibles bound in beautiful colors, and
hymnals, and horse liniment, and fountain-pens,
and vases, and other bric-à-bracs. He was particularly strong on bric-à-brac of all sorts and
sizes, but these were not for sale. They were
gifts, souvenirs, mementoes of visits to Hiram's

store. In order to get a bric-à-brac all you had
to do was to buy a dollar's worth of goods, and
receive as a present ten pale écru trading-stamps.
When you got a thousand stamps you cashed 'em
in at Hiram's little money-counter—and Hiram
would let you take your pick of his windowful of
glass vases and china match-boxes.

Now, there was no objection to all that—bar-
ring the cigars, of course—and the custom is generally followed by highly esteemed merchants
everywhere. If Hiram Yupsilon Biswel had
known when he was well off he would have
stopped right there, for he was doing a mighty
satisfactory business in butter, cheese, hair-oil,
eggs, rubber boots, prepared flour, chest-pro-
tectors, and other luxuries. But of course competition sprang up, and old Smith (who has had
a store here for thirty years) laid in several miles
of blue trading-stamps, and for a while some of
his lifetime customers came back to him; but not
for long.

Hiram had been in town about seven minutes
when he learned that, besides smaller ones, there
were two important churches here — the old
original body called the First, and the younger,
called the Second. The people had split off several years previous over the question as to
whether a missionary box should be sent to North
Dakota or South Dakota, and half the congraga-
tion walked out of the First Church and organized the Second. They were so all-fired mad at

the other congregation that they put their hands
deep into their pockets without any urging, and
erected a fine modern building, engaged a chipper
young minister, and started off with a bang.
Old Mr. Smith went with the new crowd, and although he sent half his family regularly to the
First Church, yet he was always regarded as belonging to the Second.   So when Hiram landed
in town he opened his store for business and
promptly identified himself with the old congregation—also for business.

It was astonishing how active Hiram became
in that First Church.   He was in the choir the
second Sunday; he attended every prayer-meeting, and took part earnestly.   After the church
service, morning and evening, he would step up
to the minister and shake hands, and say what a
fine sermon it was, and what a privilege he felt it
to listen to such words of comfort and encourage-
ment.   Hiram was a white alley, all right, and
there weren't any nicks on him, either, to impede
the smoothness of his progress.   He was generous
in his contributions, too, and took such an interest in the money affairs of the church that by
Thanksgiving they made him chairman of the
finance committee.   The old chairman was mighty
glad to resign (although Hiram didn't know it
then); for the First Church had been having a
mighty hard struggle to get along for a year or
two, and the outlook was so poor that half the
time the fire in the stove got discouraged and

went out. But as soon as Hiram had skimmed over the books and old envelopes and scraps of brown paper on which the church's accounts were kept, he sized up the situation. Then he sat down to think; but soon he got up with a smile on his face and a well-defined plan in his head, and called a special meeting of the finance committee for that evening, which was Saturday.

At the close of the service next morning the minister stepped to one side of the pulpit and remarked:

"We are all requested to remain in the church for a few minutes while the chairman of the finance committee makes an important announcement. I do not know just what Mr. Biswel has to say, but I'm sure we shall all listen with interest and profit."

Then he walked down to the floor of the church and sat in a pew, while Hiram mounted the pulpit steps and began without any urging.

"You all know, of course," he said, "that it's been hard work to raise funds to keep going here. But now we've sort of struck on a plan which will undoubtedly set our minds at rest, and provide all the cash we need—and," he added, with emphasis, "nobody 'll have to spend any more'n they do now.

"At considerable expense to myself," he went on, without even stopping to clear his throat, "I have arranged with the greatest supply-house in the country to give me a mail-order agency here, so that in addition to the luxurious and substantial stock I already carry, I will be able after this to provide everything on earth for man, woman, or beast to eat, wear, smell, look at, hear, or think of.   Now, don't make any mistake in your own mind about this until I finish.   Commencing with the service to-night, each woman who comes to church will receive free, gratis, for nothing, a yellow ticket with her name written on it to show that she really was here in church this Sunday. The ticket will be good for one week only.   And every lady getting one can come to my store as often as she wants for the next six days, and upon buying goods there and showing the yellow ticket she will get twice the usual number of trading-stamps as she's received heretofore, which is ten trading-stamps for every dollar's worth purchased.   But if she has the yellow ticket she gets twenty stamps.

"In view of the fact that I am willing to give double the ordinary value on all purchases, it is expected, of course, that holders of the yellow tickets will increase their church contributions. That's all."

Then Hiram skeetered down the pulpit steps, and left the church by the back door.

All that afternoon the village fairly buzzed with excitement.   Everybody told everybody else, and when Hiram arrived at church that evening, half an hour ahead of time, he found the vestibule jammed with women, children, and

babies, all anxious—and most of them hollering
—for yellow tickets.   Before he got this crowd
fixed up properly, a lot of others came streaming
in, many belonging to the Second Church; but a
lot more from the Methodist, Baptist, Presby-
terian and Episcopal congregations.   Hiram certainly did have his hands full, and after that he
made it a rule to write the names out beforehand,
and on Sunday swap new cards already prepared
for the old ones that had been in use a week.   Of
course, the service was delayed that first evening,
and it was an hour late in beginning, but every
pew was filled, and the collection jumped from
an average of twelve dollars to thirty-eight dollars.   Mighty few were willing to accept Hiram's
yellow cards without dropping a nickel or a dime
in the collection-box, and Hiram had counted on
just that thing.   He had schemed it all out in
advance, and he knew human nature like a book.

The idea naturally created no end of a row in
the community.   When the elders and deacons
and trustees and various officers of the other
churches heard of that scheme they simply ripped
and reared up on their hind feet.   People down
in the Second Church tried to get Hiram and the
pastor of the First Church indicted on a charge
of running a gambling-house, and named the First
Church as the place of gambling.   But the wives
of three grand jurors, and of the foreman and the
public prosecutor, had yellow tickets; so no in-
dictment was found.   By Wednesday afternoon

7

Hiram had sold for cash pretty nearly everything in his store except twenty-seven lamp-chimneys that were cracked, and Wednesday evening an old lady bought these on her way to prayer-meeting. It was awful, the business Hiram Yupsilon did those few days, and he had to telephone for a car-load of assorted stock to come by fast freight, or he'd have had to close his shop by Friday. As it was, he hired all of old Smith's clerks at a big advance in their wages, or nobody could have handled the gangs of women that infested his store, shaking money in the air, clamoring to buy, and demanding trading-stamps by the barrel. Hiram couldn't attend to them; it was all he could do to rake in the cash they shoved at him and give back what little change was needed.

That first week he increased his sales about seven hundred per cent., while poor old Smith used to shut up his store at three o'clock in the afternoon and go out in the woods and cuss. He was particularly and enthusiastically mad, was old Smith, because Hiram took on an agency for a coal-yard, and lots of women induced their husbands to lay in a winter's supply at once. The young man sold about two hundred tons that week, and took in one thousand dollars from that alone. The next week he added a piano agency and life-insurance and fire-insurance, and bought a burglar-proof safe seven feet high. He needed it, too, for the nearest bank was twelve miles distant.

The third Sunday that old First Church was so jammed with people that they sat all over the pulpit steps, and stood in the aisles packed like herring. The road in front of the church for one-quarter of a mile in each direction was jammed with all sorts of wagons and buggies and carryalls from farms and surrounding villages; it seemed as if the whole township was turned loose in the direction of the First Church. Hiram appeared promptly, as he always did, but pale and hag-gard, for he was pretty nearly exhausted with business; and he absolutely refused to help take up the collection.

"I just can't stand it!" he gurgled, passing the box to another deacon. "I'm so sick of money that the sight of it fairly turns my stomach."

So the others gathered in one hundred and ninety-six dollars and twenty-five cents that evening, and turned it over to the chairman of the finance committee. The next day—Monday —there were seventy-five women waiting at his store when he opened the doors for business, and they kept coming in such numbers that he didn't shut up shop until 1 A.M. Tuesday. Then he started in to count receipts, and had barely got through when he had to open up again at seven o'clock or see his glass smashed in by the throng outside. Goods kept arriving on every train, and every wagon in the village was busy hauling them to his store, where they would remain a few hours and then be taken away to purchasers.

Thursday night Hiram sent for the doctor, and on Friday morning the village learned that he was a wreck from nervous prostration and had started for Colorado to regain his health. Then the city papers got hold of the news, and by night Hiram's creditors began to arrive. They broke into the store, and found nothing there but empty shelves and a safe weighing three tons, which contained a good deal of air and some dust.

We don't look forward very hopefully to seeing Hiram Yupsilon Biswel in our midst again—at least not in the near future. And a good many wouldn't be at all surprised to hear any day that the State of Colorado was missing from its accustomed place in the Union.

MRS. NOAH'S ARK

BY GELETT BURGESS

Mrs. Noah Figtry stood upon the huge front gallery, between the Doric columns of the "big house," her hands clasped beneath her blue gingham apron, dispiritedly regarding the main road, a hundred yards away. Her pursed New England lips expressed disapproval. It was March, and March is disconsolate enough anywhere, but the cold gray day made the down-at-the-heels plantation seem more ruinous than ever. Mrs. Noah was alone, in temporary possession of the house, having come from New England to take charge during her son-in-law's absence. The prospect of two weeks' loneliness in this dreary environment was, to a person of her lively temperament, depressing.

"If the Lord would only send *something* interesting, I wouldn't mind, if it was only a plaid pig," she mused.

As if in answer to this prayer, at that moment a little procession appeared coming round a turn of the road. It was led by a pleasant-looking man in blue overalls, who guided with his hands

the shafts of a highly decorated circus cage on
gilded wheels, which was pushed by a solemn,
wrinkled, muddy elephant, bending his forehead
to the rear of the car. The beast was directed
in his labors by a barelegged Oriental-looking person with a turban and white blouse, who walked
alongside. Behind this group stalked a giraffe,
who bore, seated perilously astride, a buxom,
smiling woman of some forty years.

"For the land sakes!" Mrs. Noah ejaculated,
"if that don't beat the Book of Revelation! I
wonder if I'm dreamin' 'em, or are they really
alive? If that ain't the tag-end of a circus, I
never see a wild-beast show in *my* life. I do believe they're turnin' in here, and me in my apron
and curl-papers!"

Directly in front of the door the elephant, at a
word from his driver, stopped, and the procession
came to a stand-still. The woman slid gracefully
down from her perch, with a sigh of relief; the
man in blue overalls dropped his shafts and came
up to the front steps, taking off his hat.

"Good-afternoon," he said, politely. "Pretty
muddy roads you have along here."

"What in the world did you bring them critters
in here for?" was Mrs. Noah's rejoinder. "If
you expect to set up a show in my front yard, I
may as well tell you that it ain't worth the trouble.
They ain't nobody here but me and the malaria."

"Lady, I'd like to introduce the Princess Ziffio,
the snake-charmer and contortionist, and Ramo

Bung, the elephant-driver, late of Sorrowtop's Circus," the man explained. "My name is Steggins, and I'm a lion-tamer from the same show."

"I'm proud to know you. It ain't often I meet celebrities in these parts," was Mrs. Noah's welcome, as she placidly awaited further developments.

"You see, it's this way, lady," Mr. Steggins went on, affably: "The show's bust up on account of a small financial difficulty, bringing on a seizure by the sheriff. Now, as me and my partners 'ain't been paid our salaries for two months, we just laid our hands on what we could find last night and are holding them as security for the money that's due us. It ain't our fault that the manager was crooked, and we don't propose to pay his debts; so what we want you to do is to let us hide the animals in your place until we can find a scow to take 'em down the river and sell 'em."

"What in the world do you mean?" Mrs. Noah exclaimed. "I 'ain't got any tent, nor even a barn. I'm real sorry for you, but I don't see what I can do— There's the old mill down by the river."

"That won't do at all," said Steggins, uneasily; "the sheriff will look there first thing. It ain't so easy to hide an elephant and a giraffe. We got to put 'em in some place where people won't be likely to suspect. See here; if you'll let us hide our property in your house for a week, we'll agree to pay you two hundred and fifty dollars as soon as we've sold the beasts."

"Why, you can't ever get that critter through the front-door, much less up-stairs," said Mrs. Noah, pointing to the elephant.

Ramo Bung now broke in, excitedly. "Oh yes, yes!" he exclaimed; "it is a just perfection of sizes. You regard with pleasure?" He snatched a hoe from the ground by the front steps and applied it to the elephant's side in measurement. The creature was not a large one, being only one and a half hoe-handles in height. Running up to the double front-doors, the Hindu demonstrated the possibility of entrance. "You accept the certainty? Even he can with kneeling crawl, I guiding in wisdom!"

Mrs. Noah Figtry had already rapidly estimated what two hundred and fifty dollars could do to improve her son-in-law's place. In an instant her mind was made up, her cool, practical head defeated by her childlike emotions and kind, indulgent heart.

"Well," she said, "when Ebeneezer left I didn't calculate to take in no boarders, but if you think you can get that elephant into the parlor, I don't know but what I'll let you try it, just to see how you come out. I can't think what you can do with a giraffe, unless you put his head up a chimney somewheres. But perhaps he can be made to go in the bath-room with a little squeezin'. What you got in that bag, anyway? Looks like

it was boilin'. I won't tolerate no rabbits! Of
all things, I do hate a rabbit."

The Princess Ziffio was already loosening the
ropes which bound the sack, and at this moment
the mass fell to the ground and began to squirm
convulsively.

"Snakes, I do declare! I can't abide snakes.
I couldn't sleep a wink at night! You just take
that bag of varmints as far away from the house
as you can get it."

"Oh, he won't hurt you," asserted the Princess;
"he's only a boy-constrictor, and he's got thawed
out in the sun, that's all. We'll just put him in
a cool place, and he won't give you a bit of
trouble."

"There ain't no cellar to this house, and the
coolest place I know is the ice-chest. He might
possibly scrouge in there, though I can't say as
I'd be at all easy in my mind about it. They
ain't any lock on the door." Mrs. Noah was still
holding her skirts raised, and kept at a safe distance.

Hardly had she said this, when a terrific and
prolonged roar of blood-curdling intensity shook
the shutters of the cage. Mrs. Noah was inside
the house in an instant, behind barred doors.
She reappeared later at the parlor window, which
she gently raised a quarter of an inch. "You
never said nothin' about lions," she cried, hys-
terically. "I consider I'm doin' considerable to
welcome an elephant into my front-parlor, and a

giraffe in the bath-room, but roarin' lions is al-
together *too* much. You go along and don't
bother me any more."

Mr. Steggins reassured her with a laughing
voice. "Why, lady," he said, "Joshua wouldn't
hurt a fly. He was born in captivity, and he's
forty years old, without a tooth in his head.
He's tame as a puppy. I can have him right in
my room. He wouldn't roar if he wa'n't so
hungry, but he hasn't been fed for two days, and
then only bones and sawdust."

Mrs. Noah˙ timidly emerged again. "You
'ain't got any seven-horned beasts or nothin',
have you? That roar did give me a start, but I
don't know but I might as well be hung for a
sheep as a lamb if I've got to keep house for a
whole menagerie. It does seem a shame to leave
a dumb animal outside without a roof to help himself to, don't it? I'll go up and sit on the ridge-
pole while you get that critter into the house;
and mind you lock the door after him when you
get him up-stairs. I ain't goin' to be devoured
by a ragin', rampin' lion at *my* time of life." At
that she scurried up-stairs, and, a little later,
appeared on the flat roof, from which post of
security she surveyed the installation over the
eaves.

One shutter was removed from the side of the
cage, and Joshua—a tawny, dignified Numidian
lion—was discovered, his eyes blinking with the
unaccustomed glare. Into his den Steggins en-

tered nonchalantly by a door in the rear, and threw a noose round the beast's neck. The lion arose and shook himself like a dog, and then, urged by a slap on the rump, slowly descended from the cage and was dragged unresistingly into the house.

Mrs. Noah, who had been gazing in terror, now breathed freer. After the interval her caution demanded she descended from the roof, and hurrying breathlessly down-stairs, joined the perspiring group on the portico. Princess Ziffio informed her that the serpent had already been safely removed to its new abode.

All the lighter pieces of furniture having been moved into the back room, proceedings were now begun with the elephant, who was manœuvred clumsily up the creaking front steps under the guidance of Ramo Bung, who emitted a stream of directions in Hindustani. A violent percussion against the door-jambs, the crash of a newel-post, and the overturning of a hat-rack marked his progress into the front-parlor, where he rested quietly, exploring the precincts within range of his trunk.

Only the giraffe now remained, patiently grazing on the Virginia-creeper that grew over the columns.

His entrance was effected with a grotesque awkwardness that made Mrs. Noah laugh, in spite of her fear for the transom. His neck was bent stiffly down like a pump-handle by the

weight of Steggins, who was forced to climb a
chair to reach the animal's horns. But once inside the hallway, he was propelled rapidly, though
reluctantly, into the bath-room. The upper sash
of the window was dropped, and the animal took
advantage of the aperture to gaze at the levee on
the bank of the Mississippi, about a mile distant.

The four conspirators entered the house at
last, fairly safe against discovery. The lion-
tamer and the Hindu left to complete their preparations for the animal's comfort, while Mrs. Noah
and Princess Ziffio set about getting dinner in the
kitchen.

"Well," said the hostess, when the quartet was
assembled about the dining-room table, "I've
often seen 'Entertainment for Man and Beast'
on tavern sign-boards, but the last thing I ever
thought I'd be doin' was that! What do you feed
the critters, anyway?"

"Those sucking-pigs will do just right for the
lion. One a day is enough," Mr. Steggins said.
"Hay or corn-husks for the elephant and giraffe."

"Do tell! Why, I thought you fed elephants
on peanuts!" was Mrs. Noah's comment. She
turned to the Princess: "What do you want to
give your snake in the ice-box? Eggs, I s'pose."

"Oh, he won't need anything at all. He was
fed only last New Year's Day."

"My land! He'd make a prime husband for
a lazy woman, wouldn't he?" said Mrs. Noah.
Then she looked curiously at the woman.

"Whatever are you princess of, anyway?" she inquired, regarding the snake-charmer's good-natured, stupid face, her heavy coils of straight black hair and the elaborate curl swinging over her nose. "I'd never suspect your father was a king, though they *do* say emperors and sultans and such are as thick as flies in August out in them heathen lands of Asia."

"Oh, Mr. Gentry, our advertising man, made up that name for me. I'm really Mrs. Bung. Ramo here is my husband, though we was married only last month."

Ramo Bung showed a score of glittering white teeth as he clasped his wife's fat, pudgy hand ecstatically. "Yes, yes, we are allies quite undoubtedly!" he proclaimed. "Even the honeymoon is not yet out, and our hearts are packed to tightening with quite absolute blisses!"

"By-the-way, don't you think you could get your elephant's feet out the side window, one at a time, and wash them off with a pail of water?" Mrs. Noah asked the Hindu, anxiously. "I'm afraid he's goin' to make dreadful unsightly work of that body-Brussels carpet in spite of the straw, stompin' around."

Ramo Bung bowed with immense deference. "It shall doubtless be experimented at, Mrs. Lady. I will be endeavoring to Jumbo the Junior with the next morning. He is being at this time unremittingly fastened against the leg of piano. Only to-night with careless training he shall acquire the machination of the folding-bed for helpfulness of myself. It can be opened and shut easily, assisted by proboscis, doubtlessly."

Steggins, who felt an unfeigned fondness for his own charge, now spoke up: "Mrs. Figtry, you really ought to know Joshua better. You'd learn to like him like I do when you see how affectionate he is. Why, if you rub his neck, he'll purr like a kitten, and I'd sleep with him if only he didn't snore so. I left him all curled up on that fourpost bed of yours, and I'll be darned if he didn't wave his paw at me like a baby when I left."

"I suppose lions ain't really no more than great big cats, after all," said Mrs. Noah, "but I never looked at 'em in that light before. I expect he might like some milk to-night. I could spare you a washbowl full just as well as not, if you promised he wouldn't spill it. I would like to have him get after the rats in the woodshed. They do beat all Greely out there."

The Hindu interposed, excitedly. "Have a fear! have a fear!" he cried; "Jumbo the Junior is distracted of mice from out his brains, yes! Even in the number of one small mouse his insides turn, and he trumpets of extremest caution. Two mouses will he break his constriction —very so, indeed! How say further what mices of three will obtain by him? It is of fury certainly. I must be vigilant with candles all inside the night-time."

Mrs. Noah gasped. "Dear me suz!" she exclaimed, "elephants are just as bad as women-folks, ain't they? I do hope he won't jump on that parlor-table if he's frightened. They ain't nothin' can happen to your snake, is they?" she inquired of the Princess. "I do believe I left a lot of broilers in the ice-chest. Well, never mind; I expect they are about half a mile down his throat by this time."

After dinner, their extraordinary live stock having been fed and watered and the dishes washed, Mrs. Noah was persuaded to visit her four-footed guests. She waited outside the up-per bedroom door until Steggins had entered, lighted a lamp, and tied the lion to the bed-post. Then she went in on tiptoe, as if visiting a sick-room, speaking in a hushed whisper.

"Well, of all things! Ain't he too cute for any-thing?" she said. "I never thought a wild lion could feel so much to home in a back bedroom."

Joshua was crouching in a kittenish pose upon the braided rag rug, lazily licking his paws. He raised his heavy head to blink with yellow eyes at his landlady.

"Well, as I'm a sinner, he's getting bald!" she exclaimed. "I'll bet a hairpin I could cure him and keep his mane from falling out!" In her in-terest she approached the brute fearlessly and laid a hand upon his neck. Joshua purred with a basso-profundo church-organ vibration. "Dan-druff! I thought so. Looks like a snow-storm. Here, Mr. Steggins, you just reach me that bottle of Paderewski Hirsutine in the medicine-closet over your head, and I'll have a good growth of new hair started in less than a week. Say, does lion's hair ever turn gray? I've got some Brunette Rejuvenator that 'll fix his color just as natural as life. Or I don't know but what you'd call him a blond, after all. Seems to me he's kind o' betwixt an' between. He's sandy-complected, I should say." She regarded him judicially. "I believe I'll look up a ball of yarn for him to play with," she said, as she left. "I had no idea lions behaved so clever. Why, they're as much like folks as second cousins."

Her next visit was to the front-parlor, where Jumbo Junior stood rocking to and fro like a ship at anchor in a swell, his lithe trunk questing the air with sinuous curves. He held it out to her inquisitively. She attempted to shake hands with him, but he drew back. "You ought to teach that critter better manners," she remarked to the Hindu. "Though, to be sure, I never did quite know whether an elephant's trunk was most like a hand or a nose. *Will* you look at them toenails! I do hope there aren't any of them ingrowin'. What does he want, anyway?"

Jumbo Junior himself answered her question by deftly removing her stick-pin from the front of her dress and carefully inserting it in the ceiling. After this, he waved his trunk aloft, broke a piece of glass from the hanging-lamp shade, and threw it on the floor.

"My stars and garters, ain't he sassy! Now I've always heard that elephants had more intelligence than all the other animals put together. You'd think he'd know he'd got to walk round this room barefoot. How much do you suppose he could lift?"

"Entire immenseness, past eight horses," said the Hindu. "In Cawnpore, I did see a lonesome elephant push a house downside."

Mrs. Noah gazed musingly upon the elephant's bulk: "I've often wished that piano could be moved into the back room, but these niggers here ain't no more use than woodchucks. If you want to give him a stint, there's lots of chores round the house he'll be real handy at. . . . But I expect you hadn't ought to require a parlor-boarder to exert himself too much. If he's cold in the night, I've got a spare bedspread up in the garret. Now try to shake hands again, Jumbo. You must act genteel when you're in my parlor." And after shaking the elephant's trunk cordially, she left the room.

Then she visited the giraffe in the bath-room. Accompanied by the Princess, she opened the door, to find the animal still standing at the window, gazing pensively out into the night. As they entered, the giraffe's head turned in their direction, and a pair of melting brown eyes gazed down at them. Her mouth opened and emitted a noise that was something between a wheeze and a whinny.

8

"Now I was *afraid* that giraffe was going to catch his death of cold!" cried Mrs. Noah, her quick benevolence instantly aroused.

The Princess Ziffio laughed. "Oh, Milly, she's all right. I reckon she just smells the hay, that's all."

"Hay-fever! Just what I thought! I can't see a dumb beast suffer under my roof. I've got some of Dr. Surenuff's Celebrated Specific handy, and I'm goin' to rub it on his throat. It may take seven or eight bottles, but it's fortunate I've got plenty of it in the house. Just move in that step-ladder you'll see in the hall closet, please, and I'll go and get the remedy."

In a few minutes more she had mounted a somewhat unsteady perch and began to administer the lotion. "Strange how much this creature's eyes favor Lucy's," she said to herself, massaging energetically. "I always *did* admire brown eyes. Ebeneezer always used to say you can get a black eye too easy for 'em to be pretty. Lucy admires to get herself up in low-cut gowns; I s'pose she would even if she had a neck like this. Say, Princess, hand me up a couple of them crash bath-towels, will you? I think Milly ought to have a regular bandage. I'll take my needle and thread and sew em on good. Don't you think I might tie the top onto his horns so it won't slip down? Hold your head still, won't you, please! My land! the airs this critter puts on! Bridles like a girl of sixteen. There! I guess that 'll keep her from

gettin' any worse.   She does look ridiculous, don't
she?   If I once stop to laugh, I'll fall off this step-
ladder.''

The Princess gazed stolidly at the result.   "You
got an awful good heart, Mrs. Figtry,'' she said,
"but I don't reckon dumb animals suffer much
like us folks.''

"What! With all that throat to be sore?''
cried Mrs. Noah, descending the steps.   "Don't
you believe it!   Animals have got organs and
innerds just like ours.   If you'd cleaned and
drawn as many chickens as I have, you'd known
that.   Now what that animal wants is a good hot
bath and then be well wrapped up.   But I don't
suppose we could get her in the tub; that zinc's
too slippery; and then the water 'd never reach
up beyond her knees, anyway.   But I tell you
what I'm goin' to do, I'm goin' to fill a hot-water
bottle and fasten it on this giraffe's chest.   That 'll
do more good than anything else.   But where in
the world her neck leaves off and her chest begins I'm jiggered if I can tell!   I hope your snake
won't get sick, Princess, for I consider I'd have
to draw the line at reptiles.   They don't hardly
seem to deserve even pity from a Christian, but I
hope I won't be tempted to allow him to suffer.''

Mrs. Noah's ministrations were at last finished
by means of a complicated net of tapes, and the
two women bade the men good-night and prepared
for bed.   Their repose was somewhat broken, however, by the snoring of the trio of quadrupeds.

Joshua's almost continuous performance reverber-
ated through the night. Occasionally the plaintive
wheezing of the giraffe in the bath-room awoke
Mrs. Noah, and she made several trips of visitation
in her night-gown to renew the temperature of the
hot-water bottle by means of an alcohol-lamp and
a tea-kettle. The Princess, however, slept on
serenely. A heavy jar at midnight and a rattle of
window-panes at four o'clock in the morning
marked the limits of Jumbo Junior's deep sleep.
From the ice-chest no sound was heard.

So a few days passed, during which time Mr.
Steggins scoured the neighborhood to find some
raft or barge upon which to make his voyage to
Memphis. During his absence his hostess's acquaintance with the three animals and the married couple progressed towards friendship.

A feature of Mrs. Noah's methodical habits was
her diary—a small octavo bound in faded morocco
—the week-days laboriously altered from 1887,
the year of its publication, to the current calen-
dar. A few excerpts from this volume would indi-
cate the progress of events in her household.

"*Tuesday, March 27.*—Last night I heard Jumbo Junior whining in his sleep. Thought he might
have a tuskache. Went down-stairs with a bottle
of oil of clove and a wash-rag. Stepped on something at foot of stairs. Felt just like a big sausage,
only more energetic. Screamed. The Princess
(found out she really comes from Hoboken) come
down in her shawl. It was the big snake. Sat

on banisters while she gave it two soup-ladles full
of soothing-syrup. Ramo came out in Ebeneezer's
smoking-jacket and helped lift the snake into the
ice-chest. Elephant didn't have toothache, after
all.

"*Wednesday, March 28.*—Cloudy, S.W. wind.
Giraffe still enjoying poor health. Tried hot ap-
plications and tied two pairs of bed-socks on her
feet. Wrapped Ebeneezer's flannelette bathrobe
round her shoulders. Found later she had succeeded in getting a packet of pennyroyal, four
moth-balls, and a cigar out of the left-hand pocket
and was chewing them. Her swallow is 'way up
on top of her neck, not half-way down as I naturally expected. Have been trying to teach Jumbo
Junior to shake hands. He can drink a tumbler
of molasses very nicely. Joshua's hair seems to
be improving. Tried a little Hirsutine on his tail,
at the end. He got into my room and woke me
up at 3 A.M. Must have left his door open. Only
two pigs left.

So a week passed without Mrs. Noah's interesting family having been discovered by the sheriff,
and each day she became more fond of her new
friends. She watched, as with a doting mother's
eye, the improvement which she believed was apparent in Joshua's coat and the gentle Milly's
voice, while Jumbo Junior's adaptability to instruction pleased her beyond words. The silent,
inscrutable Princess baffled her, but the Hindu's

vocabulary and diction kept her in a continual glee.

"Oh, there is so muchness!" cried Ramo Bung, when he was shown the Mississippi. "Oh, be astonished beyond utterness!"

And so, when at last Steggins procured a raft and moored it to the pier by the molasses-shed, the kind-hearted hostess wiped away the tears that came to her eyes. The boa-constrictor she was indeed glad to be rid of, for it was the one cloud on her week of happiness, but when Milly's plaintive eyes had looked their last at her, and Joshua had been dragged, whining, aboard, it was all she could do to speak. It only remained for Jumbo Junior, of his own accord, to offer her his trunk for her to break down with emotion.

"I don't know *when* I've had such a pleasant time," she said. "I do hope you'll get to Memphis all right; and be sure and send me word how you get along and how Joshua stood the trip. Now here's four bottles of Smiley's Embrocation for Milly's neck and feet. Be sure you rub it well in, night and morning. If I only had a bottle of aconite pills, I'd like her to have them."

Steggins took her hand with a fierce grip. "Good-bye, Mis' Figtry," he said. "You treated us square, and we'll treat you square. Just as soon as I get to Memphis and sell the animals I'll send you the money. You've been a good friend to Joshua, and he'll never forget you, I know."

Ramo Bung prostrated himself before her in an

elaborate salaam. "Good-bye with condescen-
sion," he cried. "Bung family are in salutement
to your home with excellence. There is a doubtless explosion of violent heart on my interior.
Ever so much blessing come against you."

"Well," said Mrs. Noah, "now you've found
the way, I hope you'll come again sometime. The
world ain't such a big place but that we may meet
again."

Mrs. Noah sobbed as she watched the little ex-
pedition sweep away. Then, just as they were
abreast of the house, a long, muffled roar came to
her over the rushing waters, as Joshua lifted up
his voice in mournful lament. In spite of herself
she smiled through her tears.

Soon the barge was far away, rapidly diminish-
ing in the distance. When at last it drifted out
of her sight she turned to her cook-stove and
brewed a pot of strong tea.

"Well," she said, over the third cup, "what
can't be cured must be endured. I must say this
place looks like Sam Patch in a hail-storm—I
guess it 'll do me good to go to spring cleanin'!"

The month of April, a year later, found Mrs.
Noah Figtry home again in Duxbury, immersed
in the quiet of New England life. From the quaint
collection of friends that she had made in Tennes-
see no word had come, except a draft for two hundred and fifty dollars and a short misspelled letter
from Mr. Steggins, announcing their safe arrival

in Memphis, and subsequent sale of the animals, and employment by Wilder's Triplex Conglomeration.

It was with a feeling of keen disappointment, then, that, returning late one Saturday night from a week's visit in Boston, she learned that Wilder's circus had been in town. It was breaking camp that very night, and would on Sunday proceed to Plymouth. Mrs. Noah, eagerly interrogating her neighbors, found scant satisfaction in their reports. The show, it was true, boasted a small menagerie, including a lion, a giraffe, and two elephants, but it was not easy to identify the animals from the meagre description she received.

"I should know Joshua anywhere by a scar on his left cheek," Mrs. Noah declared, "but as for Jumbo Junior and Milly, I ain't so sure I'd recognize them, unless I met a wheezing giraffe and an elephant that volunteered to shake hands with me. But it seems strange that nobody saw that mealy-mouthed Hindu and the snake-princess. As for Mr. Steggins, he ain't the kind of man that's likely to keep any job long, and maybe he's in Terra del Fuego by this time. Howsomever, I'm determined to go over to Plymouth on Monday to see the show. I'll spear around, and if I don't see any folks or critters I know, I'll inquire. They say these show-people all know each other."

On Sunday morning Mrs. Noah Figtry proceeded decorously to church. As she approached the meeting-house, she observed an unusual stir among the villagers on the street, and upon the steps of the edifice were groups of church-members excitedly discussing some surprising piece of news. A band of small boys charged by her on the run, their faces lighted by adventurous anticipation. Deftly capturing one by the arm, Mrs. Noah demanded information. The answer was sufficiently alarming. Wilder's Triplex Conglomeration, en route for Plymouth, had discovered that the door of the lion's cage had been left open and its occupant was missing. Somewhere between Kingston and Duxbury a lion was at large, and a party of searchers from the circus was now on the animal's trail.

The second bell had already rung, but no one felt in a devotional mood, and the minister himself soon came out to learn the latest developments of the situation. A dozen plans for the capture of the beast were offered and debated. Mrs. Noah, an acknowledged authority on lions, was at her best, and became the centre of an admiring audience, to whom she described, as one with experience, the power of the human eye, the influence of kindness.

She was in the midst of her discourse, when of a sudden came a chorus of shrieks from down the road. A stampede of small boys swept back towards the growing concourse of people, and a prolonged roar in the distance proclaimed that the approach of the lion was imminent. In an instant the street was cleared. The crowd scuttled into the church, slammed the doors, and flew to the windows. On the steps only the bolder members of the congregation remained, anxiously peering down the road. Among these men and boys Mrs. Noah stood calm and dignified, the only woman who dared venture out.

Then around the curve by the post-office came a galloping tawny brute, scattering the dust in clouds as he ran. The watchers on the church steps, terrified by the sight, burst inside the church, leaving Mrs. Noah alone to confront the situation. She grasped the handle of her parasol tighter, and waited with supreme confidence till the last possible moment. The lion had now settled into a stealthy trot, and seemed about to pass the building without molesting its occupants, when Mrs. Noah, who had been gazing intently at him, took a step forward.

"It *is* Joshua, as I live!" she exclaimed; "there's that self-same scar on his cheek, I declare!"

At the sound of her voice, the lion stopped immediately and stood lashing his tail. Then his heavy muzzle was raised, his fangless jaws opened, and he emitted a mournful roar. Mrs. Figtry stood her ground.

"Joshua, Joshua," she called to him, as one calls to a stray poodle; "don't you know me, Joshua?" and she started down the steps.

From the windows and through a hazardous slit of half-opened door the astonished members of the congregation stared upon a marvel. They

SHE SPOKE KINDLY AND PLEASANTLY TO THE LION

saw her boldly approach the beast and lay her
hand calmly upon his head. They saw his blood-
thirsty rage wilt into docility as Joshua recognized
his former benefactor. One by one the church-
goers crept out upon the steps to witness this unwonted scene, the men first, the women following,
timid but curious, ready at a moment's notice to
bolt back into their refuge.

"You needn't be a bit scared," Mrs. Noah was
saying. "I'll tend to this lion," grabbing him by
the ear and swinging him round. "He's all heat
up, anyhow. Deacon Skinner, can't you let me
take your overcoat to wrap him up with? This
southwest wind isn't like what he's used to in the
tropics of Sahara, and I'm afraid he'll catch cold,
perspiring so."

She took the overcoat that was hesitatingly
offered her, spread it carefully on Joshua's back,
pinning the sleeves around his neck. Then she
sat herself upon his hind-quarters as he lay in the
middle of the road, and proceeded to give further
orders.

"Now, Deacon Skinner, I want you should
bring your buggy round here. I've got to take
this lion home. It wouldn't do for him to stay
here, and if he walks I'm afraid he'll be run into
by some team. He ain't much used to travellin'
afoot."

Deacon Skinner was meekly obedient, and going
round to the sheds, untied his horse and led him
back. But at the first sight of the lion the horse

became paralyzed with terror.   Nothing could in-
duce him to move forward.   The dilemma seemed
unsolvable.   Mrs. Figtry looked up and down the
road in despair.   Then the rhythmic thud of ma-
chinery was heard as an automobile touring-car
came rapidly towards them.

Without a word, but with lips compressed, Mrs.
Figtry stepped directly into its path.   There, hold-
ing her parasol in front of her, she opened and shut
it rapidly, making frantic signals to the chauffeur.
He came to a stop a few feet away from her.
There was no one else in the car.

"See here," she cried to him; "can't you take
me and this lion back to the circus in your steam-
engine?   It's nothing more nor less than cruelty to
animals to let him stay here, and horses are scared
to death of him."   She paused for his reply.

The chauffeur, with a grin, pulled off his mask
of goggles.   It was Steggins.   "Why, how-de-do,
Mis' Figtry?" he cried.   "I'm proud to see you!
Step right in.   I never calculated to see you or
Joshua again, least of all together.   Come, Josh-
ua," he commanded.

At the sound of his master's voice the old lion
leaped into the automobile.   Here he was pushed
into a back seat.   Mrs. Figtry, after seeing that
the overcoat was well wrapped about the animal's
shoulders, got in beside him.   In another instant
the car had bounded off down the road.   The awe-
struck congregation watched its heroine well round
the turn and then filed into church.

TOM'S AUNT

BY MARK TWAIN

TOM SAWYER's Aunt Polly was one of those people who are infatuated with patent medicines and all new-fangled methods of producing health or mending it. She was an inveterate experi-menter in these things. When something fresh in this line came out she was in a fever, right away, to try it; not on herself, for she was never ailing, but on anybody else that came handy. She was a subscriber for all the "Health" periodicals and phrenological frauds; and the solemn ignorance they were inflated with was breath to her nostrils. All the "rot" they contained about ventilation, and how to go to bed, and how to get up, and what to eat, and what to drink, and how much exercise to take, and what frame of mind to keep one's self in, and what sort of clothing to wear, were all gospel to her, and she never observed that her health journals of the current month customarily upset everything they had recommended the month before. She was as simple-hearted and honest as the day was long, and so she was an easy victim. She gathered together her quack periodicals and her quack medicines, and thus armed with death, went about on her pale horse, metaphorically speaking, with "hell following after." But she never suspected that she was not an angel of healing, and the balm of Gilead in disguise, to the suffering neighbors.

The water treatment was new, now, and Tom's low condition was a windfall to her. She had him out at daylight every morning, stood him up in the woodshed, and drowned him with a deluge of cold water; then she scrubbed him down with a towel like a file, and so brought him to; then she rolled him up in a wet sheet and put him away under blankets till she sweated his soul clean and "the yellow stains of it came through his pores"—as Tom said.

Yet notwithstanding all this, the boy grew more and more melancholy and pale and dejected. She added hot baths, sitz baths, shower baths, and plunges. The boy remained as dismal as a hearse. She began to assist the water with a slim oatmeal diet and blister plasters. She calculated his capacity as she would a jug's, and filled him up every day with quack cure-alls.

Tom had become indifferent to persecution by this time. This phase filled the old lady's heart with consternation. This indifference must be broken up at any cost. Now she heard of Painkiller for the first time. She ordered a lot at once. She tasted it and was filled with gratitude. It was simply fire in a liquid form. She dropped the water treatment and everything else, and pinned her faith to Pain-killer. She gave Tom a teaspoonful, and watched with the deepest anxiety for the result. Her troubles were instantly at rest, her soul at peace again; for the "indifference" was broken up. The boy could not have shown a wilder, heartier interest, if she had built a fire under him.

Tom felt that it was time to wake up; this sort of life might be romantic enough, in his blighted condition, but it was getting to have too little sentiment and too much distracting variety about it.

So he thought over various plans for relief, and finally hit upon that of professing to be fond of Pain-killer. He asked for it so often that he became a nuisance, and his aunt ended by telling him to help himself and quit bothering her. If it had been Sid, she would have had no misgivings to alloy her delight; but since it was Tom, she watched the bottle clandestinely. She found that the medicine did really diminish, but it did not occur to her that the boy was mending the health of a crack in the sitting-room floor with it.

One day Tom was in the act of dosing the crack, when his aunt's yellow cat came along, purring, eying the teaspoon avariciously, and begging for a taste. Tom said:

"Don't ask for it unless you want it, Peter."

But Peter signified that he did want it.

"You better make sure."

Peter was sure.

"Now you've asked for it, and I'll give it to you, because there ain't anything mean about *me;* but if you find you don't like it, you mustn't blame anybody but your own self."

Peter was agreeable. So Tom pried his mouth open and poured down the Pain-killer. Peter sprang a couple of yards in the air, and then delivered a war-whoop and set off round and round the room, banging against furniture, upsetting flower-pots, and making general havoc. Next he rose on his hind feet and pranced around, in a frenzy of enjoyment, with his head over his shoulder and his voice proclaiming his unappeasable happiness. Then he went tearing around the house again, spreading chaos and destruction in his path. Aunt Polly entered in time to see him throw a few double summersets, deliver a final mighty hurrah, and sail through the open window, carrying the rest of the flower-pots with him. The old lady stood petrified with astonishment, peering over her glasses; Tom lay on the floor expiring with laughter.

"Tom, what on earth ails that cat?"

"*I* don't know, aunt," gasped the boy.

"Why, I never see anything like it. What *did* make him act so?"

"'Deed I don't know, Aunt Polly: cats always act so when they're having a good time."

"They do, do they?" There was something in the tone that made Tom apprehensive.

"Yes'm. That is, I believe they do."

"You *do?*"

"Yes'm."

The old lady was bending down, Tom watching with interest emphasized by anxiety. Too late he divined her "drift." The handle of the tell-tale teaspoon was visible under the bed-valance. Aunt Polly took it, held it up. Tom winced, and dropped his eyes. Aunt Polly raised him by the usual handle — his ear — and cracked his head soundly with her thimble.

"Now, sir, what do you want to treat that poor dumb beast so for?"

"I done it out of pity for him—because he hadn't any aunt."

"Hadn't any aunt!—you numskull. What has that got to do with it?"

"Heaps. Because if he'd a had one she'd a burst him out herself! She'd a roasted his bowels out of him 'thout any more feeling than if he was a human!"

Aunt Polly felt a sudden pang of remorse. This was putting the thing in a new light; what was cruelty to a cat *might* be cruelty to a boy, too. She began to soften; she felt sorry. Her eyes watered a little, and she put her hand on Tom's head and said, gently:

"I was meaning for the best, Tom. And, Tom, it *did* do you good."

Tom looked up in her face with just a perceptible twinkle peeping through his gravity.

9

"I know you was meaning for the best, aunty, and so was I with Peter. It done *him* good, too. I never see him get around so since—"

"Oh, go 'long with you, Tom, before you aggravate me again. And you try and see if you can't be a good boy, for once, and you needn't take any more medicine."

THE FABLE OF SPRINGFIELD'S FAIREST FLOWER AND LONESOME AGNES WHO WAS CRAFTY

BY GEORGE ADE

SPRINGFIELD had a Girl who was being Courted by a Syndicate. She was the Girl who took First Prize at the Business Men's Carnival. When the Sunday Paper ran a whole Page of Typical Belles she had the Place of Honor.

If a Stranger from some larger Town was there on a Visit and it became necessary to Knock his Eye out and prove to him that Springfield was strictly In It, they took him up to call on Mazie. Mazie never failed to Bowl him over, for she was a Dream of Loveliness when she got into her Glad Raiment. Mazie had large mesmeric Eyes and a Complexion that was like Chaste Marble kissed by the Rosy Flush of Dawn. She carried plenty of Brown Hair that she Built Up by putting Rats under it. When she sat very straight on the edge of the Chair, with the queenly Tilt of the Chin and the Shoulders set back Proudly and the Skirt sort of Whipped Under so as to help the General Outline, she was certainly a Pleasing Ob-

ject to size up. She did not Fall Down at any
Point.

Mazie had such a Rush of Men Callers that the
S. R. O. Sign was out almost every Night, and
when the Weather permitted she had Overflow
Meetings on the Veranda.

Right across the Street from Beautiful Mazie
there lived a Girl named Agnes, who was Fair to
Middling, although she could not Step it Off within twenty Seconds of Mazie's regular Gait.   Sometimes when she happened to get the right Combination of Colors and wore a Veil and you did
not get too Close, she was not Half Bad, but as
soon as she got into the same Picture with Mazie,
the Man Charmer, she was faded to a Gray Bleach.

All the plain, every-day XX Springfield Girls,
designed for Family Use and not for Exhibition
Purposes, used to wish that Mazie would go away
somewhere and forget to come back.

The Other Girls had to Admit that Mazie was
a good deal of a Tangerine, but they did not
Enthuse the same as their Brothers did. You
cannot expect a lot of Spirited Girls to strike a
Chord in G and sing any Anthem of Praise to a
Friend who is trying to make Wall Flowers of
them. When some Poor Man who was off his
Dip on Matchless Mazie, the Sprite of Springfield,
would start a Rhapsody to some other Girl, the
Other Girl would say Yes, that Mazie was a Sweet
and Lovely Girl, but when she said it she would
look as if she had just tasted a Lemon.

But Agnes, who lived across the Street from the Pearl of Springfield, tried to be Cheerful and Keep her Hammer hidden, although goodness knows she had Reason to feel Put Out. It is Hard Lines for a Sociable Girl to sit around the House and practise Finger movements on the Piano and see everything Lighted Up across the Street.

Agnes felt sometimes as if she would just have to Up and Tell the Boys what a deceitful, two-faced old Thing this Mazie really was. But she knew better than to do it, for Mazie had all of them Zizzy and they would have said that Agnes was Miffed because of Mazie's Popularity.

Agnes understood that Men always show a Strong Preference for a Feather-Headed Girl, if she has the Looks and a Circus Style, and particularly if all the sedate, well-read, plain, intellectual Girls are trying to Close Up ahead of her, so as to throw her into a Pocket.

So long as Mazie was the Reigning Fad, and while Mazie's Front Room was the Mecca for Golf Players and Glee - Club Undergraduates, Agnes sat back, a trifle Forlorn, but not so Rattled that she took any Chances of Queering her own Game.

Sometimes when there was such a Push at Mazie's Home that the Late Comers could not get up to within Rubbering Distance of the celebrated Siren of Springfield, and it was too Early to go Home, one or two of the Young Men would

drift over to pay a little Attention to Agnes.
Here was the chance for Agnes to make the Mistake of her Life. But she never asked them if
they had been to see Mazie first, and she never
made any of these unwelcome Cracks about being Second Choice. She received them with the
long Hand - Clasp and the Friendly Smile, and
threw herself to Entertain them, wotting well
that now and then a Girl must pocket her Pride
and she Laughs Best who postpones her Laughing until after the Banns have been Published.

Instead of seeking to undermine the Un-
crowned Queen of Springfield and put the Skids
under her, she lauded Mazie to the Skies. She
asked the Boys if they did not think that Mazie
was a Dashing Beauty and by far the Swellest
in Town, and was it any Wonder that the whole
Crowd was Dotty about her. When she talked
like that, Beaux who had been getting the gleam-
ing Cold Shoulder from Mazie were inclined to
Demur and say that Mazie was unquestionably
an Artist on the Make-Up and a Caution when it
came to Coquettish Wiles, but there were Others
just as Nice.

In this Town of Springfield there was a Steady
Young Fellow who wrote Junior after his Name,
and was Prospective Heir to an Iron Foundry.
He was Foolish about Mazie for quite a Spell,
but when he went up to see her and try to make
it worth her Time to look him over, the Door-
Bell kept ringing, and he found that instead of

conducting a Courtship he was simply getting in on a Series of Mass-Meetings. So he dropped out of the Competition and took to calling on Agnes, and found that he was the Whole Thing. She treated him Kindly and never disagreed with him except on one Point. Whenever he would say that Mazie was getting the Big Head and put on too many Frills to suit him, and had been Spoiled by having so many on her Staff at one time, Agnes would stick up for her Friend, and say that she could hardly blame any Man for giving in to the Superlative Charms of One who had Julia Marlowe set back a Mile.

She kept that Talk going until he was good and tired of having Mazie dingdonged at him. One Evening he stopped her right in the middle of an Eulogium and suggested that they let up on the Mazie Topic and talk about Themselves for a while. And although she Protested, he convinced her that she was worth a Ten-Acre Field full of Mazies.

So they were Married and went to Niagara Falls and came Home and still Mazie remained Single.

She was supposed to be several Notches too High Up for any One Man in Springfield. After getting such Job Lots of Adulation and having at least six pulsating Courtiers kneeling on her Sofa Pillows every Evening it would have been a Tame Let-Down for her to splice up with one lone Business Man and settle down to a dull Existence in some Apartment House.

So it came about that there was a General Impression in Springfield that Mazie was the Unattainable. She was a kind of Public Character to be Idolized, but not removed from the Pedestal. The discouraged Suitors fell away one by one, and married the ordinary Girls who were willing to Play Fair and not keep the Applicants dangling. Mazie took up with a new Generation and seemed to believe that she could reign Forever, the same as the Elfin Queen in the Fairy Tale.

But the Peach Crops come and go.

After a few Years Mazie's Door-Bell did not Tinkle with its whilom frequency, and right down the Street there was a Seventeen-Year-Older who had shot up out of Short Dresses like a Willow Sprout, and it was her Picture that went into the Special Illustrated Edition as Springfield's Fairest Daughter.

Mazie saw that the Vernal Season had passed and the Harvest Time was at Hand, so she decided to chop the Philandering and pick one for Keeps. But when she began to encourage the Eligibles they took it to mean that she was prolonging the same old String Game. The Men who knew that she had turned down at least Fifty figured that there was no Possible Chance for them, so they were Leery and would not be led into Committing themselves. Besides, Mazie had been handed around by so many that she was beginning to be Graded as Second Hand, and

there was not the same keen Anxiety to capture
her that there had been along about the Year of
the World's Fair.

At last Accounts she was supposed to be Guess-
ing. Agnes is doing Nicely, with a well-trained
Husband.

MORAL: *Cheer Up, Girls.*

THE FABLE OF THE FATAL ALBUM AND THE LEAP FOR LIFE

BY GEORGE ADE

ONE Evening a Girl named Eclaire had her Steady in the Parlor and was trying to keep him from falling Asleep. She had told him all the Scandal she could think of and Wished a Ring on his Finger and played Philopene, and at last she had to call in that Stop-Gap of revered Memory, the Family Album.

She showed him the Picture of Uncle Tibbetts who lived in Iowa, and Cousin Jess who married the Music-Teacher et cetera, finally coming to the Likeness of a slender and attractive Damsel in an out-of-date Costume.

"Why, this is a Ringer for you," said the Regular Fellow.

"It is a Picture of Mommer before she was married," said Eclaire. "Every one says I am the perfect Image of her."

The Young Man got busy with his Thinks. He had seen Mommer. She was a good, moral Woman, but she had a Face that suggested Dill Pickles and a Shape that no Straight Front could regulate.

THE "STEADY"

"If It 25 years ago looked exactly as Daughter does at present, then it is an 8 to 1 Bet that Daughter in 25 years will be what Mommer is to-day," he said to himself.

So he jumped through the Window and carried the Sash with him.   No one ever saw him on that Corner again.

MORAL: *It is not on Record that the Family Album ever proved a Help.*

A PLEASURE EXERTION

BY MARIETTA HOLLEY

WAL, the very next mornin' Josiah got up with
a new idee in his head. And he broached it to
me to the breakfast-table. They have been havin' sights of pleasure exertions here to Jonesville
lately. Every week a'most they would go off on
a exertion after pleasure, and Josiah was all up
on end to go too.

That man is a well-principled man as I ever
see, but if he had his head, he would be worse
than any young man I ever see to foller up picnics
and 4th of Julys and camp-meetin's and all
pleasure exertions. But I don't encourage him
in it. I have said to him time and again: "There
is a time for everything, Josiah Allen, and after
anybody has lost all their teeth and every mite
of hair on the top of their head, it is time for 'em
to stop goin' to pleasure exertions."

But good land! I might jest as well talk to the
wind! If that man should get to be as old as
Mr. Methusler, and be goin' on a thousand years
old, he would prick up his ears if he should hear
of a exertion. All summer long that man has

beset me to go to 'em, for he wouldn't go without
me. Old Bunker Hill himself hain't any sounder
in principle than Josiah Allen, and I have had to
work head-work to make excuses and quell him
down. But last week they was goin' to have one
out on the lake, on a island, and that man sot his
foot down that go he would.

We was to the breakfast-table a-talkin' it over,
and says I:

"I sha'n't go, for I am afraid of big water,
anyway."

Says Josiah: "You are jest as liable to be
killed in one place as another."

Says I, with a almost frigid air, as I passed
him his coffee: "Mebby I shall be drownded on
dry land, Josiah Allen, but I don't believe it."

Says he, in a complainin' tone: "I can't get you
started onto a exertion for pleasure anyway."

Says I, in a almost eloquent way: "I don't believe in makin' such exertions after pleasure. As
I have told you time and agin, I don't believe in
chasin' of her up. Let her come of her own free
will. You can't ketch her by chasin' after her
no more than you can fetch up a shower in a
drowth by goin' out-doors and runnin' after a
cloud up in the heavens above you. Sit down
and be patient, and when it gets ready the re-
freshin' rain-drops will begin to fall without none
of your help. And it is jest so with pleasure,
Josiah Allen; you may chase her up over all the
oceans and big mountains of the earth, and she

will keep ahead of you all the time; but set down and not fatigue yourself a-thinkin' about her, and like as not she will come right into your house unbeknown to you."

"Wal," says he, "I guess I'll have another griddle-cake, Samantha."

And as he took it, and poured the maple-syrup over it, he added, gently, but firmly:

"I shall go, Samantha, to this exertion, and I should be glad to have you present at it, because it seems jest to me as if I should fall overboard durin' the day."

Men are deep. Now that man knew that no amount of religious preachin' could stir me up like that one speech. For though I hain't no hand to coo, and don't encourage him in bein' spoony at all, he knows that I am wrapped almost completely up in him. I went.

Wal, the day before the exertion Kellup Cobb come into our house of a errant, and I asked him if he was goin' to the exertion, and he said he would like to go, but he dassent.

"Dassent!" says I. "Why dassent you?"

"Why," says he, "how would the rest of the wimmin round Jonesville feel if I should pick out one woman and wait on her?" Says he, bitterly: "I hain't perfect, but I hain't such a cold-blooded rascal as not to have any regard for wimmin's feelin's. I hain't no heart to spile all the comfort of the day for ten or a dozen wimmen."

"Why," says I, in a dry tone, "one woman would be happy, accordin' to your tell."

"Yes, one woman happy, and ten or fifteen gauled—bruised in the tenderest place."

"On their heads?" says I, inquirin'ly.

"No," says he, "their hearts. All the girls have probable had more or less hopes that I would invite 'em—make a choice of 'em. But when the blow was struck, when I had passed 'em by and invited some other, some happier woman, how would them slighted ones feel? How do you s'pose they would enjoy the day, seein' me with another woman, and they droopin' round without me? That is the reason, Josiah Allen's wife, that I dassent go. It hain't the keepin' of my horse through the day that stops me. For I could carry a quart of oats and a little jag of hay in the bottom of the buggy. If I had concluded to pick out a girl and go, I had got it all fixed out in my mind how I would manage. I had thought it over, while I was onde-cided and duty was a-strugglin' with me. But I was made to see where the right way for me lay, and I am goin' to foller it. Joe Purday is goin' to have my horse, and give me seven shillin's for the use of it and its keepin'. He come to hire it just before I made up my mind that I hadn't ort to go.

"Of course it is a cross to me. But I am will-in' to bear crosses for the fair sect. Why," says he, a-comin' out in a open, generous way, "I would be willin', if necessary for the general good of the fair sect—I would be willin' to sacrifice ten cents for 'em, or pretty nigh that, I wish so well to 'em. I *hain't* that enemy to 'em that they think I am. I can't marry 'em all, Heaven knows I can't, but I wish 'em well."

"Wal," says I, "I guess my dish-water is hot; it must be pretty near bilin' by this time."

And he took the hint and started off. I see it wouldn't do no good to argue with him that wimmen did't worship him. For when a feller once gets it into his head that female wimmen are all after him, you might jest as well dispute the wind as argue with him. You can't convince him nor the wind—neither of 'em—so what's the use of wastin' breath on 'em. And I didn't want to spend a extra breath that day, anyway, knowin' I had such a hard day's work in front of me, a-finishin' cookin' up provisions for the exertion, and gettin' things done up in the house so I could leave 'em for all day.

We had got to start about the middle of the night; for the lake was fifteen miles from Jonesville, and the old mare bein' so slow, we had got to start an hour or two ahead of the rest. I told Josiah in the first on't, that I had just as lives set up all night as to be routed out at two o'clock. But he was so animated and happy at the idee of goin' that he looked on the bright side of everything, and he said that we would go to bed before dark, and get as much sleep as we commonly did.

So we went to bed the sun an hour high. And I
was truly tired enough to lay down, for I had
worked dretful hard that day—almost beyond
my strength. But we hadn't more'n got settled
down into the bed, when we heard a buggy and a
single wagon stop at the gate, and I got up and
peeked through the window, and I see it was
visitors come to spend the evenin'—Elder Bamber and his family, and Deacon Dobbinses'
folks.

Josiah vowed that he wouldn't stir one step out
of that bed that night. But I argued with him
pretty sharp, while I was throwin' on my clothes,
and I finally got him started up. I hain't deceitful, but I thought if I got my clothes all on
before they came in, I wouldn't tell 'em that I
had been to bed that time of day. And I did get
all dressed up, even to my handkerchief pin.
And I guess they had been there as much as ten
minutes before I thought that I hadn't took my
night-cap off. They looked dreadful curious at
me, and I felt awful meachin'. But I jest ketched
it off, and never said nothin'. But when Josiah
come out of the bedroom with what little hair he
has got standin' out in every direction, no two
hairs a-layin' the same way, and one of his gal-
luses a-hangin' most to the floor under his best
coat, I up and told 'em. I thought mebby they
wouldn't stay long. But Deacon Dobbinses'
folks seemed to be all waked up on the subject
of religion, and they proposed we should turn it

10

into a kind of a conference meetin'; so they never went home till after ten o'clock.

It was most eleven when Josiah and me got to bed agin. And then jest as I was gettin' into a drowse, I heerd the cat in the buttery, and I got up to let her out. And that roused Josiah up, and he thought he heered the cattle in the garden, and he got up and went out. And there we was a-marchin' round most all night.

And if we would get into a nap, Josiah would think it was mornin', and he would start up and go out to look at the clock. He seemed so afraid we would be belated, and not get to that exertion in time. And there we was on our feet most all night. I lost myself once, for I dreampt that Josiah was a-drowndin', and Deacon Dobbins was on the shore a-prayin' for him. It started me so, that I jist ketched hold of Josiah and hollered. It skairt him awfully, and says he: "What does ail you, Samantha? I hain't been asleep before, to-night, and now you have rousted me up for good. I wonder what time it is!"

And then he got out of bed again, and went and looked at the clock. It was half-past one, and he said he didn't believe we had better go to sleep again, for fear we would be too late for the exertion, and he wouldn't miss that for nothin'.

"Exertion!" says I, in a awful cold tone. "I should think we had had exertion enough for one spell,"

But as bad and wore out as Josiah felt bodily, he was all animated in his mind about what a good time he was a-goin' to have. He acted foolish, and I told him so. I wanted to wear my brown-and-black gingham and a shaker, but Josiah insisted that I should wear a new lawn dress that he had brought me home as a present, and I had jest got made up. So, jest to please him, I put it on, and my best bonnet.

And that man, all I could do and say, would put on a pair of pantaloons I had been a-makin' for Thomas Jefferson. They was gettin' up a milatary company to Jonesville, and these pantaloons was blue, with a red stripe down the sides —a kind of uniform. Josiah took a awful fancy to 'em, and says he:

" I will wear 'em, Samantha; they look so dressy."

Says I: " They hain't hardly done. I was goin' to stitch that red stripe on the left leg on again. They hain't finished as they ort to be, and I would not wear 'em. It looks vain in you."

Says he: " I will wear 'em, Samantha. I will be dressed up for once."

I didn't contend with him. Thinks I: we are makin' fools of ourselves by goin' at all, and if he wants to make a little bigger fool of himself, by wearin' them blue pantaloons, I won't stand in his light. And then I had got some machine-oil onto 'em, so I felt that I had got to wash 'em, anyway, before Thomas J. took 'em to wear. So he put 'em on,

I had good vittles, and a sight of 'em. The basket wouldn't hold 'em all, so Josiah had to put a bottle of red rossberry jell into the pocket of his dress-coat, and lots of other little things, such as spoons and knives and forks, in his pantaloons and breast pockets. He looked like Captain Kidd armed up to the teeth, and I told him so. But good land! he would have carried a knife in his mouth if I had asked him to, he felt so neat about goin', and boasted so on what a splendid exertion it was goin' to be.

We got to the lake about eight o'clock, for the old mare went slow. We was about the first ones there, but they kep' a-comin', and before ten o'clock we all got there.

The young folks made up their minds they would stay and eat their dinner in a grove on the main-land. But the majority of the old folks thought it was best to go and set our tables where we laid out to in the first place. Josiah seemed to be the most rampant of any of the company about goin'. He said he shouldn't eat a mouthful if he didn't eat it on that island. He said, what was the use of goin' to a pleasure exertion at all if you didn't try to take all the pleasure you could. So about twenty old fools of us sot sail for the island.

I had made up my mind from the first on't to face trouble, so it didn't put me out so much when Deacon Dobbins, in gettin' into the boat, stepped onto my new lawn dress and tore a hole

in it as big as my two hands, and ripped it half
offen the waist. But Josiah havin' felt so animated and tickled about the exertion, it worked
him up awfully when, jest after we had got well
out onto the lake, the wind took his hat off and
blew it away out onto the lake. He had made
up his mind to look so pretty that day that it
worked him up awfully. And then the sun beat
down onto him; and if he had had any hair onto
his head it would have seemed more shady.

But I did the best I could by him. I stood by
him and pinned on his red bandanna handkerchief onto his head. But as I was a-fixin' it on,
I see there was suthin' more than mortification
ailed him. The lake was rough and the boat
rocked, and I see he was beginnin' to be awful
sick. He looked deathly. Pretty soon I felt
bad, too. Oh, the wretchedness of that time! I
have enjoyed poor health considerable in my life,
but never did I enjoy so much sickness in so
short a time as I did on that pleasure exertion to
that island. I s'pose our bein' up all night
a'most made it worse. When we reached the
island we was both weak as cats.

I sot right down on a stun and held my head
for a spell, for it did seem as if it would split
open. After a while I staggered up onto my
feet, and finally I got so I could walk straight
and sense things a little; though it was tejus
work to walk, anyway, for we had landed on a
sand-bar, and the sand was so deep it was all we

could do to wade through it, and it was as hot
as hot ashes ever was.

Then I began to take the things out of my
dinner-basket. The butter had all melted, so we
had to dip it out with a spoon. And a lot of
water had washed over the side of the boat, so
my pies and tarts and delicate cake and cookies
looked awful mixed up. But no worse than the
rest of the company's did.

But we did the best we could, and the chicken
and cold meats bein' more solid, had held together
quite well, so there was some pieces of it con-
side'able hull, though it was all very wet and
soppy. But we separated 'em out as well as we
could, and begun to make preparations to eat.
We didn't feel so animated about eatin' as we
should if we hadn't been so sick to our stomachs.
But we felt as if we must hurry, for the man that
owned the boat said he knew it would rain before
night, by the way the sun scalded.

There wasn't a man or a woman there but
what the presperation and sweat jest poured
down their faces. We was a haggard and melancholy lookin' set. There was a piece of woods
a little ways off, but it was up quite a rise of
ground, and there wasn't one of us but what
had the rheumatiz more or less. We made up
a fire on the sand, though it seemed as if it was
hot enough to steep the tea and coffee as it
was.

After we got the fire started, I histed a umberell

and sot down under it, and fanned myself hard, for I was afraid of a sunstroke.

Wal, I guess I had set there ten minutes or more, when all of a sudden I thought, Where is Josiah? I hadn't seen him since we had got there. I riz up and asked the company, almost wildly, if they had seen my companion, Josiah.

They said: "No, they hadn't."

But Celestine Wilkin's little girl, who had come with her grandpa and grandma Gowdy, spoke up, and says she:

"I seen him goin' off towards the woods. He acted dretful strange, too; he seemed to be a-walkin' off sideways."

"Had the sufferin's he had undergone made him delerious?" says I to myself; and then I started off on the run towards the woods, and old Miss Bobbet, and Miss Gowdy, and Sister Bamber, and Deacon Dobbinses' wife all rushed after me.

Oh, the agony of them two or three minutes! my mind so distracted with fourbodin's, and the presperation and sweat a-pourin' down. But all of a sudden, on the edge of the woods, we found him. Miss Gowdy weighin' a little less than me, mebby a hundred pounds or so, had got a little ahead of me. He sot backed up against a tree, in a awful cramped position, with his left leg under him. He looked dretful uncomfortable. But when Miss Gowdy hollered out: "Oh, here you be! We have been skairt about you. What is the matter?" he smiled a dretful sick smile, and says he: "Oh, I thought I would come out here and meditate a spell. It was always a real treat to me to meditate."

Just then I come up a-pantin' for breath, and as the wimmen all turned to face me, Josiah scowled at me, and shook his fist at them four wimmen, and made the most mysterious motions of his hands towards 'em. But the minute they turned round he smiled in a sickish way, and pretended to go to whistlin'.

Says I: "What is the matter, Josiah Allen? What are you off here for?"

"I am a-meditatin', Samantha."

Says I: "Do you come down and jine the company this minute, Josiah Allen. You was in a awful takin' to come with 'em, and what will they think to see you act so?"

The wimmen happened to be a-lookin' the other way for a minute, and he looked at me as if he would take my head off, and made the strangest motions towards 'em; but the minute they looked at him he would pretend to smile—that deathly smile.

Says I: "Come, Josiah Allen, we're goin' to get dinner right away, for we are afraid it will rain."

"Oh, wal," says he, "a little rain, more or less, hain't a-goin' to hender a man from meditatin'."

I was worn out, and says I: "Do you stop meditatin' this minute, Josiah Allen."

Says he: "I won't stop, Samantha. I let you

have your way a good deal of the time; but when
I take it into my head to meditate, you hain't
a-goin' to break it up."

Jest at that minute they called to me from the
shore to come that minute to find some of my
dishes. And we had to start off. But oh, the
gloom of my mind that was added to the lame-
ness of my body! Them strange motions and
looks of Josiah wore on me. Had the sufferin's
of the night, added to the trials of the day, made
him crazy? I thought more'n as likely as not I
had got a luny on my hands for the rest of my
days.

And then, oh, how the sun did scald down onto
me! and the wind took the smoke so into my face
that there wasn't hardly a dry eye in my head.
And then a perfect swarm of yellow wasps lit
down onto our vittles as quick as we laid 'em
down, so you couldn't touch a thing without
runnin' a chance to be stung. Oh, the agony of
that time! the distress of that pleasure exertion!
But I kep' to work, and when we had got dinner
most ready, I went back to call Josiah again.
Old Miss Bobbet said she would go with me, for
she thought she see a wild turnip in the woods
there, and her Shakespeare had a awful cold, and
she would try to dig one to give him. So we
started up the hill again. He set in the same
position, all huddled up, with his leg under him,
as uncomfortable a lookin' creeter as I ever see.
But when we both stood in front of him, he pre-

tended to look careless and happy, and smiled
that sick smile.

Says I: "Come, Josiah Allen; dinner is ready."

"Oh, I hain't hungry," says he. "The table
will probable be full. I had jest as lieves wait."

"Table full!" says I. "You know jest as well
as I do that we are eatin' on the ground. Do
you come and eat your dinner this minute!"

"Yes, do come," says Miss Bobbet; "we can't
get along without you!"

"Oh," says he, with a ghastly smile, a pretend-
in' to joke, "I have got plenty to eat here—I can
eat muskeeters."

The air was black with 'em, I couldn't deny it.

"The muskeeters will eat you, more likely,"
says I. "Look at your face and hands; they are
all covered with 'em."

"Yes, they have eat considerable of a dinner
out of me, but I don't begrech 'em. I hain't
small enough, nor mean enough, I hope, to begrech 'em one good meal."

Miss Bobbet started off in search of her wild
turnip, and after she had got out of sight Josiah
whispered to me with a savage look, and a tone
sharp as a sharp axe:

"Can't you bring forty or fifty more wimmen
up here? You couldn't come here a minute,
could you, without a lot of other wimmen tight
to your heels?"

I begun to see daylight, and after Miss Bobbet
had got her wild turnip and some spignut, I made

some excuse to send her on ahead, and then Josiah told me all about why he had gone off by himself alone, and why he had been a-settin' in such a curious position all the time since we had come in sight of him.

It seems he had sot down on that bottle of rossberry jell. That red stripe on the side wasn't hardly finished, as I said, and I hadn't fastened my thread properly, so when he got to pullin' at 'em to try to wipe off the jell, the thread started, and bein' sewed on a machine, that seam jest ripped from top to bottom. That was what he had walked off sideways towards the woods for. But Josiah Allen's wife hain't one to desert a companion in distress. I pinned 'em up as well as I could, and I didn't say a word to hurt his feelin's, only I jest said this to him, as I was fixin' 'em; I fastened my gray eye firmly, and almost sternly, onto him, and says I:

"Josiah Allen, is this pleasure?" Says I: "You was determined to come."

"Throw that in my face agin, will you? What if I was? There goes a pin into my leg! I should think I had suffered enough without your stabbin' of me with pins."

· "Wal, then, stand still, and not be a-caperin' round so. How do you s'pose I can do anything with you a-tossin' round so?"

"Wal, don't be so aggravatin', then."

I fixed 'em as well as I could, but they looked pretty bad, and there they was all covered with

jell, too. What to do I didn't know. But finally I told him I would put my shawl onto him.
So I doubled it up corner-ways as big as I could,
so it almost touched the ground behind, and he
walked back to the table with me. I told him it
was best to tell the company all about it, but he
just put his foot down that he wouldn't, and I
told him, if he wouldn't, that he must make his
own excuses to the company about wearin' the
shawl. So he told 'em he always loved to wear
summer shawls; he thought it made a man look
so dressy.

But he looked as if he would sink, all the time
he was a-sayin' it. They all looked dretful curious at him, and he looked as meachin' as if he had
stole sheep—and meachin'er—and he never took
a minute's comfort, nor I nuther. He was sick
all the way back to the shore, and so was I. And
jest as we got into our wagons and started for
home, the rain began to pour down. The wind
turned our old umberell inside out in no time.
My lawn dress was most spilte before, and now I
give up my bonnet. And I says to Josiah:

"This bonnet and dress are spilte, Josiah Allen,
and I shall have to buy some new ones."

"Wal, wal! who said you wouldn't?" he snapped
out.

But it were on him. Oh, how the rain poured
down! Josiah, havin' nothin' but a handkerchief on his head, felt it more than I did. I had
took a apron to put on a-gettin' dinner, and I

tried to make him let me pin it on his head.   But
says he, firmly:

"I hain't proud and haughty, Samantha, but
I do feel above ridin' out with a pink apron on
for a hat."

"Wal, then," says I, "get as wet as sop, if you
had ruther."

I didn't say no more, but there we jest sot and
suffered.   The rain poured down; the wind howled
at us; the old mare went slow; the rheumatiz laid
holt of both of us; and the thought of the new
bonnet and dress was a-wearin' on Josiah, I
knew.

There wasn't a house for the first seven miles,
and after we got there I thought we wouldn't go
in, for we had got to get home to milk, anyway,
and we was both as wet as we could be.   After I
had beset him about the apron, we didn't say
hardly a word for as much as thirteen miles or
so; but I did speak once, as he leaned forward,
with the rain drippin' offen his bandanna handkerchief onto his blue pantaloons.   I says to him
in stern tones:

"Is this pleasure, Josiah Allen?"

He give the old mare a awful cut, and says he:
"I'd like to know what you want to be so aggravatin' for."

I didn't multiply any more words with him,
only as we drove up to our door-step, and he
helped me out into a mud puddle, I says to
him:

"Mebby you'll hear to me another time, Josiah Allen."

And I'll bet he will. I hain't afraid to bet a ten-cent bill that that man won't never open his mouth to me again about a pleasure exertion.

SPEECH ON WASHINGTON'S BIRTHDAY

BY SIMEON FORD

IF ever a man lived who was justified in being stuck on himself, it was G. Washington, late of Mount Vernon. He has since been stuck on a good many things—principally letters—or, rather, his likeness has. You have all noticed George's likeness as it appears on the two-cent postage-stamps, wearing a look of entire self-satisfaction and a collar cut somewhat lower in the neck than is now considered *de rigeur* among the *beau monde*. It has frequently and truly been re-marked that George was never licked until he got on a postage-stamp, and then only when his back was turned. It may not be considered amiss for to suggest, in connection with this fond Revolutionary joke, that any one who would lend his countenance to some of the recent issues of two-cent stamps deserves to be licked; and I firmly believe that, if the person who compounds the flavoring extract used on the back thereof could be located, his name would go thundering down the ages linked with that of Benedict Arnold, J. Iscariot, and other gentlemen whose popularity is on the wane.

But to revert to G. Washington. I repeat he
had just cause to throw bouquets at himself, for
certainly he possessed to a pre-eminent degree the
gift of getting his name in the papers and histories
and third readers, and having streets and pies
named after him, without its costing him a cent.
Look at that tale of the little hatchet and the
cherry-tree, with which you are doubtless familiar!
Think of the free advertising he got out of that
comparatively trifling incident! I used to have
that story rubbed into me when a child until it
warped and soured a naturally sunny and lovely
nature. That George was startled into telling
the truth upon this occasion we are bound to admit; but note the forced and ostentatious way in
which he did it, as though saying to the grand-
stand, "Look at me knock the cover off it for
three bases." Think, my hearers, how often you
yourselves have inadvertently been betrayed into
telling the truth, and yet you never set up a
claim to be "first in war, first in peace, and first
in the hearts of your countrymen."

How a man's whole life may be influenced by a
trifling circumstance. Suppose George's father,
instead of being a sentimental old cuss, on hearing that his son had been monkeying with edged
tools, had hastily removed him to the seclusion of
the wood-shed, and had then and there, with a
shingle or other convenient weapon, proceeded to
tan that portion of George's anatomy which the
British were never permitted to gaze upon. In-

stead of growing up to be the father of his country, he might have become morose and sullen, and
developed into a life insurance solicitor or an advertising agent or a map peddler, or even fallen
to still greater depths of depravity. The moral
of all this is, that one should ever strive to tell
the truth, even at some personal inconvenience,
especially when one is likely to be found out anyhow.

Much has been made of the incident of crossing
the Delaware. Every one is sick of the picture
presenting that aquatic feat. George stands, as
you remember, right in the prow, in the full glare
of the calcium, in such a position that, had the
boat bumped into one of the numerous cakes of
ice which were floating about, he would have
taken a tumble into the turgid tide. But George
never tumbled! George never took water! His
features wear an expression, as Bill Nye says,
as though he had just become aware of the presence of a glue factory on the opposite shore.
His massive brow is crowned with a neat, tri-
angular hat of a new, happily obsolete, pattern,
and his cloak is carelessly thrown back over
his shoulder so as to best display the cute red
lining. His whole demeanor is that of innate
majesty, commingled with *dolce far niente*, *nux
vomica*, and *pro bono publico*, and the likeness
is so speaking that we can almost hear George
say: "It may be a little chilly around here,
but it's a cold day when the father of his coun-

try gets left; and, cold as it is, I'm not the only pebble on the beach — there's other coons as warm as me."

I have sometimes fancied that the artist did not depict George as he actually appeared on that occasion, for the chances are he wore earmuffs and chilblains, had a piece of pork bound around his throat with a red flannel rag, and had his feet tied up in hay; because research shows us that it was a cold winter and George got the frozen face ever and anon or even oftener. Crossing the Delaware was all well enough in its way, but to one accustomed to crossing Amsterdam Avenue on the way home from the Colonial Club, in all stages of sobriety, with the Elevated road thundering overhead and the trolley cars swooping up and down with clanging bells on the dead level, it seems as if crossing the Delaware would be a mere frolic.

But Valley Forge was tough—I must admit that. When I think of those ragged Continentals waltzing up and down, leaving bloody foottracks in the snow, I am greatly moved. I've often had cold feet myself, and have even dallied with cold hands, but I never yet have been called upon to let my rich red heart's-blood flow out through my feet at my country's call, and I trust I never shall.

I never go down into our café and gaze upon the free lunch which is there displayed in all its colonial simplicity and severity, but I am forcibly reminded of the sufferings of the starving soldiers at Valley Forge.

I hate to stand up here and shatter a public idol, and ruthlessly yank George off the lofty perch where he has been enshrined in history's pages, but I can't help thinking that in some things he showed a singular indifference to the rights of posterity. Take a little thing, now, like the selection of the date of his birth. Could he possibly have hit upon a more disagreeable date? What is the use of a holiday on the twenty-second of February? It's too late for sleighing or skating and too early for golf or bicycling. The only thing it is good for is to break up the business week and give a man an opportunity to hang around the house and smoke too many cigars and aggravate his poor, patient wife, and exasperate his children, and make himself generally obnoxious to all with whom he comes in contact.

Perhaps it will not be considered meet for me to sound my own praises, but when the time comes that the anniversary of my natal day will be made the occasion of public rejoicings, it is a satisfaction for me to know that I picked out a date when a man can go fishing, or swimming, or shooting, or sailing, or indulge in other pleasant summer pastimes, and not a bleak, miserable day at the fag end of the most cussed month of the year. And yet, simple justice demands that I should say that perhaps the father of his country was not consulted, and that at that early portion of his career his parents arranged his dates for him.

And yet far be it from me to withhold from George that meed of praise which is his due. George certainly had his strong points, and the manner in which he played tag with the British army, always managing to be on the hunk when they caught up with him, and to be "it" most of the time, incontestably proves that he was a smooth article. Take him for all and all, he was a great and good man, and I trust that nothing which I have said about him will detract from his fame.

"It's a wise child that knows its own father," and if you want to know that father of your country you must hear both sides. Possibly you have heard it said that faith will move mountains, but it will never lift a chattel mortgage, and what is more, you know you can't believe everything you hear.

To look at the noble Washington as he appears in that beautiful portrait in the Colonial Club — one of the eight hundred and seventy-five genuine portraits for which he sat — you would think he was just waiting to feel his wings sprout, but don't you believe he was so slow as his appearance implies. During my brief yet ignominious career I have already seen some eight hundred and fifty different houses in which George temporarily sojourned, and he must have been pretty quick in order to have played all these one - night stands and still preserve his reputation unspotted. My experience has led me to believe that in order to preserve an un-spotted reputation you have got to look out that nobody spots you.

NO UNCLE OF OURS

BY CHARLES B. DE CAMP

My youngest son, Malcolm, not yet thirteen, persuaded me, a year ago, to buy him a printing-press. For some weeks after it was installed the house was deluged with queer-looking laundry lists, jelly-glass labels, calling-cards, and other startling evidences of its presence. Malcolm was much hurt that his mother and I used engraved visiting-cards, so to console him I ordered a hundred business cards. When he brought them to me I read:

Cordon Livingso

Attorney at Law.   *Safe and Reliable.*

"I added that on," he explained, engagingly. "Lots of 'em have it, and it fills out better."

While I had to admit the force of the latter point, I could not agree that there were "lots of 'em" in the profession who would so far commit themselves in print.

And by mistake I used one of those cards! Sent it up to one of the best-known and wealthiest men in town that I hoped some day would become a client of mine. Let us draw a timely veil over this occurrence.

The project of a newspaper to be edited and printed by Malcolm Livingso originated in an article describing the success of two Indiana boys in publishing a small journal. Malcolm was instantly aglow with the idea. We discussed at length the question of a name for the new moulder of opinion. I suggested the *Orange Blossom* (we live in Orange). Malcolm regarded me sharply.

"That's what brides wear, ain't it?" he asked, with scorn. And he repudiated it.

It was finally decided to call the paper the *Mosquito*, the *Orange Mosquito*. I think it was my suggestion; I know my wife thought the name silly. For two weeks I rarely saw my youngest son. He came to his dinner long after the soup with a preoccupied air and a portentous frown. After bolting a few necessaries and the dessert he would disappear until dragged from the garret at bed-time. During this period he wore a perpetual war-paint of printer's ink, fresh, fierce daubs overlying pale, brush-scrubbed stains that would yield to time alone. The initial number of the *Mosquito* finally appeared on a Saturday afternoon. I found it on sale at the station when I returned from the city. A red-headed boy whom I had occasionally seen escape from my house at dinner-time was crying it in blissful imitation of the little news rats across the river: "Yere y'are! The *Orange Mosquito*—just out—five cents a copy! The *Mosquiter!*" Waiving my official connection with the publication, I purchased a copy, whereat the red-headed boy grinned. "I'm the company," he announced.

The *Mosquito* was a five-by-eight-inch sheet on which the printing was set somewhat on the bias. At the head of the first page, beneath the date-line, bold-faced type announced that Malcolm Livingso was "soal editor," and that "Malcolm Livingso and Co." were the publishers. I now understood the remark of the red-headed boy. Appended to the rates was this honest announcement: "If the editor goes to Nantucket next summer the *Mosquito* will cost 30 cents a year less." Beneath this and heading the reading-matter was the quatrain, suitably printed in "Old English":

> "𝕷ife is real, life is earnest
> 𝔄ndthegrave is not its goal
>   𝔇ust thou art to dust returnest!
> 𝔚as not spoken of the soul."

Then came in orderly brevier:

" It has rained a lot lately.
" James Hollis dog was poisoned last Sunday.   Jim
would just like to catch the fellow that did it.
" Subscribe for the MOSQUITO!!!"

The second page was headed "Personal," and
leading the list of mention, I read:

" Gordon Livingso, the celebrated lawyer, went to
Boston some time ago."

It had been six months ago.
The third page of the paper was devoted to fiction of a rather gory sort, and recounted the death
from Indians of "Dick, The Terror of the Plains."
It was concluded with the enthralling line:

" Death! death? exclaimed Dick as he Felt the arow
in hls hart.,,

My advertisement occupied a prominent place
on the last page, together with that of a butcher
with whom I had threatened to sever business re-
lations because of disreputable steaks.   Whether
Malcolm had blackmailed the butcher to secure
his ad. I know not, but it was a master-stroke.

When I arrived at the house my son, the editor,
had just returned from a door-to-door sale of the
Mosquito, and was flushed and jubilant over the
ten nickels in his trousers-pocket.   I called him
Horace Greeley, and complimented him on his
initial number.

"Ah, gee," he replied, panting, "wait till you

see the next one. There wasn't any big things to tell in this one. We just had to get her out any old way."

The *Mosquito* appeared with pardonable irregularity every fortnight, and became quite an institution in the neighborhood. The personal column especially grew to be a feature; and it was a long one, as Malcolm faithfully chronicled the arrivals and departures of cooks and maids. Once, indeed, I discovered that the "company" was compiling a series of back-door interviews with servants as to the merits or demerits of their "places." I suppressed the article in my capacity of official censor.

One evening as I unfolded my New York paper by the library table, my eye rested on a despatch from Kansas describing the extraordinary case of one John Livingso on trial for bigamy, some eight women, ranging in age from eighteen to fifty, having sworn that he had been their lawfully wedded husband.

"I declare!" I exclaimed. "I rarely see that name. John, too — and under such circumstances!" I read the despatch to my wife.

"It is your uncle!" she cried, with absurd conclusiveness.

"Your grandmother!" I retorted, impolitely.

Now I have an uncle John, supposed to be living in the West, lost to the family years ago. My wife's remark had confirmed a suspicion in my breast, and I resented it.

"My uncle John," I said, with dignity, "was a
—a—gentleman."

"But he owed your father money," said my
wife, resuming her fancy-work.

"That's true," I assented, "but Heaven save
us if a man who owes money is no gentleman!
No," I continued, with less heat, "Uncle John
could never have gotten into such a scrape. He
didn't go to Kansas, anyway [this was weak]; he
went to Dakota. Besides, he never had a cent,
and was afflicted with heart trouble. He wouldn't
dare have married. He was a little, bald-headed
man, too, with a cast in his eye. No woman would
look at him, let alone eight."

"Some women are awful fools," said my
wife.

"Good Heavens, Ethel!" I cried, "do you want
to prove that this bigamist is my uncle? If so,
let it go at that. John Livingso, my father's
brother, bigamist, sent up for ten years. We
might get out announcement cards."

"Your sarcasm is such a treat, Gordon," said
my wife.

"Moreover," I continued, picking up the paper, "this despatch says the man is past middle
age, and my uncle John can't be more than—
let's see—1885—seventeen years—can't be more
than—fifty-five."

"No, dearest," said my wife, coming over to
me, "it couldn't possibly be. Even if the description was exact, I know no brother of your

noble father could be such a wretched, low creature as a bigamist."

"It's hard to tell, though, what different conditions and environment will do to a man," I murmured, thoughtfully.

This is quite the usual way in which arguments between Mrs. Livingso and myself develop and conclude.

I said, savagely: "Outrage, though, that a decent family paper should give space to a story of that sort. There'll be no end to the guying that I'll receive."

It was at this moment that I observed our youngest sitting listening to our conversation with his mouth open above his school-books. I had forgotten his presence, and this nettled me.

"Malcolm," I said, sternly, "attend to your studies. They receive little enough of your time since that paper was started."

"Yes, papa," replied Malcolm, meekly. He busied himself for a while with a pad and pencil, and then guessed he would go to bed. Soon I heard him in the garret, and summoned him to his bedroom. He received my sharp rebuke with the spirit of a Christian martyr.

I retired that night thinking evil of Uncle John and John the bigamist, whether they were two individuals or one.

I was not "guyed" about the bigamist, however. By evening, as I proceeded homeward, I had dismissed the story from my thoughts. Even

if my Uncle John was the wholesale deceiver, I
argued, finally, either my friends had not seen the
despatch or had given no thought to the name in
that connection. That ended it. Ah, little did I
wot of a positive and vigorous defender of a
family legacy of good repute!

When I got down from the train I saw a man
smiling at me. It was a good-natured smile, and
I returned it, though somewhat vaguely. Then
I saw a poster on the waiting-room wall. It said:
"Extra *Mosquito*. Today. Buy it!" Then I
heard a shrill crying, and recognized the "company." He was surpassing himself. "Yere's yer
extra *Mosquiter!* All about the bigermust. Just
out! Extry!"

I went to him, and plucked one of the copies
from his wrist. Beneath the date line were three
enormous "extras" in a row, and below I read:

NO UNCLE OF OURS!

**Bigermist arrested in Kansas not a relation
of the Editor's.**

By Our Special Reporter On The Spot.

"A man is getting tried in Kansas for being married
to eight wives. His name is John Livingso, which is the
same as the editors, thatis, the last name is. But he
aint an uncle of the editor's father, Mr. Gordon Livingso, the well-known and reliable lawyer, because Mr.
Livingso said last night that he could not be his uncle
because his uncle john who went away a long time ago
went to Dakota and did not go to Kansas. besides Mr.
Livingso said his uncle never had a cent and had hart

trouble and had a cock eye so as he couldnt marry eight
women.   If people say hes my fathers uncle there telling lies."

That was all.   The second and last pages of
the *Mosquito* were blank.   On the third page was
a short anecdote from the *Fireside Guardian*, very
properly credited in brackets with, "By curtesy
of the publishers."   This was evidently intended
to mollify those who took the "extra" home for
family reading.

I walked home.   Malcolm was with his mother
in her bedroom.   I paused outside the closed
door.   Malcolm was talking:

"But it was news, mamma; don't you see?
News that [sob] people ought to know."

I went back down-stairs.   I saw that I had
been anticipated.

THE IDIOT AND THE LANDLADY

BY JOHN KENDRICK BANGS

"GOOD-MORNING!" said the Idiot, cheerfully, as he entered the dining-room.

To this remark no one but the landlady vouchsafed a reply. "I don't think it is," she said, shortly. "It's raining too hard to be a very good morning."

"That reminds me," observed the Idiot, taking his seat and helping himself copiously to the hominy. "A friend of mine on one of the newspapers is preparing an article on the 'Antiquity of Modern Humor.' With your kind permission, Mrs. Smithers, I'll take down your remark and hand it over to Mr. Scribuler as a specimen of the modern antique joke. You may not be aware of the fact, but that jest is to be found in the rare first edition of the *Tales of Bobbo*, an Italian humorist, who stole everything he wrote from the Greeks."

"So?" queried the Bibliomaniac. "I never heard of Bobbo, though I had, before the auction sale of my library, a choice copy of the *Tales of Poggio*, bound in full crushed Levant morocco, with gilt edges; and one or two other Italian *Joe Millers* in tree calf. I cannot at this moment recall their names."

"At what period did Bobbo live?" inquired the School-master.

"I don't exactly remember," returned the Idiot, assisting the last potato on the table over to his plate. "I don't know exactly. It was subsequent to B.C., I think, although I may be wrong. If it was not, you may rest assured it was prior to B.C."

"Do you happen to know," queried the Bibliomaniac, "the exact date of this rare first edition of which you speak?"

"No; no one knows that," returned the Idiot. "And for a very good reason. It was printed before dates were invented."

The silence which followed this bit of information from the Idiot was almost insulting in its intensity. It was a silence that spoke, and what it said was that the Idiot's idiocy was colossal, and he, accepting the stillness as a tribute, smiled sweetly.

"What do you think, Mr. Whitechoker," he said, when he thought the time was ripe for renewing the conversation—"what do you think of the doctrine that every day will be Sunday by-and-by?"

"I have only to say, sir," returned the Dominie, pouring a little hot water into his milk, which was a bit too strong for him, "that I am a firm believer

in the occurrence of a period when Sunday will be
to all practical purposes perpetual."

"That is my belief, too," observed the School-
master. "But it will be ruinous to our good landlady to provide us with one of her exceptionally
fine Sunday breakfasts every morning."

"Thank you, Mr. Pedagog," returned Mrs.
Smithers, with a smile. "Can't I give you another cup of coffee?"

"You may," returned the School-master, pained
at the lady's grammar, but too courteous to call
attention to it save by the emphasis with which
he spoke the word "may."

"That's one view to take of it," said the Idiot.
"But in case we got a Sunday breakfast every day
in the week, we, on the other hand, would get
approximately what we pay for. You may fill
my cup, too, Mrs. Smithers."

"The coffee is all gone," returned the landlady,
with a snap.

"Then, Mary," said the Idiot, gracefully, turning to the maid, "you may give me a glass of ice-
water. It is quite as warm, after all, as the coffee,
and not quite so weak. A perpetual Sunday,
though, would have its drawbacks," he added,
unconscious of the venomous glances of the landlady. "You, Mr. Whitechoker, for instance,
would be preaching all the time, and in consequence would soon break down. Then the effect
upon our eyes from habitually reading the Sunday
newspapers day after day would be extremely bad;

12

nor must we forget that an eternity of Sundays means the elimination 'from our midst,' as the novelists say, of baseball, of circuses, of horse-racing, and other necessities of life, unless we are prepared to cast over the Puritanical view of Sunday which now prevails. It would substitute Dr. Watts for 'Annie Rooney.' We should lose 'Ta-ra-ra-boom-de-ay' entirely, which is a point in its favor."

"I don't know about that," said the genial old gentleman. "I rather like that song."

"Did you ever hear me sing it?" asked the Idiot.

"Never mind," returned the genial old gentleman, hastily. "Perhaps you are right, after all."

The Idiot smiled, and resumed: "Our shops would be perpetually closed, and an enormous loss to the shop-keepers would be sure to follow. Mr. Pedagog's theory that we should have Sunday breakfasts every day is not tenable, for the reason that with a perpetual day of rest agriculture would die out, food products would be killed off by un-pulled weeds; in fact, we should go back to that really unfortunate period when women were with-out dress-makers, and man's chief object in life was to christen animals as he met them, and to abstain from apples, wisdom, and full dress."

"The Idiot is right," said the Bibliomaniac. "It would not be a very good thing for the world if every day were Sunday. Wash-day is a neces-sity of life. I am willing to admit this, in the face of the fact that wash-day meals are invariably atrocious. Contracts would be void, as a rule, because Sunday is a *dies non*."

"A what?" asked the Idiot.

"A non-existent day in a business sense," put in the School-master.

"Of course," said the landlady, scornfully. "Any person who knows anything knows that."

"Then, madam," returned the Idiot, rising from his chair, and putting a handful of sweet crackers in his pocket—"then I must put in a claim for $104 from you, having been charged at the rate of one dollar a day for 104 *dies nons* in the two years I have been with you."

"Indeed!" returned the lady, sharply. "Very well. And I shall put in a counter-claim for the lunches you carry away from breakfast every morning in your pockets."

"In that event we'll call it off, madam," returned the Idiot, as with a courtly bow and a pleasant smile he left the room.

"Well, I call him 'off,'" was all the landlady could say, as the other guests took their departure.

And of course the School-master agreed with her.

THEIR FIRST QUARREL

BY WILLIAM DEAN HOWELLS

"WE shall have time for the drive round the mountain before dinner," said Basil, as they got into their carriage again; and he was giving the order to the driver, when Isabel asked how far it was.

"Nine miles."

"Oh, then we can't think of going with one horse. You know," she added, "that we always intended to have two horses for going round the mountain."

"No," said Basil, not yet used to having his decisions reached without his knowledge. "And I don't see why we should. Everybody goes with one. You don't suppose we're too heavy, do you?"

"I had a party from the States, ma'am, yesterday," interposed the driver; "two ladies, real heavy ones; two gentlemen, weighin' two hundred apiece, and a stout young man on the box with me. You'd 'a' thought the horse was drawin' an empty carriage, the way she darted along."

"Then his horse must be perfectly worn out

to-day," said Isabel, refusing to admit the poor fellow directly even to the honors of a defeat. He had proved too much, and was put out of court with no hope of repairing his error.

"Why, it seems a pity," whispered Basil, dispassionately, "to turn this man adrift, when he had a reasonable hope of being with us all day, and has been so civil and obliging."

"Oh yes, Basil, sentimentalize him; do! Why don't you sentimentalize his helpless, overworked horse?—all in a reek of perspiration."

"Perspiration! Why, my dear, it's the rain!"

"Well, rain or shine, darling, I don't want to go round the mountain with one horse; and it's very unkind of you to insist now, when you've tacitly promised me all along to take two."

"Now, this is a little too much, Isabel. You know we never mentioned the matter till this moment."

"It's the same as a promise, your not saying you wouldn't. But I don't *ask* you to keep your word. *I* don't want to go round the mountain. I'd *much* rather go to the hotel; I'm tired."

"Very well, then, Isabel, I'll leave you at the hotel."

In a moment it had come, the first serious dispute of their wedded life. It had come, as all such calamities come—from nothing; and it was on them in full disaster ere they knew. Such a very little while ago, there in the convent garden, their lives had been drawn closer in sympathy than ever before; and now that blessed time seemed ages since, and they were further asunder than those who have never been friends. "I thought," bitterly mused Isabel, "that he would have done anything for me!" "Who would have dreamed that a woman of her sense would be so unreasonable!" he wondered. Both had tempers, as I know my dearest reader has (if a lady), and neither would yield; and so, presently, they could hardly tell how, for they were aghast at it all, Isabel was alone in her room amid the ruins of her life, and Basil alone in the one-horse carriage, trying to drive away from the wreck of his happiness. All was over; the dream was past; the charm was broken. The sweetness of their love was turned to gall; whatever had pleased them in their loving moods was loathsome now, and the things they had praised a moment before were hateful. In that baleful light, which seemed to dwell upon all they ever said or did in mutual enjoyment, how poor and stupid and empty looked their wedding-journey! Basil spent five minutes in arraigning his wife and convicting her of every folly and fault. His soul was in a whirl:

> "For to be wroth with one we love,
>   Doth work like madness in the brain."

In the midst of his bitter and furious upbraidings he found himself suddenly become her ardent advocate, and ready to denounce her judge as a

DURING THEIR FIRST QUARREL

heartless monster. "On our wedding-journey, too! Good Heavens, what an incredible brute I am!" Then he said, "What an ass I am!" And the pathos of the case having yielded to its absurdity, he was helpless. In five minutes more he was at Isabel's side, the one-horse carriage driver dismissed with a handsome *pour-boire*, and a pair of lusty bays with a glittering barouche waiting at the door below. He swiftly accounted for his presence, which she seemed to find the most natural thing that could be, and she met his surrender with the openness of a heart that forgives but does not forget, if indeed the most gracious art is the only one unknown to the sex.

She rose with a smile from the ruins of her life, amid which she had heart-brokenly sat down with all her things on. "I knew you'd come back," she said.

"So did I," he answered. "I am much too good and noble to sacrifice my preference to my duty."

"I didn't care particularly for the two horses, Basil," she said, as they descended to the barouche. "It was your refusing them that hurt me."

"And I didn't want the one-horse carriage. It was your insisting so that provoked me."

"Do you think people *ever* quarrelled before on a wedding-journey?" asked Isabel, as they drove gayly out of the city.

"Never! I can't conceive of it! I suppose,

if this were written down, nobody would believe it."

"No, nobody could," said Isabel, musingly; and she added, after a pause, "I wish you would tell me just what you thought of me, dearest. Did you feel as you did when our little affair was broken off, long ago? Did you hate me?"

"I did, most cordially; but not half so much as I despised myself the next moment. As to its being like a lover's quarrel, it wasn't. It was more bitter; so much more love than lovers ever give had to be taken back. Besides, it had no dignity, and a lover's quarrel always has. A lover's quarrel always springs from a more serious cause, and has an air of romantic tragedy. This had no grace of the kind. It was a poor, shabby little squabble."

"Oh, don't call it so, Basil! I should like you to respect even a quarrel of ours more than that. It was tragical enough with me, for I didn't see how it could ever be made up. I knew *I* couldn't make the advances. I don't think it is quite feminine to be the first to forgive, is it?"

"I'm sure I can't say. Perhaps it *would* be rather unlady-like."

"Well, you see, dearest, what I am trying to get at is this: whether we shall love each other the more or the less for it. *I* think we shall get on all the better, for a while, on account of it. But I should have said it was totally out of character. It's something you might have expected of a very young bridal couple; but after what we've been through, it seems too improbable."

"Very well," said Basil, who, having made all the concessions, could not enjoy the quarrel as she did, simply because it was theirs; "let's behave as if it had never happened."

"Oh no; we can't. To me, it's as if we had just won each other."

TIM CRANE AND WIDOW BEDOTT

BY FRANCES M. WHICHER

"Oh no, Mr. Crane, by no manner o' means, 'tain't a minnit tew soon for you to begin to talk about gittin' married ag'in. I am amazed you should be afeerd I'd think so. See—how long's Miss Crane ben dead? Six months!—land o' Goshen! why, I've know'd a number of individ-diwals get married in less time than that. There's Phil Bennett's widder 't I was a talkin' about jest now (she 't was Louisy Perce) her husband hadn't been dead but *three* months, you know. I don't think it looks well for a *woman* to be in such a hurry—but for a *man* it's a different thing—cir-cumstances alters cases, you know. And then, sittiwated as you be, Mr. Crane, it's a turrible thing for your family to be without a head to superintend the domestic consarns and tend to the children—to say nothin' o' yerself, Mr. Crane. You dew need a companion, and no mistake. Six months! Good grievous! Why, Squire Titus didn't wait but *six* weeks arter he buried his fust wife afore he married his second. I thought ther wa'n't no partickler need o' his hurryin' so, seein' his family was all grow'd up. Such a critter as he pickt out, tew! 't was very onsuitable—but every man to his taste—I hain't no dispersition to meddle with nobody's consarns. There's old Farmer Dawson, tew—his pardner hain't ben dead but ten months. To be sure he ain't married yet—but he would 'a' ben long enough ago if somebody I know on 'd gin him any incurridgement. But 'tain't for me to speak o' that matter. He's a clever old critter and as rich as a Jew—but—lawful sakes! he's old enough to be my father. And there's Mr. Smith—Jubiter Smith—you know him, Mr. Crane —his wife (she 't was Aurory Pike) she died last summer, and he's been squintin' round among the wimmin ever since, and he *may* squint for all the good it 'll dew him so far as I'm consarned—tho' Mr. Smith's a respectable man—quite young and hain't no family—very well off, tew, and quite intellectible—but I'm purty partickler. Oh, Mr. Crane! it's ten year come Jinniwary sence I witnessed the expiration o' my belovid companion!— an oncommon long time to wait, to be sure—but 'tain't easy to find anybody to fill the place o' Hezekier Bedott. I think *you're* the most like husband of ary individdiwal I ever see, Mr. Crane. Six months! murderation! curus you should be afeard I'd think 'twas tew soon — why, I've know'd—

Mr. Crane. Well, widder—I've been thinking about taking another companion—and I thought I'd ask you—

Widow. Oh, Mr. Crane, egscuse my commotion, it's so onexpected. Jest hand me that are bottle of camfire off the mantletry shelf—I'm ruther faint—dew put a little mite on my handkercher and hold it to my nuz. There—that 'll dew—I'm obleeged tew ye—now I'm ruther more composed—you may proceed, Mr. Crane.

Mr. Crane. Well, widder, I was agoing to ask you whether—whether—

Widow. Continner, Mr. Crane—dew—I know it's turrible embarrissin'. I remember when my dezeased husband made his suppositions to me, he stammered and stuttered, and was so awfully flustered it did seem as if he'd never git it out in the world, and I s'pose it's ginnerally the case, at least it has been with all them that's made suppositions to me—you see they're ginerally oncerting about what kind of an answer they're agwine to git, and it kind o' makes 'em narvous. But when an individdiwal has reason to suppose his attachment's reperated, I don't see what need there is o' his bein' flustrated—tho' I must say it's quite embarrissin' to me—pray continner.

Mr. Crane. Well, then, I want to know if you're willing I should have Melissy?

Widow. The dragon!

Mr. Crane. I hain't said anything to her about it yet—thought the proper way was to get your consent first. I remember when I courted Trypheny, we were engaged some time before mother Kenipe knew anything about it, and when she

found it out she was quite put out because I
didn't go to her first. So when I made up my
mind about Melissy, thinks me, I'll dew it right
this time and speak to the old woman first—

Widow. *Old woman*, hey! that's a purty name
to call me!—amazin' perlite, tew! Want Melissy,
hey! Tribbleation! gracious sakes alive! well,
I'll give it up now! I always know'd you was
a simpleton, Tim Crane, but I *must* confess I
didn't think you was *quite* so big a fool—want
Melissy, dew ye? If that don't beat all! What
an everlastin' old calf you must be to s'pose she'd
look at *you*. Why, you're old enough to be her
father, and more tew—Melissy ain't only in her
twenty-oneth year. What a reedickilous idee for
a man o' your age! as gray as a rat, tew! I wonder what this world *is* a-comin' tew! 'tis aston-
ishin' what fools old widdiwers will make o' themselves! Have Melissy! Melissy!

Mr. Crane. Why, widder, you surprise me—I'd
no idee of being treated in this way after you'd
ben so polite to me, and made such a fuss over me
and the girls.

Widow. Shet yer head, Tim Crane—nun o' yer
sass to me. *There's* yer hat on that are table,
and *here's* the door—and the sooner you put on
one and march out o' t'other, the better it 'll be
for you. And I advise you afore you try to git
married ag'in, to go out West and see 'f yer wife's
cold—and arter ye're satisfied on that pint, jest
put a little lampblack on yer hair—'twould add

to yer appearance, undoubtedly, and be of sarvice tew you when you want to flourish round among the gals—and when ye've got yer hair fixt, jest splinter the spine o' yer back—'twould'nt hurt yer looks a mite—you'd be intirely unresistible if you was a *lettle* grain straiter.

Mr. Crane. Well, I never!

Widow. Hold yer tongue—you consarned old coot, you. I tell ye *there's* your hat, and *there's* the door—be off with yerself, quick metre, or I'll give ye a hyst with the broomstick!

Mr. Crane. Gimmeni!

Widow (rising). Git out, I say—I ain't agwine to stan' here and be insulted under my own ruff—and so git along—and if ever you darken my door ag'in, or say a word to Melissy, it 'll be the woss for you—that's all.

Mr. Crane. Treemenjous! What a buster!

Widow. Go 'long — go 'long — go 'long, you everlastin' old gum. I won't hear another word (stops her ears). I won't, I won't, I won't.

[*Exit Mr. Crane.*

Enter Melissa, accompanied by Captain Canoot.

"Good-evenin', Cappen! Well, Melissy, hum at last, hey? Why did'nt you stay till mornin'? Purty business keepin' me up here so late waitin' for you—when I'm eny most tired to death ironin' and workin' like a slave all day—ought to ben abed an hour ago. Thought ye left me with agree-able company, hey? I should like to know what arthly reason you had to s'pose old Crane's was

agreeable to me? I always despised the critter;
always thought he was a turrible fool—and now
I'm convinced on't. I'm completely dizgusted
with him—and I let him know it to-night. I gin
him a piece o' my mind 't I guess he'll be apt to
remember for a spell. I ruther think he went off
with a flea in his ear. Why, Cappen—did ye ever
hear of such a piece of audacity in all yer born
days! for *him—Tim Crane*—to durst to expire to
my hand—the widder o' Deacon Bedott! jest as if
I'd condescen' to look at *him*—the old numskull!
He don't know B from a broomstick; but if he'd
a-stayed much longer, I'd a-teached him the difference, I guess. He's got his *walkin' ticket* now—I
hope he'll lemme alone in futur.

THE SETTLEMENT OF DRYDEN *vs.* SHARD

BY W. O. INGLIS

It was with deep relief that Theron Slocum fell into the easy-chair before his library fire. After two weeks of slavish delving, night and day, he had finished the preparation of the plantiff's case in Gormley *vs.* Glendinning.

As Slocum's eyes rested upon the glowing bank of red coals he felt as if Nirvana could bring no finer joy than this consciousness of good work faithfully done. Dreamily he heard the tinkling chime of the quarter past midnight. Then—oh, too ridiculous! Yet as he tried to give himself once more to reverie he distinctly heard again an apologetic cough behind him.

"Out with you! How did you get in here?" he exclaimed, as he whirled towards a thin man, very tall, and with a face the color of ashes, who stood regarding him mournfully. Slocum's hand grasped at the man's shoulder and swept through empty air. He staggered. He could feel his hair spring erect and bristle as a clump of dry sedge. He could not articulate.

"Pardon this intrusion," said the stranger,

"but I've come to ask you to take my case. I have no card, but you may put down in your diary to-morrow that the ghost of Clark Dryden has called upon you."

Slocum's heart began to beat again. The necessity of impressing a client revived him. He lit a cigar. The late Dryden inhaled the fumes gratefully.

"The only way we ghosts can enjoy tobacco," he explained, "is by getting to leeward of a live smoker. Let me tell you the saddest instance of treachery you have ever heard. I want you to sue Teunis G. Shard for $10,000 for professional services. Please don't interrupt me. My claim is quite regular. I worked for him—worked hard, too—as a haunter. He cheated me.

"Mr. Slocum, Shard is the worst man on earth. I was his confidential clerk for ten years. When he found a little shortage in my accounts he held it over me like a whip, and made me work for small wages: he and drink soon made an end of me. The first midnight I was allowed to revisit earth I crept up behind him just as he turned off the lights in his bedroom, and I uttered the most awful moan I could manage. What do you think the old brute did? He laughed at me. He knew my voice.

"'Don't go 'way mad, Dryden,' the old robber said to me. 'I think we can do some business. How'd you like a little drink?'

"Now you see, Mr. Slocum, the only way we

13

ghosts can drink is to inhale the fumes of burning alcohol. I was just dying— Well, I mean, I wanted a drink pretty badly. The old fellow must have seen me jump, for he lit the lamp of a chafing-dish and went on:

"'You and I can do a neat turn in real estate, and I'll supply you with drink. You know the Shepherd place in Montvale, on the Gun Hill road? Shepherd has built him a new house at Montclair, and the old one's on the market. I've offered him $18,500 for it, but he wants $25,000. You go over there and groan and meander through the place a few nights, and I guess he'll be glad to let it go for $15,000.'

"I won't try to excuse what I did; but please remember I needed a drink more than anything else in the world—the next world. Old Shard promised to reward me with half a pint of flaming alcohol every night, and I fell into the bargain.

"My efforts were successful. Mrs. Shepherd saw me first, and her screams woke her husband, and I wailed, and he dived into a wardrobe and pinched his fingers in the door in his hurry to lock it. Then old Shard dropped in casually next day, and Shepherd was glad to sell out to him for $13,500.

"Shard sold the house in less than three months for $20,000. First he ordered me to quit haunting. Then he coaxed the Psychical Research committee to investigate, gave 'em punch and supper for three or four nights—that stood him

"MRS. SHEPARD SAW ME FIRST"

in only $80 or $90—and got their written certificate that there was no ghost on the place.

"Within three years I wrecked more happy
homes than any other individual you ever heard
of. Plaindale, Somerville, Montclair, Morristown,
and all the Oranges were my stamping-ground.
Old Shard went around picking up property for
half its value and selling it soon afterwards at a
big advance. He was deep enough not to let
me wreck two homes in one town, so no one suspected him. He used to give me my flaming
half-pint of alcohol at three o'clock every morning as I was on my way home from a hard night's
haunting, groaning, and clanking. Clank? Certainly. Next time I call on you I'll bring over
the clanker I've invented. It is far more terrifying than all the old ancestral gyves and common
chain clankers you ever heard of.

"When Shard had made enough money out of
me to thrust himself into a lumber company and
the silk business, and get himself made president
of the Plaindale First National Bank, he deserted
me. Said it was dangerous to burn alcohol in
his library at that time of night. Think of it,
Mr. Slocum—that man's made $138,000 out of
me, and he's cut off my alcohol! You go ahead
and sue him for $10,000 for my professional services."

"But, my dear sir," said Slocum, who was now
puffing comfortably at his cigar, and had forgotten that he was talking with a ghost—"my

dear sir, this is all very irregular—decidedly interesting, but highly irregular. I couldn't think
of going into such a case."

"You won't?" exclaimed the ghost. "Why,
your balance at the bank is down to $200 or less.
You owe the tailor, the butcher, the baker. You
need the money—"

"Get out! Run away, or I'll scatter you!"
cried Slocum, who had now lost all sense of fear.
The ghost involuntarily leaped back, but soon
advanced again.

"You take my case," he wailed, "or I'll haunt
your wife into hysterics. You don't think you
can convince her I'm harmless, do you? You've
tried explaining things to your wife, haven't you?
Ha! ha! Just wait till she hears me gibber!"

Slocum surrendered. Before he fell asleep he
had roughly draughted a method of action.

Teunis G. Shard, expanded from a man of mean
affairs in New Jersey to an unscrupulous man of
affairs in New York, sat in his Pine Street office. His secretary handed him a letter, saying it
seemed new and important, and discreetly with-
drew. He had read only one line when he bounded out of his big chair with an agility surprising in one of his bulk, and snapped the latches
of both doors of his private office. Then he
read carefully the letter, which was from Theron
Slocum.

"Clark Dryden's claim," the lawyer wrote,

"for $10,125.55 for professional services rendered to you has been placed in my hands for collection. He claims to have assisted you in acquiring certain parcels of real estate, on which the commissions due are set forth in the schedule I enclose. If the claim is not settled forthwith, I shall feel obliged to begin an action to recover the commissions."

Can Dryden recover? thought Shard. Surely not. How can a ghost sue or get judgment? A ghost is not a person. The Thing clearly has been able to consult counsel—the schedule showed that. But how could a ghost testify in court, when his hours on earth were limited from midnight to cock-crow? With a groan Shard remembered that Judge Deane, who presided in his district, was a member of the Psychical Society, and would hold sessions of court at any hour to hear evidence against him.

There was nothing for Shard to do but call on the ghost's lawyer. He hated lawyers — they took none of the risks and they always got part of the profits.

"Tell Mr. Slocum I must see him at once. Tell him it's Mr. Shard!" roared a bullying voice on the sixteenth floor of the Warren Arcade building.

"Ask the gentleman to come in," was Mr. Slocum's reply.

Mr. Shard entered and slammed the door. Then, with his best bullying, apoplectic manner:

"How dare you, sir?" he began, shaking the lawyer's letter high in air. "How dare you—"

"Mr. Shard," interrupted the lawyer, with a calmness that was wonderful when we consider his straits—"Mr. Shard, if you want a bill of particulars in this action, you had better let your attorney apply for it in the regular way. I am prepared to give every detail."

Only too well the financier understood. Great beads came out on his brow.

"I—I'll make you a proposition," he stammered. "I'll pay your client $5000 and take his general release."

"That's something," mused Theron, with great gravity; "still, I wouldn't miss the fun of trying this case for any consideration. I am moved, I must admit, by the spectacle of suffering respectability that you present. I will do this: I will accept $7000 in settlement of my client's just claim. I am his attorney in fact as well as at law, and I can give you your general release at once."

Teunis G. Shard hastily drew a check-book from his pocket, filled out a form and signed it— not without a groan—and handed it to the lawyer. Slocum, in turn, filled all the blanks in a formidable-looking document, which to this day witnesseth that Clark Dryden, late of the State of New Jersey, doth release the said Teunis G. Shard, of the State of New Jersey, him and his heirs and assigns forever, of any and all claims of whatsoever kind and of whatsoever cause arising. When it was signed the financier read it and put it in his pocket.

Success burned in Slocum like a fever until Saturday night. For two hours before midnight he sat in his tiny library. Then he turned off the gas and lit the lamp of the chafing-dish, and instantly became aware of his friend Dryden hovering over the wavering blue, gold-threaded flame and murmuring, "Here's how!" For minutes the shade enjoyed the slaking of his posthumous thirst.

"How's our suit?" he asked at last.

"Settled out of court for this," replied Theron, tossing the check on a table remote from the alcohol.

"Um-m-m! You're a wonder," cried the ghost. "Well, you can keep the money. It's no use to me, you know. All I ask is one half-pint of alcohol every Monday night for three months and two nights. By that time I hope to get the better of the habit. Is it a bargain?"

"Surest thing in the world," replied Theron, lighting a Carolina perfecto for his own and his disembodied client's benefit, and presently regarding him over a tinkling glass in which was an exhibition of something Scotch and mellow: "Surest thing in the world. Dryden, here's to you!"

A BARN-YARD MYSTERY

BY EDWINA STANTON BABCOCK

I NEVER knew the Suicide Club existed until Faustine joined it. When she began going to roost at the top of the tallest poplar-tree with some of her bosom friends—"so as to be as near as possible to the stars," she explained—I tried to talk her out of it. "What good does being near the stars do you?" I asked. "Can you eat them? No. Can you hatch them out? No. Leave them alone, I say; they don't expect you to notice them." .

Faustine looked hurt. She said all the members of the Suicide Club had taken a vow to roost starward. "You see, we've gotten so interested in the Unattainable," said she. "We're just crazy about it; and to be up to date nowadays one has to be a little bit ahead of the date. "Want the thing you can't get," that's our motto—you can't think how progressive a motto like that makes you."

"What a motto!" I said, scornfully. "That motto's lost its tail-feathers; that motto couldn't get higher than a step-ladder; anyway, one motto doesn't make a moral. I'll give you some my grandfather taught me. He was all mottoes. He used to allow me a grasshopper with each one: 'Half a grain is worse than no corn,' 'A little chaff is no harm to good seed,' 'Never swallow before you taste.' My! that was a good one! 'Never swallow before you taste.' We don't have mottoes like that nowadays, Faustine."

Faustine looked at me with a grave eye. She's very critical, Faustine is; if she doesn't like a thing she doesn't take long to let you know it. "Duck's wisdom!" she muttered, contemptuously, and flew to the top of the rain-barrel. I always hate to see Faustine on the rain-barrel. It's not the place for her; once she gets up there she's so affected and self-conscious it's all she can do to keep her balance. It's my opinion that if it were not for her dislike of water she'd have let herelf fall in and be drowned long ago, merely for the excitement of the thing. She told me once that the reason she liked the rain-barrel was that it was gloomy and had Depth. But the real reason is that she can see herself in it. She began looking at her reflection in the water, and said, "If you really want to help me, please listen while I go through with my Theory."
"What's a Theory?" I asked.

"Oh, I don't know," she replied, hurriedly; "it's the explanation of the Symbol, you know. You're a Theory, I'm a Theory, everybody's a Theory."

I ate a fly. "I'd like to argue that with you,"
I said, under my breath. "Well, go on; say your
Theory; only first come down off that rain-
barrel."

"Never!" returned Faustine, firmly. "What I
need is Poise. You don't get Poise until you've
achieved something you're sure you can't do
standing on the edge of something you've always
been afraid of," and tightly clutching the rim of
the rain-barrel, she began to recite her Theory.
No sooner did she begin speaking than I heard a
lot of fussing and clamor; and looking up, I saw
the whole Suicide Club coming around the corner.
I knew them in an instant by their clothes. Such
a turnout! Feather boas wet and dribbly; beaks
smeared with yellow Indian and cold porridge;
rags tied around legs. Of all the dull-eyed, sad,
cynical, utterly cold and worldly gatherings! I
turned away; they made me sick. I ate some
plantain. But when she saw them crowding up,
Faustine was as happy as a cricket. She shook
out her white boa; she kissed her claw to them
as they came dawdling and yearning around the
rain-barrel.

"You're just in time to hear my Theory," she
said. "Shall I go on?"

"Oh, do!" "So good of you!" murmured the
Suicide - Clubbists. Then, behind their claws —
"Awfully brave of her." "Is studying Poise, you
know!" "Sweet-looking, don't you think?" "Mr.
Gawk—my daughter's friend—says she has tal-

ent," "A great deal of character, I should say,"
"Do you like the way she dresses?"

Faustine recommenced the Theory: "Do not
eat green worms," she said, soulfully; "they might
turn out to be blue butterflies!"

"Wonderful!" pronounced the Suicide Club;
"such intuition, such delicacy; she expresses my
ideas exactly. Are those her own feathers?"

I stepped forward. "I must argue that with
you, Faustine," I interrupted. "Ladies, if I in-
trude, forgive me; but, surely, this idea is as dangerous as it is fallacious. True, there are some
who question the complete identity of caterpillars.
I do not challenge these idealists; but when it
comes to a serious question like eating—a bug is
a bug and a worm is a worm, you'll admit that?"

"Well! I like that! Did you ever hear anything
so insulting? Disgusting!" said the Suicide Club,
nudging and muttering. "Isn't he terrible? So
awkward. Is he her husband? Wife-beater!"

"Cultivate Oneness at every opportunity," resumed Faustine, firmly. "It is difficult to realize
the Ultimate Ego without concentration!"

There was a rustle of approval. "So piquant,
so true!" sighed the Suicide Club. In asides, "Do
you believe that story that she was engaged to a
Mascot before she married?"

I was getting a little angry at this gossip. I
stepped forward again. "You're 'way beyond
your depth, Faustine," I said, crossly. "We don't
need to cultivate ultimate ego; it's bound to crop

up in everybody—spiders have it, potato-bugs
have it.   The thing is for a select few to get rid of
it—or we'll all be eating one another!"

"Pessimist! Brute!" whispered the Suicide
Club, in low tones, ruffling up and scratching nervously at the ground.

Faustine looked coldly down at me, sighed, and
glanced at her reflection in the rain-barrel.   "We
are born to soar; try flying a little higher every
day!" she declaimed, in a rapt manner.

"Broad, true, sublime," muttered a bedraggled
Suicide-Clubbist.   "She's certainly not a day over
thirty.   If she only wore a pompadour, now, how
much better-looking she'd be!"   This irritated me
more.   I determined that Faustine should cease
speaking to the vulgar rabble that was pushing
and shuffling around the rain-barrel.   There was
only one way to stop it.   Mounting to its rim myself, I waved my arms for silence.   "As for flying
a little higher," I said, in stern tones, "I advise
you not to try that! Who was it—I name no
names—I indulge in no personalities—but who
was it"—I addressed Faustine—"who, while trying to fly higher yesterday, got caught on the
clothes-line and was with the greatest difficulty
rescued from an absurd and undignified position?
who was it, I say?"   I glared at Faustine.

She put out her claw appealingly.   "Don't,
don't," she faltered; "it is cruel to disgrace me
here. Oh, if Mr. Gawk were to hear of it!"
Then she gasped and swayed, and I saw she was

losing her poise, so I pushed her off the rain-
barrel.

Now I'd been putting up with a good deal from
Faustine. I'd allowed her to give up eating angle-
worms because she said they were spoiling her
figure. I'd allowed her to give lectures on the
"Esoterics of Oyster-shells" and "How to Distin-
guish a Wasp from a Beetle without Being Stung."
I had let her teach the young pullets to roost in
circles and figure sevens to establish what she
called "Planetary Harmony in the Home." I had
even been persuaded to let her join the Defiance
Circles—groups consisting of hysterical creatures
who sit in the middle of the road all day vowing
that they will not submit to being run over. But
I was determined that I would no longer allow her
to give her refined thoughts to the Suicide Club,
and so, as I say, I pushed her off the rain-barrel.

She stood on the ground, looking about her
vaguely, and said, "Where am I?" Then she let
her eyelids fly up in a terrifying manner. The
Suicide Club were gathered around her, crowding
and peering over one another's necks, and talking
in low, scandalized tones. I, myself, at last came
down, and procured a black beetle and urged
Faustine to swallow it, for I really was worried
about her; but she turned away from me wist-
fully, saying, brokenly: "What would he say if
he knew? What would he say if he knew? Oh,
Mr. Gawk! Mr. Gawk!"—this in a heartrend-
ing voice that terrified me.

"For Heaven's sake!"—I turned to the Suicide Club—"whom does she mean by Mr. Gawk? Not the old duffer that leads the Plymouth Rocks?" The bedraggled clubbist whom I had noticed before stopped her sympathetic moans to answer: "She means Mr. Gawk, the Grand Master of the Plymouth Rock Defiance Circle; our dear leader; he's done *everything* for Faustine; he's lifted her up to his plane; he told her she had insight; oh, he's so intuitive! He has Mag—" She broke down, coughing and choking, and, followed by the lamenting Suicide Club, went slowly down the garden path. All of them appeared utterly dejected. They held their heads so low I could not tell whether they were crying or looking for ants.

"Old Gawk and his Mag?" I repeated to myself. "I don't care a green gooseberry for Old Gawk, but Mag is different. Mag is evidently some designing creature who is influencing Faustine and trying to win her away from her simple secluded life. Mag and Mr. Gawk indeed! I'll take care of them!" I edged up to Faustine, who stood silent and drooping. "The time has come," I said, loudly and impressively. Faustine started. She backed away nervously. "Oh no—no—no—no—it hasn't," she said, thickly; "I'm sure it hasn't. Look out, there's a worm!" Of course I turned to see if there really was a worm, and Faustine took this opportunity to elude me. Without a spark of honorable feeling she made her way rapidly down the garden path. When I

turned from a fruitless search for the worm, I saw
her afar off being received in the middle of the
largest Defiance Circle, whose members were
striking aggressive and reckless attitudes in the
roadway, raising their customary cry that they
would not be run over.

Turning over in my mind the events of the
morning, I walked restlessly up and down under
the currant-bushes, picking up a slight snack of
spiders as I proceeded, though after the scene
with Faustine my appetite had become rather
jaded. While I was lifting my foot preparatory
to taking an important step, I happened to see
the Widow coming towards me. The Widow is
rather small, plump as a cherry, and always
dresses in a stylish black costume that shows off
her figure. She is of a bouncing, brisk disposi-
tion, and keeps a sharp eye forward. "I'll ask
her who 'Mag' is," I thought, for the Widow
knows everybody.

I diagonalled over towards her, and, turning my
back on her, began to pick up seeds. It seemed
best to let her see me before I appeared to see her.
But the Widow was absorbed with a worm she
was trying to help out of his hole, and so I was
forced to take the initiative. I advanced towards
her. "Good weather for worms," I observed,
with easy familiarity.

"It's a good deal better for slugs," she returned,
kicking out sidewise with the stylish movement
peculiar to her.

"Oh, slugs are almost all dead and eaten now," I replied. I can always talk easily with the Widow. She is very sensible, and takes care to say the things one has heard before and knows the answer to.

I concentrated upon a refreshing pink pebble, and offered it to the Widow. "Thanks; I don't take anything but broken glass just now," said she. "How's Faustine?"

It was the opportunity I wanted. I related to the Widow the rain-barrel episode; I dwelled upon the baleful influence of Old Gawk and his assistant "Mag" upon my wife. I went on to recount the episode of the worm and Faustine's ruse to escape my righteous indignation. The Widow settled down in a comfortable dust-hole and considered the matter gravely. "What made her act like that?" she said. "You must have talked pretty roughly to her?" "Not a word did I say but the 'Time has come,' and she was gone," said I.

The Widow stared at me in a startled way. "*You said 'The time has come'* to Faustine?" she asked, with a look of blank horror. "Why, yes," I admitted. "Well," said the Widow, "a two-day-old gosling with softening of the brain is nothing to you for idiocy—reminding poor, delicate, mercurial Faustine of—what's that place that's all knives and chopping-blocks?"

"The future?" I suggested.

"Exactly," said the Widow. "The idea of talking about a *time coming* to a weak, helpless thing like Faustine—so imaginative, too, poor dear!" She sighed heavily.

"Can she not trust her future to her husband's strength and sagacity?" I argued.

"Ah!" said the Widow, somewhat bitterly, "what good does any one else's strength and sagacity do you when you're walking around a chopping-block in the dark, looking for your own head?"

I was silent. I could give no answer. At this moment a meal-call sounded. Somewhat subdued by our reflections, the Widow and I turned our steps thitherward. I had learned nothing about the enchantress "Mag" from the Widow. It now occurred to me to look about the assemblage at the meal-call and see if any such person was present. I mingled with the throngs, but in vain. After a time I encountered Faustine wearily sipping from a water-pan. As she did not look up at my approach, I paused and observed her closely. She seemed distraught and dazed, and drank as if unconscious of her own act. "Faustine," I said, gravely, "who is Mag? Is she not having a bad effect upon you? Give up her morbid friendship, cut loose from her society."

I paused. Faustine murmured, vaguely: "Individuality; my curse! I often think you and I and others suffer because we are so inimitably Ourselves."

"Good Heavens, Faustine!" I ejaculated, going up to her and trying to read her inscrutable ex-

14

pression. "You rave; you've never found any fault with your individuality before. You have been insulted by some one. I see it all. 'Mag' is at the bottom of this!"

"I cannot tell why this frightful hunger is put into our hearts," Faustine went on, hoarsely. "All day, after the morning's great strain, has seemed so gray and desolate and I so mistaken and feeble."

She staggered into the water-pan unseeingly, and walked past me, muttering and looking at each foot as she raised it with an inquiring air of such unutterable pathos that I nearly lost my reason.

"Gracious powers!" I gasped. "There is something on your mind, Faustine. You reel, you stagger. Is this some of Mag's fiendish work? Who is she? Where is she? Confide in me!"

But more and more incoherently Faustine raved, until I thought I heard the words "Mr. Gawk." I leaned forward eagerly. "Expelled! Expelled!" repeated Faustine, with dull distinctness— "for lack of enthusiasm. Oh, it can't be! It's too cruel, too cruel. And I thought the world of him. I was influenced by his Mag—" She choked and was silent.

For a second my earth whirled around me. I leaned forward dizzily to pick up what I thought was a grain of corn, and found it to be but a sunbeam, but this agony lasted only a moment. With my returning senses I looked about fiercely, and, raising my right claw, registered a vow to punish the wretch who had lured my incomparable Faustine into his Defiance Circle only to expel her. As for "Mag," I swore, let her cross my path!

Like one stung by a bee or bitten by an adder, I flew over the fence and towards the roadway.

Clouds of gnats and grasshoppers scattered before me. Delicious seeds lay in my way. I spurned them furiously, for afar off I caught sight of one whose blood I sought—Old Gawk!

At twilight, after I had given the Post-Meridian Call and was perched on my lonely roost, still smarting with the vicious thrusts of the villain whom I had done for, I felt some one alight gently on the roost close beside me. I turned. Could it be? It was Faustine! She laid her head on my shoulder. "Hero! Hero! Hero!" she repeated, convulsively, between her sobs. "They have just told me— Deliverer! Oh, how can I ever live up to anything so grand!"

"Faustine," I said, somewhat austerely, "let us not allude to the past; but one question—tell me, who is Mag?"

Raising her head, Faustine regarded me with sleepy surprise. "Mag?" she questioned, drowsily—"Mag? I don't know. The Suicide Club were always saying Mr. Gawk had 'magnetism.' Maybe you mean that."

MR. BUSH'S KINDERGARTEN CHRISTMAS

BY HAYDEN CARRUTH

"SHE hailed from around Boston somewheres, and she came out here and started one of these 'ere kindling-garters," said Mr. Milo Bush. "Roped in all the small children in town and begun to learn 'em to string straws, and map out beans, and wad wet clay and such other practical things which would be useful to 'em when they growed up. Showed 'em that they had thumbkins, and told 'em 'bout Jack Frost, and Old Man East Wind, and Uncle Feeble; and had 'em singing 'Hoppery, skippery, hop, flop, pop—summer's the time to whop, whop, whop!' Well, it seemed to be a good thing, though I don't reckon our folks would 'a' took much stock in it if it hadn't been for the girl herself. That there girl was the *prettiest* girl that ever struck the country. Such eyes as she had! And that mouth of hers!—well, I b'lieve if it could 'a' been done, that every man in town would 'a' had himself reduced to eighteen inches high and gone to school to her, and strung his straw, and wadded his gob of clay with thumbkins.

A MOTHERS' MEETING

"She was the most enthusiastic girl—*and* the prettiest! She just kept us parents on the jump. Doing what, do you think? *Living for our children!* That was all, but it kept us busy. She used to call parents' meetings, and make little speeches. 'Come, let us live for our children,' she would say. It was Uncle Feeble's igee, she explained. So that's wot we done—just lived for 'em. Rekerations of the past was abandoned, such as hoss-trots. Old Major Sudley killed his game-cock, and had him for Sunday dinner, though the Major said afterwards that the next old fighting rooster he et he would do it on a week-day, as the remarks necessary in carving the j'ints wa'n't no fit language for the Sabbath.

"Well, as I said, the girl was b'iling with enthusiasm. Every week she took the young uns on a picnic, or round to see a blacksmith, or a carpenter, or a cobbler, or somewheres. 'Ticky, tick, tack; tocky, whock, whoo—this is the way to half-sole a shoe!' Then when winter got here and Jack Frost come creeping, come creeping, there was new goings-on. Finally Christmas hove in sight, and the girl got more excited than ever. Called another mothers' meeting, and we fathers was on hand. The girl made another speech. Christmas was coming. Didn't we know the little song about Christmas? and wot it said about Sandy Claus? Though Sandy Claus was a miff, wot a bootiful miff! It was well that the little ones should believe in such miffs as long as they could! Alars! the stern realities of life would confront 'em but too soon! Let us make the Christmas of the little ones of the kindling-garter a glad one. (Applause.) Did we not want to live for our children? (A voice: 'You bet!') The song told especially of Sandy Claus's reindeers, and the children were much interested in the reindeers. Wot fond parent would volunteer to show the children a team of reindeers?

"I sprung to my feet while the other parents was leaning for'ard to rise, and says I: 'Miss, if we can find a pair of reindeers in Bon Pierre County, or even one reindeer, or *half* a reindeer, or a critter that *looks* like a reindeer, I'll drive him for the children.' 'Thank you,' says the girl, smiling at me; and if she'd 'a' asked me to drive two lions tandem, *with* a hyener under the seat, I'd 'a' done it. 'And you are on the right track, Mr. Bush,' she goes on; 'there are, of course, no reindeers here. We must stimulate some reindeers, Mr. Bush.' 'Wot?' says I, thumbkin behind my ear, letting on I hadn't heard. 'We must stimulate some reindeers—counterfeit 'em, you know. Get some other likely critters and fasten some horns on 'em, and make 'em look like reindeers.' Well, we all talked the matter over, and decided that the best we could do was to take a couple of mooley steers belonging to Zeb Woodbeck, and tie some horns on 'em, hitch 'em to a light sleigh, and let 'em sizzle, with me a-holding the reins, and mebbe calling, cheerily: 'On, Prancer! Whoa, Dancer!'

"Well, there ain't much more to tell. I done it. 'Bout four o'clock in the afternoon, so's the little ones could go home and get to bed early. The plan was to have the children in front of the school-house, and I was to dash around the corner, and swing round the house a couple or three times, and then leave the sleigh and crawl through a hole in the back end of the building, and pop out behind the stove as the children come in the door, all frosty, and with flowing whiskers, and wearing pillers under my clothes, and with my nose red. It took a pile of fixing up, and when they got through with me my nose was the only thing which I could recognize as my own. Then I got in the sleigh down by the livery-barn, and drove up around, the steers trotting off pretty free, and the bells on 'em ringing lively. Then I swung 'em round the corner, and, says I: 'On, Prancer! On, Dancer!' and the children clapped their hands, and the others begun to yell, and somehow it excited them critters, and they hopped up into the air, and yanked round their heads, and their horns fetched loose and tipped back and took 'em on the shoulders, and Dancer let out an awful 'B-a-a-a-r!' and Prancer kicked sideways at a dog, and they lit out down the main street like a bloo streak, me a-sawing on the reins and a-yelling 'The Night Before Christmas' at 'em in chunks. As we tore through town, both reindeers b-a-a-a-r-ing and kicking, the bells a-ringing, every dog in town close behind making use of their own language, and my own voice not idle, we was said to 'a' presented a impressive spectacle. We tore on. After passing over six miles of prehayrie in a few minutes, I was throwed out by the sleigh striking a rock. Them stimulated reindeers went on. My knee was fractured, and I started to crawl back the six miles, singing cherrily, 'Clap, clap with glee; for Christmas is coming and merry are we!' My whiskers impeded my crawl a good deal by getting under my knees, but I reached the house of a settler about dark.

"'Didn't you go by here a spell ago sort as if you was in a kind of a hurry?' says he.

"'No,' says I; 'that was Sandy Claus.'

"'It looked like you,' says he.

"'We are one and the same,' says I; 'e pluribus unum. I was stimulating Sandy Claus. Bring in some snow and thaw out my left earkin.'

"'See here, old man,' says he; 'before I stir a step tell me wot in all creation you are making such a Tom-twisted fool of yourself for.'

"'I am living for a Boston kindling-garter teacher,' says I; 'fetch in that snow!'"

THE MYSTERY OF SPEECH

BY JOSEPHINE DASKAM

TIME, as the book used to say, rolled on, and increased the stature of Martin Brinkerhoff Wilbour, and darkened his hair, and strengthened his legs, but did not unloose his tongue. It was fondly hoped by his relatives that the occasion of his second birthday, with its attendant celebrations, might excite him to a few words of appreciation, but though he looked volumes—encyclopædias, to quote his father—and nodded his head energetically at the proper points, to say nothing of frowning expressively when circumstances forced him to disagree with any of the guests' remarks, the discreet silence of his earlier life remained unbroken.

"It's useless to pretend that he doesn't understand, Tom, for he does," Aunt Emma declared, emphatically. "You ought to have seen him when the doctor came to see Belle and was telling Susy about her in the nursery. When he said to keep her quiet for a day or two and she'd be all right—that there wasn't any need for our worrying—Martin was watching him closely all the time, and he looked just as relieved when he said that. You can't imagine. We all noticed it."

"Do I doubt it for an instant, Aunt Emma? Haven't I seen him argue for minutes together without opening his mouth? It's not that I think him brainless—be calm, Toots—but I'm afraid of him. Why shouldn't he talk? I talk, you talk, Belle talks, Norah talks, we all talk—why doesn't he?"

"He could if he chose," Susy insisted, obstinately.

"All the worse, all the worse, my dear girl. When people can talk and won't, what is behind it? They have their reasons, doubtless, but what are those reasons? Do you know them? Do I? No; if we did we should tell. Our natures are open, frank, sympathetic. Concealment is foreign to us. That is," Mr. Wilbour interrupted himself, "it is to *me*."

Meeting with no response from his audience but a slight sniff, he continued:

"Not that I would force any confidence that would be improper for me to hear. Not for a moment. I recognize that Binks has a right to his own secrets. I am not one of those unreasonable parents who think that because a certain person happens to be their child they have the right necessarily to control every thought of that person's mind. No indeed. I respect his individuality, I hope, as much as—as any of the ladies that ever wrote books about it could wish, but at the same time I am hurt—hurt and disappointed."

"Why, Tom, what do you mean?"

Susy's eyes were fastened on her husband's serious face; she was obviously uncertain as to his earnestness.

"What do I mean? Why, simply this. If Binks had taken me aside at any time and said, 'My dear father, owing to reasons which I'm not at liberty to give, I shall not be able to communicate with you verbally for some time—for an indefinite period, in fact,' should I have resented it? No. I should have said immediately: 'Why, that's all right, old fellow: don't mention it, I'm sure. Don't talk till you feel you can do so with perfect propriety.'"

"But, Tommy, he couldn't say all that!"

"No?" Mr. Wilbour rejoined. "Well, perhaps not. But a hint, a few words, would have sufficed. I hope I have a little tact, my dear."

"I hope you have a little sense," Aunt Emma retorted, severely, "though sometimes I doubt it. I should think, Susy, you would be used to Tom Wilbour by this time. You listen to him as though what he said was worth a row of pins."

Susy might have replied with some pertinence that for at least one-half of her nephew's discourse Aunt Emma's attention had been as fixed as his wife's, but she did not. Nor did she suggest that in proportion to the length of that lady's acquaintance with Mr. Wilbour she exhibited a far greater degree of credulity than any other member of his household. She only smiled absently, with a worried look at her son, who, in the temporary absence of Belle, was playing with the soup-ladle under the direction of the entire family. Having failed in the attempt, which had lasted through the morning, to put the bowl into his mouth, at the same time holding the handle firmly between his knees, he was devoting the afternoon to an equally unsuccessful endeavor to sit in it. Occasional disgusted grunts chronicled his successive disappointments, but his general attitude was one of control, though it carried a definite implication of fighting it out on this line if it took all summer.

His guardians watched him for a few moments in silence, and only the clink and ring of the elusive ladle as it slid from under the impending bulk of its young master and echoed on the floor, accompanied by the thud of his soft body, broke the stillness.

"Heavens! how nervous I am! I simply cannot watch that child another minute!" Aunt Emma exclaimed, and left the room abruptly.

"Wouldn't you think he'd swear, though?" Mr. Wilbour queried, as Binks fell over the handle and knocked his ear on the bowl.

"I'd rather he would—if he'd only talk!" Susy declared, recklessly. Her husband regarded her with admiring surprise.

"Would you, now?" he remarked. "Dear me!"

Again there was a silence, and the light, drizzling rain that hit the nursery window was for a while the only sound, for Martin had fallen asleep on the floor with the ladle clasped to his breast.

At last Tom spoke, low, on Martin's account, and confusedly, because of a discontented yawn that thickened his speech.

"I thank the Lord there's only one Memorial Day in the course of the year."

"Decoration Day, I call it," his wife suggested, in a superior tone.

"That's a provincialism, and a childish one at that. The inhabitants of New England, among whom I am proud to—"

"Oh yes, the breaking waves dashed high. I know all about that," Mrs. Wilbour interrupted, irreverently. "Anybody would think that Massachusetts was the one place where you could learn that—or anything else!"

"It is undoubtedly the best place," Mr. Wilbour replied, politely, "though I should not like to say—"

"Oh, get along, Tommy! I should think not! Decoration Day has some sense: that's what they do—decorate."

"Don't tell *me* what they do," her husband returned, snappishly, yet with a careful suppression of voice and a glance at the sleeping Binks, "I know too well! What have I been doing all the morning? They, indeed! You might as well say me, for nobody has decorated more to the

square inch than I have. Those infernal snowballs! It makes me sick to think of them!
Ugh!"

Susy's face grew involuntarily more sympathetic.

"Was it very bad this time?" she inquired.

"Bad? It was worse than ever. It makes me
nervously prostrated for the day. It would be
one thing if I ever knew any of 'em from Adam."

"You knew Uncle William Wyman," Susy reminded him, perversely.

"Uncle William Wyman!" He exploded in a
snort of rage that threatened the slumber of his
son, who turned uneasily in the midst of happy
dreams of an abject and conquered soup - ladle.
"Yes, I did know Uncle William Wyman, and
for how long? For exactly two years, when I
was fifteen years old! Besides being the most
narrow - minded man in the town, and making
me pass the plate when I had new boots that
squeaked all over the church—"

"Hush! you'll wake Martin up!"

"Very well, then, don't mention Uncle William
Wyman's name to me! Slapping down snowballs on his grave, indeed! I think Aunt Em is
perfectly morbid — it upsets her, too. Of all
idiotic holidays!"

Mr. Wilbour thrust his hands deep into his
pockets and sprawled moodily in his chair. It
had been a hard day for him.

Aunt Emma was not sentimental, but she was

as devoutly given to the yearly adornment of the
many graves of her family connection as if they
occupied any appreciable part of her thoughts
during the intermediate time.   It had been her
custom, for the ten years of her life in New York,
to arise early on the morning of May 30th, and
proceed up - town, reluctantly accompanied by
her nephew, bearing baskets of the snowballs so
distasteful to him, and secure in the consciousness
of dozens more of that obvious and solid blossom
waiting at the florist's near the great cemetery.
"Miss Wilbour's snowballs" were as regular a
part of that gentleman's income as his weekly
church orders, and he invariably spared her one
of his little sons to stagger under the two great
basketfuls that he had reserved for her.   He was
never without a young son of the proper age, and
Tom had been known to hazard a bet that he
raised them for this express purpose.

As a further concession to the solemnity of the
day, Aunt Emma attired herself in unwonted
black, even to her gloves, and whistling or light
conversation on the way was distinctly felt to be
out of keeping with the occasion.   It so happened
that with the exception of one sister, who had
been much older than she and whom she had
hardly known, none of the relatives buried at
Woodlawn were closely connected with Miss Wilbour, uncles, cousins, and an almost mythical
personage referred to by Tom as my half-step-
aunt, comprising the tale; but there were at least

eight of these, besides Tom's godmother, whom
he had never seen, and the betrothed of one of
the uncles, who was supposed to have had a most
romantic history, complicated with a vow on
somebody's part to put flowers on her grave once
a year.

One would have supposed Aunt Emma to be
the last person likely to assume such a respon-
sibility, but it was nevertheless her hand that
arranged the inevitable snowballs beneath the
young woman's tombstone, and her resigned if
somewhat vague account of the heroine that was
destined to go down to posterity.

Why the snowball should appeal to Aunt Emma
as the one and only floral offering suited to these
mortuary purposes her nephew never learned,
but its association with the tomb was definitely
fixed in his mind, and he loathed it above all the
products of nature. It was curiously connected,
too, with his married life. His first lover's quarrel with Susy had occurred on May 29th, and
with his own hands he had given to the mes-
senger-boy the enormous box of supposed roses
that proved later to be the first instalment of
Aunt Emma's yearly tribal sacrifice. Sick with
horror, for to him any faintest connection with
the hated blossom was actually fatal to life, to
say nothing of the insult of offering them as a pro-
pitiatory gift to his offended mistress, Tom had
rushed to her house with the roses scorned by
Aunt Emma, and endured agonies of mortifica-

tion at the hands of her sister, who had never
ceased to comment on the originality of his taste
in that direction.

Well did he remember the occasion of the anniversary two years ago. Martin was four months
old at that time, and had been forced to go without his supper, as Tom had so worked up Susy's
sense of humor by his dramatic recital of the cor-
tège of the morning that she had threatened a
real hysteria, and the nurse had sternly forbidden
her to assist at the approaching supper-party—
which was hard on the principal guest. Aunt
Emma's righteous wrath on this occasion and the
nurse's ill-concealed disgust had hurt his feelings
very much.

The following year he had been observed, to his
undying wrath and shame, by one of the most important clients of his firm, who, while on a tour of
inspection through the grounds, apparently, had
caught sight of the young counsel heaping snowballs upon his half-step-aunt's grave, and had un-
warrantedly decided that he was mourning over
the tomb of his wife. Being a kindly man and
having been much pleased with Mr. Wilbour's
manners and appearance in the office, where he
held the position of junior partner, this client had
walked softly to where the bereaved one knelt,
and waited reverently. As he rose to his feet
after having covered the mound neatly with the
puffy white balls (Aunt Emma was very particular that there should be no bare spots), the aston-

ished young man felt a gentle pat upon the shoulder and heard a subdued murmur implying that the speaker had shared precisely this sad experience. Filled as he was with deep self-pity, the sympathy was sweet to Mr. Wilbour, and for a few uncomprehending seconds he had accepted it silently; then as it dawned on him that the mathematical probabilities of a half-step-aunt and the consequent snowballs were, in the distinguished client's case, very slight, he had demanded an explanation. The distinguished client had mentioned softly the breaking of the closest possible tie; Tom had scornfully repudiated his vague relative in this connection. The client, surprised but obstinately unenlightened, referred definitley to his own wife, "though not so young as yours, Mr. Wilbour."

At which the disgusted Thomas, with a snort of rage, had burst forth:

"Great Scott! It's my half-step-aunt, and I never saw her in my life, and I don't want to, either!"

At this they had parted abruptly, the client divided between incredulity and displeasure, Tom resignedly convinced that he had estranged forever one of the props of the firm, and correspondingly grateful to his half-step-aunt.

Recollection of these successively unlucky anniversaries did not add to the victim's cheerfulness on the present occasion, and as the atmosphere of impersonal gloom which wrapped Aunt

Emma extended inevitably to her niece, who re-
flected to a large extent the state of mind of those
about her, the house of Wilbour was sinking slowly
into a state of dark depression.   Tom was in the
frame of mind in which a woman snatches for her
handkerchief and after a few preliminary gulps
collapses into a comfortable fit of tears, to rise
refreshed and magnanimous a little later; but
Tom was a man, and possessed of no other re-
course than to kick the floor nervously and think
unsuitable thoughts.   It occurred to him that in
this crisis his wife was notably unhelpful: far from
cheering him, she merely eyed the toe of her slip-
per morosely and scowled if his tappings and
twitchings seemed to threaten the repose of Martin, who had twisted himself into a particularly foolish attitude around the soup - ladle and
slumbered somewhat audibly, with his mouth
open.

"Oughtn't he to shut his mouth?" his father
inquired, disparagingly.   "Won't he get something or other?"

"You sleep that way sometimes, and you don't
seem to get anything," Susy returned, not without point but with a distinct lack of interest.   If
Mr. Wilbour had known that she was thinking him
perilously near the point of getting too fat, and
resenting bitterly the hideous tie he had selected
in unconscious deference to the day, he would have
felt even more aggrieved than he did.

"We should all breathe through the nose," he

announced, didactically, "everybody agrees upon that.   You have only to watch the animals—"

"A dog breathes through its mouth when it's running," Susy observed, impersonally.

Her husband frowned.

"I wasn't thinking of dogs," he said, shortly, "I—"

"Oh, of course, if you take out all the animals!"

"A dog is not the only animal, Susy."

"No, but it is the most important one."

"I don't agree with you," began Mr. Wilbour, crossly, "the horse—   Oh, what nonsense!"

And again they lapsed into silence, broken only by the audible slumber of Binks.

Suddenly Tom realized a new source of discomfort, vague at first, but growing clearer with every second.   What had been a low, indistinguishable crooning was developing into a mournful melody, and as he listened, words detached themselves from the tune:

> "*Just* BREAK *the* NEWS *to* MOTHER,
> *And* TELL *her* THAT *I* LOVE *'er,*
> *But* TELL *her* NOT *to* LOOK *for me,*
> *For I shall* NOT *come* HOME!"

It was the voice of Belle, who was solacing her convalescence with the cheerful variety of song peculiar to her temperament, and even as Mr. Wilbour began to speak, the tune returned upon itself, and the refrain started again:

> "*Just* BREAK *the* NEWS *to* MOTHER—"

"What in the d—deuce is the matter with that girl? It's enough to drive a man to drink! Why doesn't she sing something else?" he demanded, furiously.

"She always sings that kind of song, you know very well," Mrs. Wilbour responded. "I don't believe she knows any other kind."

"It might just as well be Sunday! I couldn't feel any worse," he groaned. "And day after tomorrow it *will* be Sunday! Two in a week. It's too much. Can't she be stopped?"

"I don't see how," Susy answered, unsympathetically. "I can't exactly forbid the poor girl to amuse herself."

"Amuse herself? Amuse herself? Does that ghastly howling amuse her?"

"It must, or she wouldn't do it. Nobody urged her to sing, I suppose."

"No, I suppose not," he agreed, bitterly. "Nobody in their senses. How long— Heavens! what's that?"

For a depressing alto at that moment added itself to the melody, and wandered at an unsteady distance below it. It was undoubtedly a human voice, but it occurred violently to Mr. Wilbour that no human creature capable of producing such a variety of sound could possibly have been permitted to exist within shooting-distance of any fellow-man.

"Who—*what* is that?" he exploded.

"It is Norah, probably," Susy replied. "She

said she would rather come up into Belle's room and sit with her than take her afternoon out. Which was very nice of her, of course."

"Oh, very," he muttered, with his last shred of control, gritting his teeth fiercely.

"For I shall NOT *come ho-o-o-me!"*

moaned the duet, the soprano wailing like a lost soul, the alto recalling a fog-horn on a misty afternoon at sea.

"Oh, this is too much—I swear this is too much!" Tom strode across the room in desperation.

"What are you going to do?" Susy inquired, warningly.

"Do? do? I'm going to stop that infernal noise!"

"Don't be absurd, Tom. If they want to sing, they must certainly be allowed to. It does no harm and it won't last long, probably. Belle doesn't feel well, and it would hurt her feelings very much if—"

"Well, I can tell her one thing, she'll never feel any better while she does that! She'll have a relapse. And I suppose my feelings are of no importance."

"That's a very different thing," said Mrs. Wilbour.

"All my life I have hated and despised alto!" Tom proclaimed. "From a boy it has affected

me very strangely. That's why I hate Sunday.
People will sing alto on Sunday that would never
dream of singing it any other time. It's the
beastliest thing in the world. It makes you want
to die and get it over with. They used to have a
prayer-meeting in the house next to ours in
Greenfield, and when they got singing things with
alto in 'em I used to get so blue I nearly cried.
And it's the same way now."

"Well, cry now, if you want to," Susy suggested,
coolly. "Why don't you?"

This was too much for Mr. Wilbour's self-con-
trol. In his irritable state of nerves he could bear
no more, and sitting down forcibly in the nearest
chair, he uttered an angry and unpardonable
monosyllable.

I am informed that this little monosyllable is
highly offensive to many if not all of my present
readers, and so I will go no further than to say
that it begins with a letter not far from the front
of the alphabet and is frequently encountered in
real life—probably the best of reasons for elimi-
nating it from fiction, which should rather seek to
idealize the brutality of disgraceful facts than appear to encourage them with recognition.

The utterance of the monosyllable just mentioned appeared to relieve Mr. Wilbour's feelings
to a degree, for on his wife's leaving the room with
dignity, he repeated it, not once, but three distinct times, with great energy and clearness of ar-
ticulation. Pausing in a hasty march across the

room, his hair rumpled over his ears and his eyes
narrowed with the force of his remarks, he confronted his son, who met his look with one so
knowing that it was impossible to doubt his entire appreciation of the situation.

"Well," snapped his father, "what is it? Do
you like that infernal alto? What have you got
to say?"

Binks unscrewed the soup-ladle from his mouth,
grasped it with both hands in the fashion of a
golfer about to accomplish a tremendous drive,
and, smiling cheerfully at his father, repeated
the monosyllable the gentleman had just employed.

Mr. Wilbour staggered back, his jaw dropping,
the evidence of his senses in grave doubt. He
would as soon have expected speech from the cat
as from his son. As he stared wildly at the
wielder of the ladle, that young person rose to
his feet, and again manipulating his instrument
in a manner calculated to send a ball half-way
around the links, repeated the monosyllable.
There could be no doubt—he said it, and he
meant it.

It was a terrible moment. That the great
mystery of human speech should have been re-
vealed to Binks at a time and in a manner which
admitted of no proud advertisement! He had
spoken, indeed, but how? And at whose instiga-
tion? Mr. Wilbour actually groaned.

"Stop it! stop it!" he cried. "For Heaven's

BESEECHING BABY TO REPEAT HIS RECENT ADDRESS

sake, Binks, don't say that!   What will they say?
How did I know you'd—"

But Binks, who evidently felt that some nicety
of inflection was yet to be gained, calmly repeated
his last remark again with so accurate a mimicry
of his father's tone that the unhappy man, divided
between admiration and horror, could only gasp
and glance fearfully towards the door.

At this point, Martin, fixing his eyes firmly upon
his parent and pounding the floor with the ladle
at regular intervals, recited entirely without punct-
uation, but otherwise with masterly elocution,
the following speech: "Bad kitty put 'er out
Aunty Vail hot milk up-town!"

"Wh-what?   Here, Susy, Aunt Emma, come
here!   Wh-what did you say, Binks?"

They rushed into the room, pale with fright, to
see Tom squatting eagerly before the baby, beseeching him to repeat his recent address.

"He's been talking like a streak of lightning,
I tell you!   He talks as well as anybody!   Say
it again, won't you?   It's something about hot
milk—"

"Does he want hot milk?" Aunt Emma inquired, excitedly.   "Shall I get some?"

"Oh no, he doesn't want it: he just mentioned
it—in passing," Tom returned, more at ease now
and devoutly hoping that his son's second achieve-
ment had put the first out of his mind.

"What else did he say?" Susy demanded, fever-
ishly.

"He said something about Aunty Vail and the kitty— There, he's going to again!"

And indeed he began, with the automatic effect of a phonograph, a curious suggestion of having been filled with perforated rolls and wound up:

"Bad kitty put 'er out Aunty Vail hot milk up-town!"

The delighted women screamed and squealed with joy, Binks smiled in a superior manner, and Mr. Wilbour, feeling somehow responsible for the whole thing, watched them complacently.

"Was that just the way he said it before, Tom?" Aunt Emma asked, eagerly.

"Just exactly."

"Was that all he said, every bit?" Susy added, quickly.

"Heavens! wasn't that enough?" her husband equivocated.

"Then the first word, the very first word, he said, was 'bad,'" Aunt Emma announced.

"It certainly was," her nephew announced, heartily, "it certainly was!"

And to his excited eyes it seemed that Martin winked gravely at him.

A LITTLE ESSAY ON BOOKS

BY F. PETER DUNNE

"HOGAN tells me that wan iv th' first things man done afther he'd larned to kill his neighborin' animals, an' make a meal iv wan part iv thim an' a vest iv another, was to begin to mannyfacther lithrachoor, an' it's been goin' on up to th' prisint day. Thim was times that th' Lord niver heerd about, but is as well known to manny a la-ad in th' univarsity iv southren Injyanny as if th' histhry iv thim was printed on a poster. Hogan says a pro-fissor with a shovel an' a bad bringin'-up can go out annywhere along th' dhrainage-canal an' prove to ye that th' Bible is no more thin an exthry avenin' edition iv th' histhry iv th' wurruld, an' th' Noah fam'ly was considhered new arrivals in th' neighborhood where they lived. He says he'll show ye th' earth as though 'twas a section iv a layer-cake or an archytect's dhrawin' iv a flat-buildin', an' p'int out how 'twas accumylated.

"First 'twas a mere squdge in which ne'er a livin' thing cud be found. This peryod lasted a few millyion years, an' thin th' mush caked an' become buildin'-materyal, an' threes grew out iv th' buildin'-materyal an' fell down an' become coal. Thin th' wather come—but where it come fr'm I don't know, f'r they was no God at th' time—an' covered th' earth, an' thin th' wather evaporated an' left little p'ints iv land shtickin' up with ready-made men an' women occypyin' thim, an' at that moment th' Bible begun. Ye might say we're livin' on th' roof iv a flat, with all th' apartmints beneath us occypied be th' bones iv submarine monsthers an' other tinants.

"Lasteways that's what Hogan tells me, but I don't believe a wurrud he says. Most iv th' people iv this wurruld is a come-on f'r science, but I'm not. Ye can't con-vince me, me boy, that a man who's so near-sighted he can't read th' sign on a cable-car knows anny more about th' formation iv th' earth thin Father Kelly. I believe th' wurruld is flat, not round; that th' sun moves an' is about th' size iv a pie-plate in th' mornin' an' a car-wheel at noon; an' it's no proof to me that because a pro-fissor who's peekin' through a chube all night says th' stars ar-re millyions iv miles away an' each is bigger thin this wurruld, that they're bigger thin they look, or much higher thin th' top iv th' shot-tower. I've been up tin thousand feet on a mountain, an' they seemed so near that I kept whiskin' thim off me nose as I lay there on me back, but they wasn't anny larger thin they were on th' sthreet-level. I believe what I see an' some iv th' things I'm told,

if they've been told often, an' thim facts iv science has not been hung long enough to be digist-
ible.

"But, annyhow, they say that man first begun
writin' whin he had to hammer out his novels an'
pomes on a piece iv rock, an' th' hammer has
been th' imblim iv lithrachoor iver since. Thin
he painted it on skins, hince th' publisher; thin he
played it an' danced it an' croshayed it till 'twas
discovered that ink an' pa-aper wud projooce
wurruds, an' thin th' printin'-press was invinted.
Gunpowdher was invinted th' same time, an' 'tis
a question I've often heerd discussed which has
done more to ilivate th' human race. A joke.

"Th' longer th' wurruld lasts th' more books
does be comin' out. Day be day I r-read in th'
pa-apers announcemints iv new publications that
look like th' dilinquent tax-list. They's a publisher in ivry block, an' in thousan's iv happy
homes some wan is pluggin' away at th' romantic
novel or whalin' out a pome on th' type-writer
up-stairs. A fam'ly without an author is as con-
timptible as wan without a priest. Is Malachi
near-sighted, peevish, averse to th' suds, an'
can't tell whether th' three in th' front yard is
blue or green? Make an author iv him! Does
Miranda prisint no atthractions to th' young men
iv th' neighborhood, does her overskirt dhrag, an'
is she poor with th' gas-range? Make an authoreen
iv her! Forchunitly, th' manly insthinct is often
too sthrong f'r th' designs iv th' fam'ly, an'

manny a man that if his parents had had their way might have been at this moment makin' artifical feet f'r a deformed pome is l'adin' what me fri'nd Hogan calls a glad, free, an' timpery-mintal life on th' back iv a sthreet-car.

"But lithrachoor is th' gr-reat life-wurruk iv th' modhren woman. Th' conthrol is passin' into th' hands iv th' fair sect, an' th' day will come whin th' wurrud book will mane no more to an able-bodied man thin th' wurrud gusset. Women write all th' romantic novels that ar-re anny good. That's because ivry man thinks th' thrue hayroe is himsilf, an' ivry woman thinks he's James K. Hackett. A woman is sure a good, sthrong man ought to be able to kill anny number iv bad, weak men, but a man is always wondherin' what th' other la-ad wud do. He might have th' punch left in him that wud get th' money. A woman niver cares how manny men are kilt, but a man believes in fair play, an' he'd like to see th' polis intherfere about Chapter Three.

"Women writes all th' good romantic novels, an' read thim all. If anny proud la-ad in th' gum business thinks he riprisints th' ideal iv his wife's soul, he ought to take a look at th' books she reads. He'll larn there th' reason he's where he is, is because he was th' on'y chanst, not because he was th' first choice. 'Twud humble th' haughtiest prince iv thrade to look into th' heart iv th' woman he cares most f'r an' thinks laste about, an' find that, instead iv th' photygraft iv

a shrewd but kindly man with a thriflin' absence
iv hair on his head an' a burglar-proof safe on his
watch-charm, there's a pitcher iv a young la-ad
in green tights playin' a mandolin to a high front
stoop. On th' stoop, with a rose in her hand, is
his lawful-wedded wife, th' lady Annamariar Hug-
gins iv Peotone. Ye can't keep her away fr'm a
romantic novel. No matther what Edward At-
kinson tells ye, she prefers *Th' Age iv Chivalry*
to th' mos' atthractive housewurruk. A woman's readin' is niver done. Hardly a day passes
but some lady frind iv mine stops me on me way
to catch a car, an' asks me if I don't regard Morse
Hewlett as th' gr-reatest an' mos' homicidal
writer iv our time, an' what I've got to say about
Hinnelly's attack on Stevenson. 'Madam,' says
I, 'I wudn't know Morse if I was to see him goin'
down th' sthreet axe in hand, an' as f'r Hinnelly,
his name escapes me, though his language is
familiar to anny wan who iver helped load a
scow. Stevenson,' I says, 'doesn't appeal to
me, an' if he shud, I'll revarse th' decision on
th' ground iv th' bad prevyous charackter iv th'
plaintiff, while,' I says, 'admittin' th' truth iv
what he said. But,' says I, 'th' on'y books in
me libr'y is th' Bible an' Shakespeare,' says I.
'They're gr-reat f'r ye,' says she. 'So bully f'r
th' style. D' ye read thim all th' time?' she says.
'I niver read thim,' says I. 'I use thim f'r purposes iv definse. I have niver read thim, but
I'll niver read annything else till I have read thim,'

I says. 'They shtand between me an' all modhren lithrachoor,' says I. 'I've built thim up into a kind iv breakwather,' I says, 'an' I set behind it ca'm an' contint while Hall Caine rages without,' says I.

"Yes, sir, th' readin' an' writin' iv books is as much woman's wurruk as th' mannyfacther iv tidies. A woman is a nachral writer. She don't mind givin' hersilf away if 'twill bring a tear to th' eye or a smile to th' lips. But a man does. He has more to give away. I'm not sayin' that anny man can't write betther thin a woman if he wants to. But so can he cuk betther, an' sew betther, an' paint minichoors betther, an' do annything betther but nurse th' baby — if he wants to; but he don't often want to. He despises such thrivyal pursuits. Mos' iv th' gr-reat writers I iver see th' pitchers iv was little, thin, peevish men that was always gettin' licked. Wanst in a while a sthrong man got into th' game, a bull - necked, round - headed man that might have made a fine thrack-master or boiler-maker, but was addicted to dhrink, an' niver had energy enough left in th' mornin' f'r annything more thin writin' th' best plays or th' finest novels or th' gr-reatest histhries in th' wurruld. But if ye got at th' rale feelin' iv three-meal-a-day men about writin', ye'd find they classed it with preachin', school-teachin', play-actin', dancin', an' lace-wurruk. A man iv that kind might start to write, but if he did, he'd stop an' think afther a while, an' say to himsilf: 'What's a big, sthrong, able-bodied, two hundhred-an'-tin-pound, forty-four-acrost-th'-chest crather like me doin' here, pokin' these funny hireyoglyphics into a piece iv pa-aper with a little sthick? I guess I'll go out an' shoe a horse.'

"So it is with readin'. I'm tol' I ought to read more be Hogan, who's wan iv th' best-read an' mos' ignorant men I know. Well, maybe I ought, though whin I was a young man, an' was helpin' to build up this counthry, th' principal use iv lithrachoor was as a weepin. In thim days, if a little boy was seen readin' a book, his father took it away fr'm him an' bate him on th' head with it. Me father was th' mos' accyrate man in th' wurruld with letthers. He found th' range nachrally, an' he cud wing anny wan iv us with th' *Lives iv th' Saints* as far as he cud see. He was a poor man, an' on'y had such books in his libr'y as a gintleman shud take, but if ye'd give him libr'y enough, he'd capture Giber-altor. If lithrachoor niver pinethrated me in-telleck, 'twas not his fault. But nowadays, whin I go down th' sthreet, I see th' childher settin' on th' front steps studyin' a book through double-compound-convex spectacles, lookin' like th' off-spring of a pro-fissyonal diver. What 'll they iver grow up to be? Be Hivins! that la-ad Car-naygie knows his business. He is studied th' situation, an' he undhersthands that if he builds libr'ies enough an' gets enough people readin'

16

books, they won't be anny wan left afther a while
capable iv takin' away what he's got. Ye bet
he didn't larn how to make steel billets out iv
Whin Knighthood was in Flower. He larned
it be confabulatin' afther wurrukin' hours with
some wan that knew how. I think he must be
readin' now, f'r he's writin' wan or two. 'Tis th'
way with a man who takes to readin' late in life.
He can't keep it down.

"Readin', me frind, is talked about be all readin'
people as though it was th' on'y thing that makes
a man betther thin his neighbors. But th' thruth
is that readin' is th' nex' thing this side iv goin'
to bed f'r restin' th' mind. With mos' people it
takes th' place iv wurruk. A man doesn't think
whin he's readin', or if he has to, th' book is no
fun. Did ye iver have something to do that ye
ought to do, but didn't want to, an' while ye
was wishin' ye was dead, did ye happen to pick
up a newspaper? Ye know what occurred. Ye
didn't jus' skim through th' spoortin' intillygince
an' th' crime news. Whin ye got through with
thim, ye read th' other quarther iv th' pa-aper.
Ye read about people ye niver heerd iv, an'
happenin's ye didn't undhersthand—th' fashion
notes, th' theatrical gossip, th' s'ciety news fr'm
Peoria, th' quotations on oats, th' curb market,
th' rale-estate transfers, th' marredge licenses, th'
death notices, th' want ads., th' dhrygoods bargains, an' even th' iditoryals. Thin ye r-read thim
over again, with a faint idee ye'd read thim be-

fure. Thin ye yawned, studied th' design iv th'
carpet, an' settled down to wurruk. Was ye ex-
ercisin' ye-er joynt intelleck while ye was readin'?
No more thin if ye'd been whistlin' or writin'
ye-er name on a pa-aper. If anny wan else but
me come along they might say: 'What a mind
Hinnissy has! He's always readin'.' But I wud
kick th' book or pa-aper out iv ye-er hand, an'
grab ye be th' collar, an' cry, 'Up, Hinnissy, an'
to wurruk!' f'r I'd know ye were loafin'. Believe
me, Hinnissy, readin' is not thinkin'. It seems
like it, an' whin it comes out in talk sometimes,
it sounds like it. It's a kind iv nearthought that
looks ginooine to th' thoughtless, but ye can't get
annything on it. Manny a man I've knowed has
so doped himsilf with books that he'd stumble
over a carpet-tack.

"Am I again' all books, says ye? I'm not. If
I had money, I'd have all th' good lithrachoor
iv th' wurruld on me table at this minyit. I
mightn't read it, but there it 'd be so that anny
iv me fri'nds cud dhrop in an' help thimsilves if
they didn't care f'r other stimylants. I have no
taste f'r readin', but I won't deny it's a good
thing f'r thim that's addicted to it. In modheration, mind ye. In modheration, an' afther th'
chores is done. F'r as a frind iv Hogan's says,
'Much readin' makes a full man,' an' he knew what
he was talkin' about. An' do I object to th' pursuit iv lithrachoor? Oh, faith, no. As a pursuit 'tis
fine, but it may be bad f'r anny wan that catches it."

BILLY CAMPBELL'S JUNGLE STORY

BY HUGH PENDEXTER

"SHALL it be torrid or cold storage?" inquired Billy Campbell, the strolling actor, as he knocked the heel from his pipe and crammed in some plug-cut, very strong, that he was given to consuming.

With a shiver I glanced at the strings of sleet slapping the window-panes of my rooms and replied, "Torrid."

"Then we'll have to go to Chihuahua," decided Campbell, as he settled down contentedly before the grate and drew long and deep at his brier. "And this is the only way we can visit the home of frijoles and tortillas," he added. "For ever since Tiberius Smith wrenched four of his countrymen from the rude grasp of the Aztecs that republic has been closed to us. And say, the exit of Tib from the home of the Montezumas cost him one of the best animal shows that ever growled through the streets of a country town at II A.M."

"Suppose, old chap, you begin at the beginning," I suggested.

"All right. Now, look. It was early in the

winter when we reached the southwestern circuit with a wild-animal show, and Tiberius decided to run down to Chihuahua from El Paso. His object was threefold. He wanted to obtain some Mexican specimens for his outfit, and he believed he could meet expenses by satisfying the childish curiosity of the mestizos, who, by-the-way, form one-half of the population in old Mexico, and are in almost as abject a state of slavery as were their forebears under the first passenger-list of Spaniards coming over in the *Mayflower*. And lastly, he had contracted to engage a troupe of bull-fighters and Mazeppa-like dons for a big wild West show. So much for the incentive.

"We arrived healthy and flea-bitten, and easily picked up the scenery desired by the colonel, and were considering a tempting offer to show for the winter in Mexico City, when a sun-kissed peon, with a large quantity of aguardiente concealed about his person, came to our show-tent and tried to bite his way by the rotund Vermont man without crossing our palms with silver. That's largely metaphor, as we let them in for what they had, except the alcalde, who entered deadhead. 'Take what you can,' was our motto; but the half-breed forestalled a shake-down by explaining, in badly fractured English, that he had a message for Don Hidalgo Tiberio, which he would only deliver in return for a front seat. It was written by an Americano, he said, who was in Quelta, an adjacent town.

"We yanked him within the portals and placed him perilously near the hyena's cage and then procured the note. I could see Tib was worked up over the contents, for his round face was drawn down in four curves as he digested it.

"'Too bad, Billy,'' he said, in a whisper. 'And one of them worked in Vermont once.'

"'Poor devil!' I sighed; for as Vermont was Tib's home State, I knew my irrelevant remark would make him mad.

"'Certainly it's poor devil when a white man fresh from that blessed State is in this plight,' he snapped, his brown eyes becoming two points. 'Here, read.'

"It seems there were four 'poor devils,' all Americans. They were in Quelta, the letter said, waiting to be sent to the salt-mines for life. Now a man who knows Mexico would rent the salt-mines out to his dearest enemy and live in Hades —if he owned both. The letter was a brief one, the writer merely stating his prospects, and saying he had heard from his guards of Smith's presence in Chihuahua. He begged Tiberius to rescue him if he had any love for the children of the star-spangled banner.

"Tib knew Spanish more or less, chiefly less, but he carried a gilt-headed cane that would make up the difference in effect on the average alcalde, and a quick trot to the halls of justice gave him an insight to the situation. It seems Murphy, the writer, and his friends had been foolish enough

to hire out as a train crew on the Central, and that
their train, near Quelta, had run over a big-bug's
hired man.   Now the average peon, after absorb-
ing all the visible supply of aguardiente, will hunt
all over the map for the most *outré* place in which
to sleep off his pink rabbits, and nothing appeals
to his sordid imagination so much as a busy railroad track when it comes to trundle-beds.   But
while the U. S. lines yearly cause the battle of
Gettysburg to blush when it comes to boasting
of carnage, our little brunette brother beyond the
Rio Grande has a way of making it uncomfortable
for train crews when a simple life is crushed out.
It isn't because a peon is highly prized as a bit
of social bric-à-brac, but because, I reckon, the
train crews are usually made up of, or bossed by,
Americans.

"The alcalde admitted the defendants had no
course to choose, except to run over the man, but
he added, with a graceful flirt of his hands: 'The
man is dead.   What would you have?   The lesson
must be taught.'   He also said that the three
judges who sat on the case at first were of the
inclination to let a line of bare footed rifle-
men toy with the quartet behind a 'dobe wall.
'But,' he concluded, 'we are merciful, we are
merciful.'

"After kicking the hyena to stop his howling,
Tib sat down by the bear-cage that night and
thought steady for ten minutes.   Then he jolted
his hat over his right ear, and I began to realize

we were about to become fair and merry knight-
errants.

"'Billy,' he declared, 'I could never paint polka-
dots on a greyhound and believe he was a leopard
if I left those men to go to the country of saline
pursuits. Once we can get them out of Quelta
it's a quick dash to the Rio, and farewell to the
dons of the blue Pacific.'

"That was his poetry. Whenever he was stung
into radical action he always talked in circus type.
But he had a scheme back of it all that caused
my sapphire eyes to bulge out and touch the walls
of the tent. I asked him if he were to invade a
lunatic asylum that we must indulge in such opera-
bouffe. I even doubted if Murphy and his friends
would submit to being rescued by such legerde-
main.

"'I've thought it all over and it's our only way,'
replied Tib. 'The relatives of the decedent would
go without fire-water a week if those sons of Uncle
Sam would only escape into the open and give the
bereaved family a chance to shoot them up. Why,
look! They are doing real work out-of-doors, and
I don't doubt but what their guards are yearning
for them to make a break for liberty. If they
did they would never get ten miles from Quelta.
So, my way is the only way, my bosom the only
haven of refuge.'

"The upshot of it all was I hustled back to El
Paso, where we had some greenroom effects of a
new opera stored, and as fleet-footed as possible

I hiked back to Chihuahua, accompanied by two big trunks. Meanwhile Tib had sent our bill-poster to Quelta to hang up a few valentines, advertising the coming of the show, and incidentally to slip into Murphy's hand a note of minute instructions.

"This done, Tib tried to get me to go north and sit on the farther bank of the Rio and await the last curtain Of course I wasn't for that, and he blessed me and said we would probably wind up as salt-miners. Then he directed me to throw some hardware and cartridges into the cages, and on Saturday morning, with two closed animal-wagons, we started for Quelta. We had one man who could drive chain lightning, let alone the most erratic Mexican mule, and, best of all, we could trust him. He had lived in Mexico for years, but had never forgotten he came from the land of greatness and graft. He led the way, while Tib and I did the brake act on the second tally-ho. The rest of the show we left at Chihuahua.

"It took us a day to cover the short stretch over their rotten roads, but at last we arrived at Quelta, amid a Toltec buzz of excitement, and pitched the side-show tent, as if preparing for the Sunday performance. Tib explained to the head Injun of the town, who met us two miles out of the place to make sure of the tickets, that if the rest of the treat arrived per schedule, Quelta was to enjoy a highly moral entertainment that would be the red-lettered starting-point on all Mexican calendars for all hence. And he cemented his promise with a sheaf of free passes. You can wager the mayor was there with a group of corn-fed peasants to erect the tent when we did arrive. And so the time came for us to set down and wait.

"'My plans are built like a watch, and if it don't happen in five minutes I've missed fire,' groaned Tib, as we unlocked the covers to the carts.

"Then it happened. First we heard a yell; then half a dozen champagne-bottles opened in quick succession, and the little chapel-bell began ding-donging excitedly.

"Next, with fierce panting, four men burst through the chaparral that came up to the rear of our tent and plunged inside the white walls. I had just time to notice they were haggard and unkempt, and then in a second the wooden covers were down to allow them to enter the cages, and then snapped back in place again.

"'I'm afraid, Billy,' declared Tib, calmly, as he began sorting out some posters, 'that the rest of the show won't arrive in time for to-morrow's performance.'

"Just as he said this a bevy of villagers, headed by our trusty driver, Collins, burst through the canvas, yelling and brandishing carbines and other impedimenta.

"'Four men escaped from the soldiers, Mr. Smith, and I told the guards I thought they came this way,' panted Collins, with an expressive wink.

"'What!' roared Tib, in Spanish. 'Law-breakers escaped! Free passes to the brave men who capture 'em. I believe they did pass this way behind the tent in the brush. I heard a crashing and thought it was a mule. My lion growled fiercely! Hark! He is growling now!'

"The gang paused in running away to hear the growl, and Tiberius, standing near Murphy's cage, hissed, 'Growl, you villain, growl!'

"And thereat a most blood-chilling roar came from Murphy's den, and the others, to make sure, began to throw in a series of yells that would cause a Bowery gallery-god to go home and through sheer envy take lessons. The crowd fell back in a wave; it simply swept 'em off their feet, sir. To cap the climax, Collins cried: 'Don't let 'em get excited, Mr. Smith! Remember the three men mauled to death in El Paso!'

"After they'd gone Tib turned to me and grinned. 'I think we'll win the trick. And isn't that Collins a jewel!'

"Now each cage was divided by a grating of bars, and in each cosey nook was one of the comic-opera suits I'd brought from El Paso. In designing these animal make-ups Tib had made use of air-chambers, so that when a man got tucked into one and the bicycle-pump had been agitated for padding, you had a real lifelike beast, with muscles standing out like barnacles on a forgotten dredge. Of course at the best it was a fierce counterfeit, and when the quadruped forgot and stood on his hind legs the effect was simply stupendous. First, Tib ordered Murphy to slip into the lion's pelt, and Murphy was mad. He said he was Irish and would pose as a harp, but never as the emblem of merry England. Tib talked to him like a hired man to a sick horse, and at last the metamorphosis was effected. Then the others were speedily transformed into a black bear, a tiger, and a hyena, respectively.

"After they had struggled into their masquerades and Tib had used the pump on the air-pockets we dropped the covers to get the *tout ensemble*. Dear! dear! Serious as the situation was, Tib and I sat down and cried like children. And then if you could only have heard 'em swear! All four going at once, with their front paws thrust through the bars and shaking at us. They were half starved and hysterical, you see; besides, there are cooler things in Mexico than fur suits. But Tib soothed them down at last and reminded them of what they were missing in the salt-mines, and they promised to be good and not cuss any more. As they were quieting down and we were replacing the covers, the alcalde's amazed head was thrust inside the flaps, and he said: 'I heard you shouting at the beasts, señor. Such a confusion, I had to look within. Surely, they must be devils. I must see them all to-morrow.'"

"Tib snapped the barricades in place in a jiffy, and said, stiffly: 'I never give a performance un-

less I have all my animals. These are but the
advance-wagons and tent. If the others do not
arrive, I cannot exhibit.'

"'But, señor, I have tickets. I have invited
my friends. As alcalde I shall command you to
exhibit to-morrow to prove you are not a hum-
bug,' cried the intruder.

"'That comes of profanity, Murphy,' groaned
Tib, after the alcalde left us. 'I brought these
suits along as a safeguard, so that if any one
should get a peep the fleeting glance would not
arouse suspicion. Now, hang it all! we've got to
give a performance to placate the mayor. For if
we don't we can never leave town. So you've
got to learn your wild-wood lessons, my lads.'

"'For mercy's sake, gimme a drink of water!'
moaned the bear.

"'A sup of th' crathur!' howled Murphy, and
before we could quiet them we had to pass a
bottle.

"We didn't dare allow them to remove their
disguises, and between the temperature and the
fleas I am afraid they passed a troubled night.
But early next morning we fed them up and
carefully outlined what they were to do.

"'Above all things, Murphy, don't swear,'
begged Tib. 'It's immoral, and again, lions, as
a rule, eschew profanity. And don't, Reynolds,
don't sit with folded arms. That's too much,
even in a hyena. Crouch, that's the idea, crouch!
and snarl occasionally. The tiger must lie on his

side, asleep, the lion on his stomach, dignified and solemn, and the bear should huddle up in a ball.'

"Then the unthankful beasts began to protest, and Murphy and Reynolds wanted to be the tiger and sleep, but Weisman swore he'd claw the lining out of any one that disturbed his feline ease. Burke, the bear, didn't know what kind of a noise to make, and it took Tib ten minutes to teach him to say 'woof' in a bruinesque manner. Then we took each one in turn and gave the key, and made him practise his call of the wild so there would be some individuality. Then we waited for the mayor.

"I remember Tib wore a pink shirt and a suit of clothes that reminded me of a backgammon-board. But it would have done you a world of good, sir, could you have seen him walking to the entrance in his old cheerful manner, smiling pleasantly as he confronted the rabble and explained that no show would be given until all of his menagerie had arrived. He compromised, however, by explaining that the alcalde and his friends could come in for a private inspection of the few animals now on hand, and the alcalde silenced all grumbling by telling the crowd that Don Tiberio was an honest man to refuse their money until he had his best to offer. Then Tib took up the passes and called me to stand guard while he harangued the mayor and a dozen men and women on the marvellous points of his collection.

" ' DON'T SIT WITH FOLDED ARMS. THAT'S TOO MUCH, EVEN IN A HYENA ' "

"'I can't see in the bloody thing,' growled the lion, as the party swept inside.

"'Silence!' roared Tib, to the king of beasts, in English. 'The villagers approach. 'Tis better to be a circus lion than a delver after table salt, known only by a number. Remember that, my lad.' With this admonition he began to spiel to the jabbering, half-clothed jays in his unique Spanish.

"'Fear them not, señors and señoritas. For though they rage and writhe in anger, they know their master's voice. — Look out, Burke, pull in your left leg!'—the last in English. 'They never dream of incurring my displeasure. Nero, here, your excellency, ate three men and two women before he was brought low in captivity, and has added a choice collection of thumbs and fingers to the total since then. The villagers near his wild, free home called him "Ah-Ghee-Dah," which being interpreted means, "He-Who-Eats-Men-Gladly."—Growl, Murph. Ah, not so loud. Even a lion has limitations.' And the sound of the Irishman buying freedom with a series of bull-like bellows swept by me and caused the chocolate populace without to shudder.

"'Now we come to the hyena, the most treacherous of all beasts,' continued Tib, skilfully drawing the spectators away from Murphy's cage, as that animal, I observed with horror, tried to scratch his left shoulder-blade with a most unlion-like contortion. 'His record was

kept for three years by my head trainer as to
the number of digits he has chewed off, then the
task was given up because of its monotony. So,
not too near, señors and señoritas, not too near.
See him show his teeth in vain—show your teeth,
Reynolds—repining for his native lair. Note his
antipathy to Nero, the monarch of the Abyssinian
wild, for he hates and dreads his roar.—Roar,
Murph.'

"But Nero, in desperation to escape a flea, began to clamber to his hind legs, and Tib saw the
move just in time to jump to the bars and smite
him on the nose.

"'Damn ye!' mumbled Nero.

"'By all the saints! it sounded as though he
spoke!' gasped a little, dried-up señorita.

"'Ahem! His long association with men has
given his hoarse growl an almost human quality,'
said Tib, his face going a bit white. 'Or maybe
it's because of the men he has eaten. Down, you
devil! down!' he cried, jumping to the hyena's
cage and striking him with his cane to distract
their attention. Reynolds was lying quiescent
at the time, and at the blow promptly raised his
head in amazement. 'Snarl!' hissed Tib, in English, and Reynolds made good with a long-drawn
hoot that sounded like a barn-owl suffering from
diphtheria.

"'These idiots will see their finish yet, Billy,'
cried Tib to me, in disgust. 'It's them to the
salty brine all right, I guess.'

"This caused the quartet to overdo it as they attempted to cinch freedom by cunning acting. None of them had ever read nature stories, however, and only Tib's ready cane and warning— 'Back! back! Not too near!'—saved the day. 'Where I can approach with impunity,' he explained, turning easily to the alcalde, 'you would feel their cruel fangs. Ah, bite, would you!' This to the bear, who was lying perfectly quiet, and Tib gave him a poke that brought a cloud of dust from his flanks, whereat he raised his paw to straighten his head, that now was at right angles with all the laws of nature.

"'Behold the lion about to spring!' shrieked Tib, thrusting into the ribs of the king of the forest and thus bringing him into a more reasonable posture.

·"'Fer th' love iv—o-o-o-gh!' spoke and snarled Murphy, in his rich brogue.

"'Wonderful!' gasped the alcalde and his followers.

"But I never heard a lion use such a delightful Irish accent before or since in giving his howl of rage.

"'Now we come to the royal Bengal tiger, bought by me from the Sultan of Skowhegan for $10,000,' rattled Tib, rapidly, drawing his audience to the second bin. To his horror he found the royal stretched out on his stomach, legs straight behind, while the head, turned upside down, stared complacently at the top of the cage.

17

'Notice the wonderful elasticity of his neck,'—
and snap! Tib had reached in and turned the
head-piece into place. It simply swept 'em off
their feet, sir. It didn't need a naturalist sharp
to detect that the tiger was abnormal in some
respects.

"'Thanks, mate,' growled Weisman. 'The
dust—'

"But the lion and the hyena promptly came
to the rescue and drowned the visitor's exclama-
tion of wonder in a series of prolonged yells that
put crimps in my tympanums even out at the
entrance.

"'Ah, he purrs, señors. He purrs, señoritas.—
Purr, Weisman. At last he is in good-humor,'
cried Tib. Then in sotto English: 'Group your
legs, you would-be suicide! Cluster yourself!
It's no use, Billy,' cried Tib to me. 'I would
have saved them if I could, but they won't have
it so'; and all the time he was pointing dramatically at the bear. 'Kindly throw something at
Murph. He's about to stand up.' I tossed a
tent-peg, that didn't do the harp a bit of good,
and his muttered curse was only drowned by
Tib's addressing the bear.

"Well, sir, it was the most sweaty fifteen minutes I ever put in. You see, if the game was discovered, we were in as bad a box as the fugitives.
And when the sight-seers began to file out I felt
as limp as a rag.

"'I shall come again when the whole menagerie

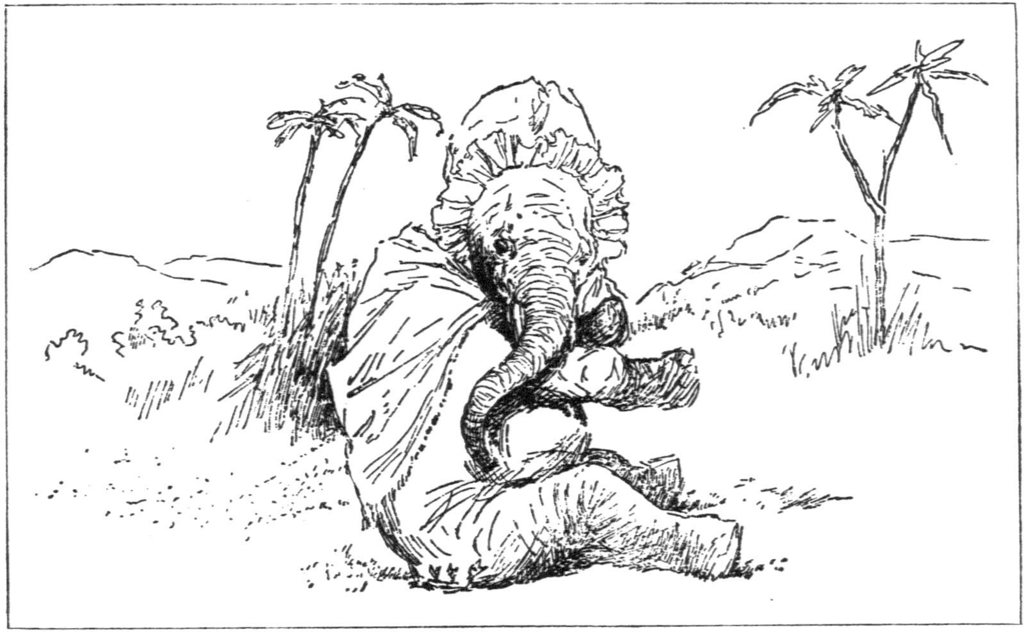

MISPLACED KINDNESS

is here,' declared the alcalde, on leaving. 'Wonderful and marvellous!'

"'Scene first and curtain,' panted Tib, closing
the tent-flaps leisurely, while I shoved bottles
and fodder to the animals. In three seconds their
disgusted faces were slipped free from the head-
pieces and were busy with food and drink.

"Then we held a council of war and decided
we would leave immediately while the alcalde
and other citizens were having their siestas. And
the way Collins and a dozen peons emulated the
Arab in striking that tent was a caution. From
the natives we learned the guards had got no
trace of the fugitives, and that Chihuahua was
being searched by inches. Tib accordingly decided to skirt the town and make for the Rio.

"We got away from Quelta all right, and whenever we met any of the home people we stopped
and inquired for the missing caravan, while the
inmates of the wagon let off a few howls to height-
en the effect. By night we were abreast of
Chihuahua and drove slowly north until morning, when we got a change of mules. Then we
crept nearer freedom, but never appearing to
hurry, and on the second night out we allowed
the four men to ride on top of their homes in their
underclothing. But with the sun they again
put on their trimmings and hopped inside. By
this time Tib and I were nearly dead for want of
sleep; for although we let Collins slumber every
little once in a while, we dared not quit our posts.

At last we neared the Rio, and the men wanted to take off their suits and make one dash for it, but Tib said nay. On inquiring from a half-breed we at last learned we had only a few miles to make.

"'Now let's go through with a rush,' I suggested, wearily.

"'We'll have to,' replied Tib. 'I see the glitter of their shields.'

"And looking back I made out a party of horse-men galloping a mile in our rear, while the sun-light played brightly on something they carried in their hands.

"With a yell to the mules we bumped and tore along, the heavy wagons swaying fearfully as we went down a decline. Nearer and nearer crept the pursuers, their shouts now reaching us, but before they could get within good shooting dis-tance we caught the glimmer of the Rio, where in the dry season the stream is a mere trickle. Smash went the head cart against a bowlder, and a wheel was broken into toothpicks. Then in a second we were all out, making for the rock-studded stream, while the soldiers coming up dismounted and began to take pot-shots at us.

"They had got wind of our game some way and did not seem to be greatly surprised at beholding four fierce denizens of the jungle scrambling, wad-ing, and swimming through the stream, each armed with a rifle or revolver.

"I reached home base first, closely followed by

Collins. And, sir, I shall never forget that spectacle. There was the lion, unable to loosen his
head-piece, swearing profusely in rich Celtic as
he sent back shot for shot. There were the hyena
and tiger, very chummy, using revolvers. And
in the rear, in the midst of the danger zone, old
Tiberius was ruining his show-clothes by sup-
porting the bear by the scruff of the neck. I
howled to the lion, and he fiercely turned and
went back to assist my patron. Once they got
Burke ashore we found a neat bullet-hole through
his neck, but no arteries or large veins were cut.
And I didn't feel a bit bad when I saw that two
of the enemy needed the kind care of a physician
when they rode away.

"Well, that's all. The fellows couldn't thank
Tib enough, for he had saved them from worse
than death. And in doing it he lost one of the
best animal shows that was ever foolish enough
to leave the States."

TWENTY MINUTES FOR REFRESHMENTS

BY OWEN WISTER

Upon turning over again my diary of that ex-
cursion to the Pacific, I find that I set out from
Atlantic waters on the 30th day of a backward
and forlorn April, which had come and done
nothing towards making its share of spring, but
had gone, missing its chance, leaving the trees as
bare as it had received them from the winds of
March. It was not bleak weather alone, but
care, that I sought to escape by a change of sky;
and I hoped for some fellow-traveller who might
begin to interest my thoughts at once. No such
person met me in the several Pullmans which I
inhabited from that afternoon until the forenoon
of the following Friday. Through that long
distance, though I had slanted southwestward
across a multitude of States and vegetations, and
the Mississippi lay eleven hundred miles to my
rear, the single event is my purchasing some cats'-
eyes of the news-agent at Sierra Blanca. Save
this, my diary contains only neat additions of
daily expenses, and moral reflections of a delicate
and restrained melancholy. They were Pecos

cat's-eyes, he told me, obtained in the rocky
cañons of that stream, and destined to be worth
little until fashion turned from foreign jewels to
become aware of these fine native stones. And
I, glad to possess the jewels of my country, chose
two bracelets and a necklace of them, paying but
twenty dollars for fifteen or sixteen cat's-eyes,
and resolved to give them a setting worthy of
their beauty. The diary continues with moral
reflections upon the servility of our taste before
anything European, and the handwriting is clear
and deliberate. It abruptly becomes hurried,
and at length wellnigh illegible. It is best, I
think, that you should have this portion as it
comes, unpolished, unamended, unarranged—hot,
so to speak, from my immediate pencil, instead
of cold from my subsequent pen. I shall disguise
certain names, but that is all.

Friday forenoon, May 5.—I don't have to gaze
at my cat's-eyes to kill time any more. I'm not
the only passenger any more. There's a lady.
She got in at El Paso. She has taken the drawing-room, but sits outside reading newspaper cut-
tings and writing letters. She is sixty, I should
say, and has a cap and one gray curl. This
comes down over her left ear as far as a purple
ribbon which suspends a medallion at her throat.
She came in wearing a sage-green duster of
pongee silk, pretty nice, only the buttons are as
big as those largest mint-drops. "You porter,"
she said, "brush this." He put down her many

things and received it. Her dress was sage-green, and pretty nice, too. "You porter," said she, "open every window. Why, they are, I declare! What's the thermometer in this car?" "Ninety-five, ma'am. Folks mostly travelling—" "That will do, porter. Now you go make me a pitcher of lemonade right quick." She went into the state-room and shut the door. When she came out she was dressed in what appeared to be chintz bedroom curtains. They hang and flow loosely about her, and are covered with a pattern of pink peonies. She has slippers— Turkish—that stare up in the air, pretty handsome and comfortable. But I never before saw any one travel with fly-paper. It must be hard to pack. But it's quite an idea in this train. Fully a dozen flies have stuck to it already; and she reads her clippings, and writes away, and sips another glass of lemonade, all with the most extreme appearance of leisure, not to say sloth. I can't imagine how she manages to produce this atmosphere of indolence when in reality she is steadily occupied. Possibly the way she sits. But I think it's partly the bedroom curtains.

These notes were interrupted by the entrance of the new conductor. "If you folks have chartered a private car, just say so," he shouted, instantly, at the sight of us. He stood still at the extreme end and removed his hat, which was acknowledged by the lady. "Travel is surely very light, Gadsden," she assented, and went on with her writing. But he remained standing still, and shouting like an orator: "Sprinkle the floor of this car, Julius, and let the pore passengers get a breath of cool. My lands!" He fanned himself sweepingly with his hat. He seemed but little larger than a red squirrel, and precisely that color. Sorrel hair, sorrel eyebrows, sorrel freckles, light sorrel mustache, thin, aggressive nose, receding chin, and black, attentive, prominent eyes. He approached, and I gave him my ticket, which is as long as a neck-tie, and has my height, the color of my eyes and hair, and my general description punched in the margin. "Why, you ain't middle-aged!" he shouted, and a singular croak sounded behind me. But the lady was writing. "I have been growing younger since I bought that ticket," I explained. "That's it, that's it," he sang; "a man's always as old as he feels, and a woman—is ever young," he finished. "I see you are true to the old teachings and the old-time chivalry, Gadsden," said the lady, continuously busy. "Yes, ma'am. Jacob served seven years for Leah and seven more for Rachel." "Such men are raised to-day in every worthy Louisiana home, Gadsden, be it ever so humble." "Yes, ma'am. Give a fresh sprinkle to the floor, Julius, soon as it goes to get dry. Excuse me, but do you shave yourself, sir?" I told him that I did, but without excusing him. "You will see that I have a reason for asking," he consequently pursued, and took out of his

coat-tails a round tin box handsomely labelled
"Nat. Fly Paper Co.," so that I supposed it was
thus, of course, that the lady came by her fly-
paper. But this was pure coincidence, and the
conductor explained: "That company's me and a
man at Shreveport, but he dissatisfies me right
frequently. You know what heaven a good
razor is for a man, and what you feel about a
bad one. Vaseline and ground shells," he said,
opening the box, "and I'm not saying anything
except it will last your lifetime and never hardens.
Rub the size of a pea on the fine side of your
strop, spread it to an inch with your thumb.
May I beg a favor on so short a meeting? Join
me in the gentlemen's lavatory with your razor-
strop in five minutes. I have to attend to a
corpse in the baggage-car, and will return at
once." "Anybody's corpse I know, Gadsden?"
said the lady. "No, ma'am. Just a corpse."

When I joined him, for I was now willing to do
anything, he was apologetic again. " 'Tis a short
acquaintance," he said, "but may I also beg
your razor? Quick as I get out of the National
Fly I am going to register my new label. First
there will be Uncle Sam embracing the world,
signifying this mixture is universal, then my
name, then the word *Stropine*, which is a novelty
and carries copyright, and I shall win comfort
and doubtless luxury. The post barber at Fort
Bayard took a dozen off me at sight to retail to
the niggers of the Twenty-fourth, and as he did

not happen to have the requisite cash on his person I charged him two roosters and fifty cents,
and both of us done well. He's after more
Stropine, and I got Pullman prices for my roosters, the buffet-car being out of chicken à la
Marengo. There is your razor, sir, and I appre-
ciate your courtesy." It was beautifully sharp-
ened, and I bought a box of the Stropine and
asked him who the lady was. "Mrs. Sedalia
Preen!" he exclaimed. "Have you never met
her socially? Why she—why she is the most intellectual lady in Bee Bayou." "Indeed!" I
said. "Why she visits New Orleans, and Charles-
ton, and all the principal centres of refinement,
and is welcomed in Washington. She converses
freely with our statesmen, and is considered a
queen of learning. Why she writes po'try, sir,
and is strong-minded. But a man wouldn't want
to pick her up for a fool, all the samey." "I
shouldn't; I don't," said I. "Don't you do it,
sir. She's run her plantation all alone since the
Colonel was killed in '62. She taught me Sunday-
school when I was a lad, and she used to catch
me at her pecan-trees 'most every time in Bee
Bayou."

He went forward, and I went back with the
Stropine in my pocket. The lady was sipping
the last of the lemonade and looking haughtily
over the top of her glass into (I suppose) the
world of her thoughts. Her eyes met mine, however. "Has Gadsden — yes, I perceive he has

been telling about me," she said, in her languid, formidable voice. She set her glass down and reclined among the folds of the bedroom curtains, considering me. "Gadsden has always been lavish," she mused, caressingly. "He seems destined to succeed in life," I hazarded. "O—h n—o!" she sighed, with decision. "He will fail." As she said no more and as I began to resent the manner in which she surveyed me, I remarked, "You seem rather sure of his failure." "I am old enough to be his mother, and yours," said Mrs. Sedalia Preen among her curtains. "He is a noble-hearted fellow, and would have been a high-souled Southern gentleman if born to that station. But what should a conductor earning $103.50 a month be dispersing his attention on silly patents for? Many's the time I've told him what I think; but Gadsden will always be flighty." No further observations occurring to me, I took up my necklace and bracelets from the seat and put them in my pocket. "Will you permit a meddlesome old woman to inquire what made you buy those cat's-eyes?" said Mrs. Preen. "Why—" I dubiously began. "Never mind," she cried, archly. "If you were thinking of some one in your Northern home, they will be prized because the thought, at any rate, was beautiful and genuine. 'Where'er I roam, whatever realms to see, my heart, untravelled, fondly turns to thee.' Now don't you be embarrassed by an old woman!" I desired to inform her that

I disliked her, but one can never do those things;
and, anxious to learn what was the matter with
the cat's-eyes, I spoke amiably and politely to
her. "Twenty dollars!" she murmured. "And
he told you they came from the Pecos!" She
gave that single melodious croak I had heard
once before. Then she sat up with her back as
straight as if she was twenty. "My dear young
fellow, never do you buy trash in these trains.
Here you are with your coat full of—what's
Gadsden's absurd razor concoction? — strut —
strup—bother! And Chinese paste buttons.
Last summer, on the Northern Pacific, the man
offered your cat's-eyes to me as native gems
found exclusively in Dakota. But I just sat
and mentioned to him that I was on my way
home from a holiday in China, and he went right
out of the car. The last day I was in Canton I
bought a box of those cat's-eyes at eight cents a
dozen." After this we spoke a little on other
subjects, and now she's busy writing again.
She's on business in California, but will read a
paper at Los Angeles at the annual meeting of
the Golden Daughters of the West. The meal
station is coming, but we have agreed to—

Later, Friday afternoon.—I have been interrupted again. Gadsden entered, removed his
hat, and shouted: "Sharon. Twenty minutes
for dinner." I was calling the porter to order a
buffet lunch in the car when there tramped in
upon us three large men of such appearance that

a flash of thankfulness went through me at having so little ready-money and only a silver watch. Mrs. Preen looked at them and said, "Well, gentlemen?" and they took off their embroidered Mexican hats. "We've got a baby show here," said one of them, slowly, looking at me, "and we'd be kind of obliged if you'd hold the box." "There's lunch put up in a basket for you to take along," said the next, "and a bottle of wine— champagne. So losing your dinner won't lose you nothing." "We're looking for somebody raised East and without local prejudice," said the third. "So we come to the Pullman." I now saw that so far from purposing to rob us they were in a great and honest distress of mind. "But I am no judge of a baby," said I; "not being mar—" "You don't have to be," broke in the first, more slowly and earnestly. "It's a fair and secret ballot we're striving for. The votes is wrote out and ready, and all we're shy of is a stranger without family ties or business interests to hold the box and do the counting." His deep tones ceased, and he wiped heavy drops from his forehead with his shirt-sleeve. "We'd be kind of awful obliged to you," he urged. "The town would be liable to make it two bottles," said the second. The third brought his fist down on the back of a seat and said, "I'll make it that now." "But, gentlemen," said I, "five, six, and seven years ago I was not a stranger in Sharon. If my friend Dean Drake was still here—" "But he ain't. Now you might as well help folks, and eat later. This town will trust you. And if you quit us—" Once more he wiped the heavy drops away, while in a voice full of appeal his friend finished his thought: "If we lose you, we'll likely have to wait till this train comes in to-morrow for a man satisfactory to this town. And the show is costing us a heap." A light hand tapped my arm, and here was Mrs. Preen saying: "For shame! Show your enterprise." "I'll hold this yere train," shouted Gadsden, "if necessary." Mrs. Preen rose alertly, and they all hurried me out. "My slippers will stay right on when I'm down the steps," said Mrs. Preen, and Gadsden helped her descend into the blazing dust and sun of Sharon. "Gracious!" said she, "what a place! But I make it a point to see everything as I go." Nothing had changed. There, as of old, lay the flat litter of the town —sheds, stores, and dwellings, a shapeless con-gregation in the desert, gaping wide every-where to the glassy, quivering immensity; and there, above the roofs, turned the slatted wind-wheels. But close to the tracks, opposite the hotel, was an edifice, a sort of tent of bunting, from which brass music issued, while about a hundred pink and blue sun-bonnets moved and mixed near the entrance. Little black Mexicans, like charred toys, lounged and lay staring among the ungraded dunes of sand. "Gracious!" said Mrs. Preen again. Her eye lost nothing; and

as she made for the tent the chintz peonies
flowed around her, and her step was surprisingly
light. We passed through the sun-bonnets and
entered where the music played. "The precious
blessed darlings!" she exclaimed, clasping her
hands. "This will do for the Golden Daughters,"
she rapidly added; "yes, this will distinctly do."
And she hastened away from me into the throng.

I had no time to look at much this first general
minute. I could see there were booths, each containing a separate baby. I passed a whole section of naked babies, and one baby farther along
had on golden wings and a crown, and was bawl-
ing frightfully. Their names were over the
booths, and I noticed Lucille, Erskine Wales,
Banquo Lick Nolin, Cuba, Manilla, Ellabelle,
Bosco Grady, James J. Corbett Nash, and Aqua
Marine. There was a great sign at the end,
painted "Mrs. Eden's Manna in the Wilderness,"
and another sign, labelled "Shot-gun Smith's
twins." In the midst of these first few impres-
sions I found myself seated behind a bare table
raised three feet or so, with two boxes on it, and
a quantity of blank paper and pencils, while one
of the men was explaining me the rules and facts.
I can't remember them all now, because I couldn't
understand them all then, and Mrs. Preen was
distant among the sun-bonnets, talking to a
gathering crowd and feeling in the mouths of
babies that were being snatched out of the
booths and brought to her. The man was in-

structing me steadily all the while, and it occurred to me to nod silently and coldly now and
then, as if I was doing this sort of thing every
day. But I insisted that some one should help
me count, and they gave me Gadsden.

Now these facts I do remember very clearly,
and shall never forget them. The babies came
from two towns—Sharon, and Rincon its neighbor. Alone, neither had enough for a good
show, though in both it was every family's pride
to have a baby every year. The babies were in
three classes: Six months and under, one prize
offered; eighteen months, two prizes; three years,
two prizes. A three-fourths vote of all cast was
necessary to a choice. No one entitled to vote
unless of immediate family of a competing baby.
No one entitled to cast more than one vote.
There were rules of entry and fees, but I forget
them, except that no one could have two exhibits
in the same class. When I read this I asked,
how about twins? "Well, we didn't kind of
foresee that," muttered my instructor, painfully;
"what would be your idea?" "Look here, you
sir," interposed Mrs. Preen, "he came in to
count votes." I was very glad to have her back.
"That's right, ma'am," admitted the man; "he
needn't to say a thing. We've only got one
twins entered," he pursued, "which we're glad
of. Shot-gun—" "Where is this Mr. Smith?"
interrupted Mrs. Preen. "Up-town, drinking,
ma'am." "And who may Mr. Smith be?"

18

"Most popular citizen of Rincon, ma'am. We had to accept his twins because—well, he come down here himself, and most of Rincon come with him, and as we aimed to have everything pass off pleasant-like—" "I quite comprehend," said Mrs. Preen. "And I should consider twins within the rule; or any number born at one time. But little Aqua Marine is the finest single child in that six months' class. I told her mother she ought to take that splurgy ring off the poor little thing's thumb. It's most unsafe. But I should vote for that child myself. "Thank you for your valuable indorsement," said a spruce, slim young man. "But the public is not allowed to vote here," he added. He was standing on the floor and resting his elbows on the table. Mrs. Preen stared down at him. "Are you the father of the child?" she inquired. "Oh no! I am the agent. I—" "Aqua Marine's agent?" said Mrs. Preen, sharply. "Ha, ha!" went the young man. "Ha, ha! Well, that's good, too. She's part of our exhibit. I'm in charge of the manna-feds, don't you know?" "I don't know," said Mrs. Preen. "Why, Mrs. Eden's Manna in the Wilderness! Nourishes, strengthens, and makes no unhealthy fat. Take a circular, and welcome. I'm travelling for the manna. I organized this show. I've conducted twenty-eight similar shows in two years. We hold them in every State and Territory. Second of last March I gave Denver—you heard of it,

probably?" "I did not," said Mrs. Preen.
"Well! Ha, ha! I thought every person up to
date had heard of Denver's Olympic Offspring
Olio." "Is it up to date to loll your elbows on
the table when you're speaking to a lady?" inquired Mrs. Preen. He jumped, and then
grew scarlet with rage. "I didn't expect to
learn manners in New Mexico," said he. "I
doubt if you will," said Mrs. Preen, and turned
her back on him. He was white now; but better
instincts, or else business, prevailed in his injured
bosom. "Well," said he, "I had no bad inten-
tions. I was going to say you'd have seen ten
thousand people and five hundred babies at Denver. And our manna-feds won out to beat the
band. Three first medals, and all exclusively
manna-fed. We took the costume prize also.
Of course here in Sharon I've simplified. No
special medal for weight, beauty, costume, or
decorated perambulator. Well, I must go back
to our exhibit. Glad to have you give us a call
up there and see the medals we're offering, and
our fifteen manna-feds, and take a package away
with you." He was gone.

The voters had been now voting in my two
boxes for some time, and I found myself hoping
the manna would not win, whoever did; but it
seemed this agent was a very capable person.
To begin with, every family entering a baby
drew a package of the manna free, and one package contained a diamond ring. Then, he had

managed to have the finest babies of all classes in his own exhibit. This was incontestable, Mrs. Preen admitted, after returning from a general inspection; and it seemed to us extraordinary. "That's easy, ma'am," said Gadsden; "he came around here a month ago. Don't you see?" I did not see, but Mrs. Preen saw at once. He had made a quiet selection of babies beforehand, and then introduced the manna into those homes. And everybody in the room was remarking that his show was very superior, taken as a whole— they all added, "taken as a whole"; I heard them as they came up to vote for the 3-year and the 18-month classes. The 6-month was to wait till last, because the third box had been accidentally smashed by Mr. Smith. Gadsden caught several trying to vote twice. "No, you don't!" he would shout. "I know faces. I'm not a conductor for nothing." And the victim would fall back amid jeers from the sun-bonnets. Once the passengers sent over to know when the train was going. "Tell them to step over here and they'll not feel so lonesome!" shouted Gadsden; and I think a good many came. The band was playing "White Wings," with quite a number singing it, when Gadsden noticed the voting had ceased, and announced this ballot closed. The music paused for him, and we could suddenly hear how many babies were in distress; but for a moment only. As we began our counting, "White Wings" resumed, and the sun-bonnets outsang their prog-

eny. There was something quite singular in the
way they had voted. Here are some of the 3-
year-old tickets: "First choice, Ulysses Grant
Blum; 2d choice, Lewis Hendricks." "First
choice, James Redfield; 2d, Lewis Hendricks."
"First, Elk Chester; 2d, Lewis Hendricks."
"Can it be?" said the excited Gadsden. "Finish
these quick. I'll open the 18-monthers." But
he swung round to me at once. "See there!" he
cried. "Read that! and that!" He plunged
among more, and I read: "First choice, Lawrence
Nepton Ford, Jr.; 2d, Iona Judd." "First
choice, Mary Louise Kenton; 2d, Iona Judd."
"Hurry up!" said Gadsden; "that's it." And as
we counted, Mrs. Preen looked over my shoulder
and uttered her melodious croak, for which I
saw no reason. "That young whipper-snapper
will go far," she observed; nor did I understand
this. But when they stopped the band for me to
announce the returns, one fact did dawn on me
even while I was reading: "Three-year-olds:
Whole number of votes cast, 300; necessary to a
choice, 225. Second prize, Lewis Hendricks, receiving 300. First prize, largest number of votes
cast, 11, for Salvisa van Meter. No award.
Eighteen-month class: Whole number of votes
cast, 300; necessary to a choice, 225. Second
prize, Iona Judd, receiving 300. Lillian Brown
gets 15 for 1st prize. None awarded." There
was a very feeble applause, and then silence for a
second, and then the sun-bonnets rushed to-

gether, rushed away to others, rushed back; and
talk swept like hail through the place. Yes, that
is what they had done. They had all voted for
Lewis Hendricks and Iona Judd for second prize,
and every family had voted the first prize to its
own baby. The Browns and van Meters happened to be the largest families present. "He'll
go far! he'll go far!" repeated Mrs. Preen. Sport
glittered in her eye. She gathered her curtains, and was among the sun-bonnets in a moment. Then it fully dawned on me. The
agent for Mrs. Eden's Manna in the Wilderness
was indeed a shrewd strategist, and knew his
people to the roots of the grass. They had never
seen a baby show. They were innocent. He
came among them. He gave away packages of
manna and a diamond ring. He offered the
prizes. But he proposed to win some. Therefore he made that rule about only the immediate
families voting. He foresaw what they would do;
and now they had done it. Whatever happened,
two prizes went to his manna-feds. "They don't
see through it in the least, which is just as well,"
said Mrs. Preen, returning. "And it's little matter that only second prizes go to the best babies.
But what's to be done now?" I had no idea;
but it was not necessary that I should.

"You folks of Rincon and Sharon," spoke a
deep voice. It was the first man in the Pullman,
and drops were rolling from his forehead, and his
eyes were the eyes of a beleaguered ox. "You

fathers and mothers," he said, and took another
breath. They grew quiet. "I'm a father myself, as is well known." They applauded this.
"Salvisa is mine, and she got my vote. The
father that will not support his own child is not
—does not—is worse than if they were orphans."
He breathed again, while they loudly applauded.
"But, folks, I've got to get home to Rincon. I've
got to. And I'll give up Salvisa if I'm met fair."
"Yes, yes, you'll be met," said voices of men.
"Well, here's my proposition: Mrs. Eden's manna
has took two, and I'm satisfied it should. We
voted, and will stay voted." "Yes, yes!" "Well,
now, here's Sharon and Rincon, two of the finest
towns in this section, and I say Sharon and Rincon has equal rights to get something out of this,
and drop private feelings, and everybody back
their town. And I say let this lady and gentleman, who will act elegant and on the square,
take a view and nominate the finest Rincon 3-
year-old and the finest Sharon 18-month they
can cut out of the herd. And I say let's vote
unanimous on their pick, and let each town hold
a first prize and go home in friendship, feeling it
has been treated right."

Universal cheers indorsed him, and he got
down panting. The band played "Union Forever," and I accompanied Mrs. Preen to the
booths. "You'll remember!" shouted the orator
urgently after us; "one apiece." We nodded.
"Don't get mixed," he appealingly insisted. We

shook our heads, and out of the booths rushed two women, and simultaneously dashed their infants in our faces. "You'll never pass Cuba by!" entreated one. "This is Bosco Grady," said the other. Cuba wore an immense garment made of the American flag, but her mother whirled her out of it in a second. "See them dimples; see them knees!" she said. "See them feet! Only feel of her toes!" "Look at his arms!" screamed the mother of Bosco. "Doubled his weight in four months." "Did he, indeed, ma'am?" said Cuba's mother; "well, he hadn't much to double." "Didn't he, then? Didn't he, indeed?" "No at you; he didn't, indeed and indeed! I guess Cuba is known to Sharon. I guess Sharon 'll not let Cuba be slighted." "Well, and I guess Rincon 'll see that Bosco Grady gets his rights." "Ladies," said Mrs. Preen, towering but poetical with her curl, "I am a mother myself, and raised five noble boys and two sweet, peerless girls." This stopped them immediately; they stared at her and her chintz peonies as she put the curl gently away from her medallion and proceeded: "But never did I think of myself in those dark, weary days of the long ago. I thought of my country and the Lost Cause." They stared at her, fascinated. "Yes, m'm," whispered they, quite humbly. "Now," said Mrs. Preen, "what is more sacred than an American mother's love? Therefore, let her not shame it with anger and strife. All little boys and girls are precious gems to me and to you. What is a cold, lifeless medal compared to one of them? Though I would that all could get the prize! But they can't, you know." "No, m'm." Many mothers, with their children in their arms, were now dumbly watching Mrs. Preen, who held them with a honeyed, convincing smile. "If I choose only one in this beautiful and encouraging harvest, it is because I have no other choice. Thank you so much for letting me see that little hero and that lovely angel," she added, with a yet sweeter glance to the mothers of Bosco and Cuba. "And I wish them all luck when their turn comes. I've no say about the 6-month class, you know. And now a little room, please."

The mothers fell back. But my head swam slightly. The 6-month class, to be sure! The orator had forgotten all about it. In the general joy over his wise and fair proposition, nobody had thought of it. But they would pretty soon. Cuba and Bosco were likely to remind them. Then we should still be face to face with a state of things that—I cast a glance behind at those two mothers of Sharon and Rincon following us, and I asked Mrs. Preen to look at them. "Don't think about it now," said she, "it will only mix you. I always like to take a thing when it comes, and not before." We now reached the 18-month class. They were the naked ones. The 6-month had stayed nicely in people's arms; these were crawling hastily everywhere,

like crabs upset in the market, and they screamed
fiercely when taken upon the lap. The mother
of Thomas Jefferson Brayin Lucas showed us a
framed letter from the statesman for whom her
child was called. The letter reeked with gratitude, and said that offspring was man's proudest
privilege; that a souvenir sixteen-to-one spoon
would have been cheerfully sent, but four hundred and twenty-eight babies had been named
after Mr. Brayin since January. It congratu-
lated the swelling army of the People's Cause.
But there was nothing eminent about little
Thomas except the letter; and we selected Reese
Moran, a vigorous Sharon baby, who, when they
attempted to set him down and pacify him, stif-
fened his legs, dashed his candy to the floor,
and burst into lamentation. We were soon on
our way to the 3-year class, for Mrs. Preen
was rapid and thorough. As we went by the
Manna Exhibit, the agent, among his packages
and babies, invited us in. He was loudly de-
claring that he would vote for Bosco if he could.
But when he examined Cuba, he became sure
that Denver had nothing finer than that. Mrs.
Preen took no notice of him, but bade me admire Aqua Marine as far surpassing any other
6-month child. I proclaimed her splendid (she
was a wide-eyed, contented thing, with a head
shaped like a croquet mallet), and the agent
smiled modestly and told the mothers that as
for his babies two prizes was luck enough for

them; they didn't want the earth. "If that thing happened to be brass," said Mrs. Preen, bending over the ring that Aqua was still sucking; and again remonstrating with the mother for this imprudence, she passed on. The three-year-olds were, many of them, in costume, with extraordinary arrangements of hair; and here was the child with gold wings and a crown I had seen on arriving. Her name was Verbena M., and she personated Faith. She had colored slippers, and was drinking tea from her mother's cup. Another child, named Broderick McGowan, represented Columbus, and joyfully shouted "Ki-yi!" every half-minute. One child was attired as a prominent admiral; another as a prominent general; and one stood in a boat and was Washington. As Mrs. Preen examined them and dealt with the mothers, the names struck me afresh—not so much the boys; Ulysses Grant and James J. Corbett explained themselves; but I read the names of five adjacent girls—Lula, Ocilla, Nila, Cusseta, and Maylene. And I asked Mrs. Preen how they got them. "From romances," she told me, "in papers that we of the upper classes never see." In choosing Horace Boyd, of Rincon, for his hair, his full set of front teeth well cared for, and his general beauty, I think both of us were also influenced by his good, sensible name, and his good, clean, sensible clothes. With both our selections, once they were settled, were Sharon and Rincon satisfied. We were

turning back to the table to announce our choice
when a sudden clamor arose behind us, and we
saw confusion in the Manna Department. Wom-
en were running and shrieking, and I hastened
after Mrs. Preen to see what was the matter.
Aqua Marine had swallowed the ring on her
thumb. "It was gold! it was pure gold!" wailed
the mother, clutching Mrs. Preen. "It cost a
whole dollar in El Paso." "She must have white
of egg instantly," said Mrs. Preen, handing me
her purse. "Run to the hotel—" "Save your
money," said the agent, springing forward with
some eggs in a bowl. "Lord! you don't catch us
without all the appliances handy. We'd run behind the trade in no time. There, now, there,"
he added, comfortingly, to the mother. "Will
you make her swallow it? Better let me—better
let me.—And here's the emetic. Lord! why, we
had three swallowed rings at the Denver Olio,
and I got 'em all safe back within ten minutes
after time of swallowing." "You go away,"
said Mrs. Preen to me, "and tell them our
nominations." The mothers sympathetically
surrounded poor little Aqua, saying to each
other: "She's a beautiful child!" "Sure indeed
she is!" "But the manna-feds has had their
turn." "Sure indeed they've been recognized,"
and so forth, while I was glad to retire to the
voting-table. The music paused for me, and as
the crowd cheered my small speech, some one
said, "And now what are you going to do about

me?" It was Bosco Grady back again, and close
behind him Cuba. They had escaped from Mrs.
Preen's eye and had got me alone. But I pretended in the noise and cheering not to see these
mothers. I noticed a woman hurrying out of the
tent, and hoped Aqua was not in further trouble
—she was still surrounded, I could see. Then
the orator made some silence, thanked us in the
names of Sharon and Rincon, and proposed our
candidates be voted on by acclamation. This
was done. Rincon voted for Sharon and Reese
Moran in a solid roar, and Sharon voted for Rincon and Horace Boyd in a roar equally solid. So
now each had a prize, and the whole place was
applauding happily, and the band was beginning
again, when the mothers with Cuba and Bosco
jumped up beside me on the platform, and the
sight of them produced immediate silence.

"There's a good many here has a right to feel
satisfied," said Mrs. Grady, looking about, "and
they're welcome to their feelings. But if this
meeting thinks it is through with its business, I
can tell it that it ain't—not if it acts honorable,
it ain't. Does those that have had their chance
and those that can take home their prizes expect
us 6-month mothers come here for nothing? Do
they expect I brought my Bosco from Rincon to
be insulted, and him the pride of the town?"
"Cuba is known to Sharon," spoke the other
lady. "I'll say no more." "Jumping Jeans!"
murmured the orator to himself. "I can't hold

this train much longer," said Gadsden; "she's due
at Lordsburg now." "You'll have made it up
by Tucson, Gadsden," spoke Mrs. Preen, quietly, across the whole assembly from the Manna
Department. "As for towns," continued Mrs.
Grady, "that think anything of a baby that's
only got three teeth—" "Ha! Ha!" laughed
Cuba's mother, shrilly. "Teeth! Well, we're
not proud of bald babies in Sharon." Bosco was
certainly bald. All the men were looking wretched, and all the women were growing more and
more like eagles. Moreover, they were separating
into two bands and taking their husbands with
them—Sharon and Rincon drawing to opposite
parts of the tent—and what was coming I cannot say, for we all had to think of something
else. A third woman, bringing a man, mounted
the platform. It was she I had seen hurry out.
"My name's Shot-gun Smith," said the man,
very carefully, "and I'm told you've reached my
case." He was extremely good-looking, with a
blue eye and a blond mustache, not above thirty,
and was trying hard to be sober, holding himself
with dignity. "Are you the judge?" said he to
me. "Well—" I began. "N-not guilty, your
honor," said he. At this his wife looked anxious.
"S-self-defence," he slowly continued; "told you
once already." "Why, Rolfe!" exclaimed his
wife, touching his elbow. "Don't you cry, little
woman," said he; "this 'll come out all right.
Where 're the witnesses?" "Why, Rolfe! *Rolfe!*"

She shook him as you shake a sleepy child.
"Now, see here," said he, and wagged a finger at
her affectionately, "you promised me you'd not
cry if I let you come." "Rolfe, dear, it's not
that to-day; it's the twins." "It's your twins,
Shot-gun, this time," said many men's voices.
"We acquitted you all right last month." "Justi-
fiable homicide," said Gadsden. "Don't you remember?" "Twins?" said Shot-gun, drowsily.
"Oh yes, mine. Why—" He opened on us his
blue eyes that looked about as innocent as Aqua
Marine's, and he grew more awake. Then he
blushed deeply, face and forehead. "I was not
coming to this kind of thing," he explained.
"But she wanted the twins to get something."
He put his hand on her shoulder and straightened
himself. "I done a heap of prospecting before I
struck this claim," said he, patting her shoulder.
"We got married last March a year. It's our
first—first—first"—he turned to me with a confiding smile—"it's our first dividend, judge."
"Rolfe! I never! You come right down."
"And now let's go get a prize," he declared, with
his confiding pleasantness. "I remember now!
I remember! They claimed twins was barred.
And I kicked down the bars. Take me to those
twins. They're not named yet, judge. After
they get the prize we'll name them fine names, as
good as any they got anywhere—Europe, Asia,
Africa—anywhere. My gracious! I wish they
was boys. Come on, judge! You and me 'll go

give 'em a prize, and then we'll drink to 'em."
He hugged me suddenly and affectionately, and
we half fell down the steps. But Gadsden as
suddenly caught him and righted him, and we
proceeded to the twins. Mrs. Smith looked at
me helplessly, saying: "I'm that sorry, sir! I
had no idea he was going to be that gamesome."
"Not at all," I said; "not at all!" Under many
circumstances I should have delighted in Shot-
gun's society. He seemed so utterly sure that,
now he had explained himself, everybody would
rejoice to give the remaining medal to his little
girls. But Bosco and Cuba had not been idle.
Shot-gun did not notice the spread of whispers,
nor feel the divided and jealous currents in the
air as he sat, and, in expanding good-will, talked
himself almost sober. To entice him out there
was no way. Several of his friends had tried it.
But beneath his innocence there seemed to lurk
something wary, and I grew apprehensive about
holding the box this last time. But Gadsden relieved me as our count began. "Shot-gun is a
splendid man," said he, "and he has trailed more
train-robbers than any deputy in New Mexico.
But he has seen too many friends to-day, and is
not quite himself. So when he fell down that
time I just took this off him." He opened the
drawer, and there lay a six-shooter. "It was
touch and go," said Gadsden; "but he's thinking
that hard about his twins that he's not missed it
yet. 'Twould have been the act of an enemy to

leave that on him to-day.—Well, d'you say!" he
broke off. "Well, well, well!" It was the
tickets we took out of the box that set him ex-
claiming. I began to read them, and saw that
the agent was no mere politician, but a statesman. His Aqua Marine had a solid vote. I remembered his extreme praise of both Bosco and
Cuba. This had set Rincon and Sharon bitterly
against each other. I remembered his modesty
about Aqua Marine. Of course. Each town,
unable to bear the idea of the other's beating
it, had voted for the manna-fed, who had two
hundred and ninety-nine votes. Shot-gun and
his wife had voted for their twins. I looked
towards the Manna Department, and could see
that Aqua Marine was placid once more, and
Mrs. Preen was dancing the ring before her
eyes. I hope I announced the returns in a
firm voice. "What!" said Shot-gun Smith; and
at that sound Mrs. Preen stopped dancing
the ring. He strode to our table. "There's the
winner," said Gadsden, quickly, pointing to the
Manna Exhibit. "What!" shouted Smith again;
"and they quit me for that hammer-headed son-
of-a-gun?" He whirled around. The men stood
ready, and the women fled shrieking and cowering
to their infants in the booths. "Gentlemen!
Gentlemen!" cried Gadsden, "don't hurt him!
Look here!" And from the drawer he displayed
Shot-gun's weapon. They understood in a second, and calmly watched the enraged and disap-

19

pointed Shot-gun. But he was a man. He saw
how he had frightened the women, and he stood
in the middle of the floor with eyes that did not
at all resemble Aqua Marine's at present. 'I'm
all right now, boys," he said. "I hope I've
harmed no one. Ladies, will you try and forget
about me making such a break? It got ahead of
me, I guess; for I had promised the little woman—" He stopped himself; and then his eye fell
upon the Manna Department. "I guess I don't
like one thing much now. I'm not after prizes.
I'd not accept one from a gold-bug-combine-trust
that comes sneaking around stuffing wholesale
concoctions into our children's systems. My
twins are not manna-fed. My twins are raised
as nature intended. Perhaps if they were swelled
out with trash that acts like baking-powder, they
would have a medal, too—for I notice he has
made you vote his way pretty often this afternoon." I saw the agent at the end of the room
look very queer. "That's so!" said several. "I
think I'll clear out his boxes," said Shot-gun,
with rising joy. "I feel like I've got to do something before I go home. Come on, judge!" He
swooped towards the manna with a yell, and the
men swooped with him, and Gadsden and I were
swooped with them. Again the women shrieked.
But Mrs. Preen stood out before the boxes with
her curl and her chintz.

"Mr. Smith," said she, "you are not going to
do anything like that. You are going to behave

yourself like the gentleman you are, and not like the wild beast that's inside you." Never in his life before, probably, had Shot-gun been addressed in such a manner, and he too became hypnotized, fixing his blue eyes upon the strange lady. "I do not believe in patent foods for children," said Mrs. Preen. "We agree on that, Mr. Smith, and I am a grandmother, and I attend to what my grandchildren eat. But this highly adroit young man has done you no harm. If he has the prizes, whose doing is that, please? And who paid for them? Will you tell me, please? Ah, you are all silent!" And she croaked melodiously. "Now let him and his manna go along. But I have enjoyed meeting you all, and I shall not forget you soon. And, Mr. Smith, I want you to remember me. Will you, please?" She walked to Mrs. Smith and the twins, and Shot-gun followed her, entirely hypnotized. She beckoned to me. "Your judge and I," she said, "consider not only your beautiful twins worthy of a prize, but also the mother and father that can so proudly claim them." She put her hand in my pocket. "These cat's-eyes," she said, "you will wear, and think of me and the judge who presents them." She placed a bracelet on each twin, and the necklace upon Mrs. Smith's neck. "Give him Gadsden's stuff," she whispered to me. "Do you shave yourself, sir?" said I, taking out the Stropine. "Vaseline and ground shells, and will last your life. Rub the size of a pea on your strop and spread it to an inch." I placed the box in Shot-gun's motionless hand. "And now, Gadsden, we'll take the train," said Mrs. Preen. "Here's your lunch! Here's your wine!" said the orator, forcing a basket upon me. "I don't know what we'd have done without you and your mother." A flash of indignation crossed Mrs. Preen's face, but changed to a smile. "You've forgot to name my girls!" exclaimed Shot-gun, suddenly finding his voice. "Suppose *you* try that," said Mrs. Preen to me, a trifle viciously. "Thank you," I said to Smith. "Thank you. I—" "Something handsome," he urged. "How would Cynthia do for one?" I suggested. "Shucks, no! I've known two Cynthias. You don't want that?" he asked Mrs. Smith; and she did not at all. "Something extra, something fine, something not stale," said he. I looked about the room. There was no time for thought, but my eye fell once more upon Cuba. This reminded me of Spain, and the Spanish, and my brain leaped. "I have them!" I cried. "'Armada' and 'Loyola.'" "That's what they're named!" said Shot-gun; "write it for us." And I did. Once more the band played, and we left them, all calling, "Good-bye, ma'am. Good-bye, judge," happy as possible. The train was soon going sixty miles an hour through the desert. We had passed Lordsburg, San Simon, and were nearly at Benson before Mrs. Preen and Gads-

den (whom she made sit down with us) and I
finished the lunch and champagne. "I wonder
how long he'll remember me?" mused Mrs.
Preen at Tucson, where we were on time. "That
woman is not worth one of his boots."

Saturday afternoon, May 6.—Near Los Angeles. I have been writing all day, to be sure
and get everything in, and now Sharon is twenty-
four hours ago, and here there are roses, gardens,
and many nice houses at the way-stations. Oh,
George Washington, father of your country, what
a brindled litter have you sired!

But here the moral reflections begin again, and
I copy no more diary. Mrs. Preen liked my
names for the twins. "They'll pronounce it
Loyo'la," she said, "and that sounds right
lovely." Later she sent me her paper for the
Golden Daughters. It is full of poetry and sentiment and all the things I have missed. She
wrote that if she had been sure the agent had
helped Aqua Marine to swallow the ring, she
would have let them smash his boxes. And I
think she was a little in love with Shot-gun Smith.
But what a pity we shall soon have no more
Mrs. Preens! The causes that produced her—
slavery, isolation, literary tendencies, adversity,
game blood—that combination is broken forever.
I shall speak to Mr. Howells about her. She
ought to be recorded.

EXPERIENCE OF THE McWILLIAMSES WITH MEMBRANEOUS CROUP

BY MARK TWAIN

[*As related to the author by Mr. McWilliams, a pleasant New York gentleman whom the said author met by chance on a journey.*]

WELL, to go back to where I was before I digressed, to explain to you how that frightful and incurable disease, membraneous croup, was ravaging the town and driving all mothers mad with terror. I called Mrs. McWilliams's attention to little Penelope, and said:

"Darling, I wouldn't let that child be chewing that pine stick, if I were you."

"Precious, where is the harm in it?" said she, but at the same time preparing to take away the stick—for women cannot receive even the most palpably judicious suggestion without arguing it; that is, married women.

I replied:

"Love, it is notorious that pine is the least nutritious wood that a child can eat."

My wife's hand paused in the act of taking the

stick, and returned itself to her lap. She bridled perceptibly, and said:

"Hubby, you know better than that. You know you do! Doctors *all* say that the turpentine in pine wood is good for weak back and the kidneys."

"Ah—I was under a misapprehension. I did not know that the child's kidneys and spine were affected, and that the family physician had recommended—"

"Who said the child's spine and kidneys were affected?"

"My love, you intimated it."

"The idea! I never intimated anything of the kind."

"Why, my dear, it hasn't been two minutes since you said—"

"Bother what I said! I don't care what I did say. There isn't any harm in the child's chewing a bit of pine stick if she wants to, and you know it perfectly well. And she *shall* chew it, too. So there, now!"

"Say no more, my dear. I now see the force of your reasoning, and I will go and order two or three cords of the best pine wood to-day. No child of mine shall want while I—"

"Oh, *please* go along to your office and let me have some peace. A body can never make the simplest remark but you must take it up and go to arguing and arguing and arguing, till you don't know what you are talking about, and you *never* do!"

"Very well, it shall be as you say. But there is a want of logic in your last remark which—"

However, she was gone with a flourish before I could finish, and had taken the child with her. That night at dinner she confronted me with a face as white as a sheet.

"Oh, Mortimer, there's another! Little Georgie Gordon is taken."

"Membraneous croup?"

"Membraneous croup."

"Is there any hope for him?"

"None in the wide world. Oh, what is to become of us!"

By-and-by a nurse brought in our Penelope to say good-night and offer the customary prayer at the mother's knee. In the midst of "Now I lay me down to sleep," she gave a slight cough. My wife fell back like one stricken with death. But the next moment she was up and brimming with the activities which terror inspires.

She commanded that the child's crib be removed from the nursery to our bedroom; and she went along to see the order executed. She took me with her, of course. We got matters arranged with speed. A cot bed was put up in my wife's dressing-room for the nurse. But now Mrs. Mc-Williams said we were too far away from the other baby, and what if *he* were to have the symptoms in the night—and she blanched again, poor thing.

We then restored the crib and the nurse to the

nursery, and put up a bed for ourselves in a room adjoining.

Presently, however, Mrs. McWilliams said, "Suppose the baby should catch it from Penelope?" This thought struck a new panic to her heart, and the tribe of us could not get the crib out of the nursery again fast enough to satisfy my wife, though she assisted in her own person and wellnigh pulled the crib to pieces in her frantic hurry.

We moved down-stairs; but there was no place there to stow the nurse, and Mrs. McWilliams said the nurse's experience would be an inestimable help. So we returned, bag and baggage, to our own bedroom once more, and felt a great gladness, like storm-buffeted birds that have found their nest again.

Mrs. McWilliams sped to the nursery to see how things were going on there. She was back in a moment with a new dread. She said:

"What *can* make baby sleep so?"

I said:

"Why, my darling, baby *always* sleeps like a graven image."

"I know, I know. But there's something peculiar about his sleep now. He seems to—to—he seems to breathe so *regularly*. Oh, this is dreadful!"

"But, my dear, he always breathes regularly."

"Oh, I know it, but there's something frightful about it now. His nurse is too young and inexperienced. Maria shall stay there with her, and be on hand if anything happens."

"That is a good idea, but who will help *you*?"

"You can help me all I want. I wouldn't allow anybody to do anything but myself, anyhow, at such a time as this."

I said I would feel mean to lie abed and sleep, and leave her to watch and toil over our little patient all the weary night. But she reconciled me to it. So old Maria departed and took up her ancient quarters in the nursery.

Penelope coughed twice in her sleep.

"Oh, why *don't* that doctor come! Mortimer, this room is too warm. This room is certainly too warm. Turn off the register—quick!"

I shut it off, glancing at the thermometer at the same time, and wondering to myself if seventy *was* too warm for a sick child.

The coachman arrived from down-town now, with the news that our physician was ill and confined to his bed. Mrs. McWilliams turned a dead eye upon me, and said in a dead voice:

"There is a Providence in it. It is foreordained. He never was sick before. Never. We have not been living as we ought to live, Mortimer. Time and time again I have told you so. Now you see the result. Our child will never get well. Be thankful if you can forgive yourself; I never can forgive *my*self."

I said, without intent to hurt, but with heedless

choice of words, that I could not see that we had
been living such an abandoned life.

"*Mortimer !* Do you want to bring the judgment upon baby, too!"

Then she began to cry, but suddenly exclaimed:
"The doctor must have sent medicines!"

I said:

"Certainly.   They are here.   I was only waiting for you to give me a chance."

"Well, do give them to me!   Don't you know
that every moment is precious now?   But what
was the use in sending medicines, when he *knows*
that the disease is incurable?"

I said that while there was life there was hope.

"Hope!   Mortimer, you know no more what you
are talking about than the child unborn.   If you
would—   As I live, the directions say, give one
teaspoonful once an hour!   Once an hour!—as if
we had a whole year before us to save the child
in!   Mortimer, please hurry.   Give the poor per-
ishing thing a tablespoonful, and *try* to be quick!"

"Why, my dear, a tablespoonful might—"

"*Don't* drive me frantic! . . . There, there,
there! my precious, my own; it's nasty bitter
stuff, but it's good for Nelly—good for mother's
precious darling; and it will make her well.
There, there, there! put the little head on mamma's breast and go to sleep, and pretty soon—oh,
I know she can't live till morning!   Mortimer, a
tablespoonful every half-hour will— Oh, the
child needs belladonna, too; I know she does—

and aconite.   Get them, Mortimer.   Now, do let me have my way.   You know nothing about these things."

We now went to bed, placing the crib close to my wife's pillow.   All this turmoil had worn upon me, and within two minutes I was something more than half asleep.   Mrs. McWilliams roused me.

"Darling, is that register turned on?"

"No."

"I thought as much.   Please turn it on at once. The room is cold."

I turned it on, and presently fell asleep again. I was aroused once more.

"Dearie, would you mind moving the crib to your side of the bed?   It is nearer the register."

I moved it, but had a collision with the rug and woke up the child.   I dozed once more, while my wife quieted the sufferer.   But in a little while these words came murmuring remotely through the fog of my drowsiness:

"Mortimer, if we only had some goose-grease— will you ring?"

I climbed dreamily out, and stepped on a cat, which responded with a protest, and would have got a convincing kick for it if a chair had not got it instead.

"Now, Mortimer, why do you want to turn up the gas and wake up the child again?"

"Because I want to see how much I am hurt, Caroline."

"Well, look at the chair, too—I have no doubt it is ruined. Poor cat, suppose you had—"

"Now I am not going to suppose anything about the cat. It never would have occurred if Maria had been allowed to remain here and attend to these duties, which are in her line, and are not in mine."

"Now, Mortimer, I should think you would be ashamed to make a remark like that. It is a pity if you cannot do the few little things I ask of you at such an awful time as this when our child—"

"There, there, I will do anything you want. But I can't raise anybody with this bell. They're all gone to bed. Where is the goose-grease?"

"On the mantel-piece in the nursery. If you'll step there and speak to Maria—"

I fetched the goose-grease and went to sleep again. Once more I was called.

"Mortimer, I so hate to disturb you, but the room is still too cold for me to apply this stuff. Would you mind lighting the fire? It is all ready to touch a match to."

I dragged myself out and lit the fire, and then sat down disconsolate.

"Mortimer, don't sit there and catch your death of cold. Come to bed."

As I was stepping in, she said:

"But wait a moment. Please give the child some more of the medicine."

Which I did. It was a medicine which made a child more or less lively; so my wife made use of

its waking interval to strip it and grease it all over
with the goose-oil.   I was soon asleep once more,
but once more I had to get up.

"Mortimer, I feel a draught.   I feel it distinctly.
There is nothing so bad for this disease as a draught.
Please move the crib in front of the fire."

I did it, and collided with the rug again, which
I threw in the fire. Mrs. McWilliams sprang out
of bed and rescued it, and we had some words.   I
had another trifling interval of sleep, and then got
up, by request, and constructed a flaxseed poul-
tice.   This was placed upon the child's breast and
left there to do its healing work.

A wood fire is not a permanent thing.   I got up
every twenty minutes and renewed ours, and this
gave Mrs. McWilliams the opportunity to shorten
the times of giving the medicines by ten minutes,
which was a great satisfaction to her.   Now and
then, between times, I reorganized the flaxseed
poultices, and applied sinapisms and other sorts
of blisters where unoccupied places could be found
upon the child.   Well, towards morning the wood
gave out, and my wife wanted me to go down
cellar and get some more.   I said:

"My dear, it is a laborious job, and the child
must be nearly warm enough, with her extra
clothing.   Now mightn't we put on another layer
of poultices and—"

I did not finish, because I was interrupted.   I
lugged wood up from below for some little time,
and then turned in and fell to snoring as only a

man can whose strength is all gone and whose
soul is worn out.   Just at broad daylight I felt a
grip on my shoulder that brought me to my senses
suddenly.   My wife was glaring down upon me
and gasping.   As soon as she could command her
tongue she said:

"It is all over!   All over!   The child's perspiring!   What *shall* we do?"

"Mercy! how you terrify me!   *I* don't know
what we ought to do.   Maybe if we scraped her
and put her in the draught again—"

"Oh, idiot!   There is not a moment to lose!
Go for the doctor.   Go yourself.   Tell him he
must come, dead or alive."

I dragged that poor sick man from his bed and
brought him.   He looked at the child and said she
was not dying.   This was joy unspeakable to me,
but it made my wife as mad as if he had offered her
a personal affront.   Then he said the child's cough
was only caused by some trifling irritation or other
in the throat.   At this I thought my wife had a
mind to show him the door.   Now the doctor said
he would make the child cough harder and dis-
lodge the trouble.   So he gave her something that
sent her into a spasm of coughing, and presently
up came a little wood splinter or so.

"This child has no membraneous croup," said
he.   "She has been chewing a bit of pine shingle
or something of the kind, and got some little slivers
in her throat.   They won't do her any hurt."

"No," said I, "I can well believe that.   Indeed,

the turpentine that is in them is very good for certain sorts of diseases that are peculiar to children. My wife will tell you so."

But she did not. She turned away in disdain and left the room; and since that time there is one episode in our life which we never refer to. Hence the tide of our days flows by in deep and untroubled serenity.

THE KIND-HEARTED SHE-ELEPHANT

BY GEORGE T. LANIGAN

A KIND-HEARTED She-Elephant, while walking through the Jungle where the Spicy Breezes blow soft o'er Ceylon's Isle, heedlessly set foot upon a Partridge, which she crushed to death within a few inches of the Nest containing its Callow Brood. "Poor little things!" said the generous Mammoth. "I have been a Mother myself, and my affection shall atone for the Fatal Consequences of my Neglect." So saying, she sat down upon the Orphaned Birds.

MORAL: *The above Teaches us What Home is Without a Mother; also, that it is not every Person who should be intrusted with the Care of an Orphan Asylum.*

20

THE RHYMESTER'S CONFESSION

BY BURGES JOHNSON

I'd rather do rhymes of a morning betimes
Than anything else on the gamut of crimes.
Discursing with versing began with my nursing,
And chasing a metrical thought as it climbs
Is sweet, I repeat—why, e'en as I eat
The chewing I'm doing quite lyric'ly chimes.
Alas, what a pass! My head's a morass
Of singular jingular metres en masse.

Nor do they retreat at the noise of the street,
But tread through my head to the beat of my feet,
The while each particular ruption auricular
(Jars of the cars or a hubbub vehicular)
Falls into line, as though by design,
To act as a dactyl or trochee of mine.
Ah me, you can see by the force of my plea,
How troublesome bubblesome metre may be.

One hint is enough for some stuff in the rough,
And I promptly advert to my shirt-sleeve or cuff;
A word I have heard that is odd, or a name
That's odder, is fodder for feeding the flame.

Also the vernacular adds a spectacular
Shine to a line that were otherwise tame.
This shows, I suppose, as far as it goes,
A skill with the quill quite unsuited to prose.

And so, when I'm hit by a rhythmical fit,
I rhyme against time, and I don't, I admit,
Disturb with a curb any verbular bit,
But build up upon it a sonnet or skit.
I never expect its course to direct,
But let it express its excesses unchecked.
'Tis better than drinking, to my way of thinking,
For others, not I, must endure the effect.

Pray pardon this praise of my ways, but for days
I've itched to be rich in reward for my lays—
And maybe I might, so well I indite,
If only I had some ideas when I write.

AFTER THE FUNERAL

BY J. M. BAILEY

IT was just after the funeral. The bereaved and subdued widow, enveloped in millinery gloom, was seated in the sitting-room with a few sympathizing friends. There was that constrained look so peculiar to the occasion observable on every countenance. The widow sighed.

"How do you feel, my dear?" observed her sister.

"Oh, I don't know," said the poor woman, with difficulty restraining her tears. "But I hope everything passed off well."

"Indeed it did," said all the ladies.

"It was as large and respectable a funeral as I have seen this winter," said the sister, looking around upon the others.

"Yes, it was," said the lady from next door. "I was saying to Mrs. Slocum, only ten minutes ago, that the attendance couldn't have been better—the bad going considered."

"Did you see the Taylors?" asked the widow, faintly, looking at her sister. "They go so rarely to funerals that I was surprised to see them here."

"Oh yes! the Taylors were all here," said the sympathizing sister. "As you say, they go but a little: they are *so* exclusive!"

"I thought I saw the Curtises also," suggested the bereaved woman, droopingly.

"Oh yes!" chimed in several. "They came in their own carriage, too," said the sister, animatedly. "And then there were the Randalls and the Van Rensselaers. Mrs. Van Rensselaer had her cousin from the city with her; and Mrs. Randall wore a very heavy black silk, which I am sure was quite new. Did you see Colonel Haywood and his daughters, love?"

"I thought I saw them; but I wasn't sure. They were here, then, were they?"

"Yes, indeed!" said they all again. And the lady who lived across the way observed:

"The Colonel was very sociable, and inquired most kindly about you and the sickness of your husband."

The widow smiled faintly. She was gratified by the interest shown by the Colonel.

The friends now rose to go, each bidding her good-bye, and expressing the hope that she would be calm. Her sister bowed them out. When she returned, she said:

"You can see, my love, what the neighbors think of it. I wouldn't have had anything unfortunate to happen for a good deal. But nothing did. The arrangements couldn't have been better."

"I think some of the people in the neighborhood must have been surprised to see so many of the up-town people here," suggested the afflicted woman, trying to look hopeful.

"You may be quite sure of that," asserted the sister. "I could see that plain enough by their looks."

"Well, I am glad there is no occasion for talk," said the widow, smoothing the skirt of her dress.

And after that the boys took the chairs home, and the house was put in order.

THE SHOPPER

BY ROBERT JONES BURDETTE

TRAMP, tramp, tramp!
    With the morning clocks at ten,
She skimmed the street with footsteps fleet,
    And hustled the timid men;
        Tramp, tramp, tramp!
    She entered the dry-goods store,
And with echoing tread the dance she led
    All over the crowded floor.
She charged the throng where the bargains were,
And everybody made way for her;
Wherever she saw a painted sign,
She made for that spot a prompt bee-line;
Whatever was old, or whatever was new,
She had it down and she looked it through;
Whatever it was that caught her eye,
She'd stop, and price, and pretend to buy.
But 'twas either too bad, too common, or good,
So she did, and she wouldn't, and didn't, and
    would.
And round the corners and up the stairs,
In attic, and basement, and everywheres.

The salesmen fainted and cash-boys dropped,
But still she shopped, and shopped, and shopped,
And round, and round, and round, and round,
Like a winding toy with a key that's wound,
She'd weave and wriggle and twist about,
One way in and the other way out,
Till men grew giddy to see her go.
And by-and-by, when the sun was low,
Homeward she dragged her weary way,
And had sent home the spoils of the day:
A spool of silk and a hank of thread—
Eight hours—ten cents—and a dame half dead.

A ZOOLOGICAL ROMANCE

BY CHARLES FOLLEN ADAMS

Inspired by an Unusual Flow of Animal Spirits

No sweeter girl ewé ever gnu
Than Betty Marten's daughter Sue.

With sable hare, small tapir waist,
And lips you'd gopher miles to taste;

Bright, lambent eyes, like the gazelle,
Sheep pertly brought to bear so well;

Ape pretty lass, it was avowed,
Of whom her marmot to be proud.

Deer girl! I loved her as my life,
And vowéd to heifer for my wife.

Alas! a sailor, on the sly,
Had cast on her his wether eye—

He said my love for her was bosh,
And my affection I musquash.

He'd dog her footsteps everywhere,
Anteater in the easy-chair.

He'd setter round, this sailor chap,
And pointer out upon the map

The spot where once a cruiser boar
Him captive to a foreign shore.

The cruel captain far outdid
The yaks and crimes of Robert Kid.

He oft would whale Jack with the cat,
And say, "My buck, doe you like that?

"What makes you stag around so, say!
The catamounts to something, hey?"

Then he would seal it with an oath,
And say, "You are a lazy sloth!

"I'll starve you down, my sailor fine,
Until for beef and porcupine!"

And, fairly horse with fiendish laughter,
Would say, "Henceforth, mind what giraffe ter!"

In short, the many risks he ran
Might well a llama braver man.

Then he was wrecked and castor shore
While feebly clinging to anoa;

Hyena cleft among the rocks
He crept, *sans* shoes and minus ox;

And when he fain would goat to bed,
He had to lion leaves instead.

Then Sue would say, with troubled face,
"How koodoo live in such a place?"

And straightway into tears would melt,
And say, "How badger must have felt!"

While he, the brute, woodchuck her chin,
And say, "Aye-aye, my lass!" and grin.

  .   .   .   .

Excuse these steers. . . . It's over now;
There's naught like grief the hart can cow.

Jackass'd her to be his, and she—
She gave Jackal and jilted me.

And now, alas! the little minks
Is bound to him with Hymen's lynx.

OBSERVATIONS

BY JOSH BILLINGS

I AM a poor man, but i hav this consolashun: i am poor by acksident, not desighn.

Lasting reputashuns are ov a slo growth: the man who wakes up famus sum morning iz very apt to go to bed sum night and sleep it all off.

The gratest bores in the world are those who are eternally trieing to prove to yu that 2 and 2 allwuss makes 4.

Yung man, set down, and keep still—yu will hav plenty ov chances yet to make a phool ov yureself before yu die.

Truth iz sed to be stranger than fickshun; it is to most pholks.

About the hardest thing a fellow kan do iz to spark 2 gals at one time and preserve a good average.

Don't dispize your poor relashuns. They may be taken suddenly ritch sum day, and then it will be awkward to explain things to them.

If a young man hain't got a well-balanced head, I like to see him part his hair in the middle.

I don't take any foolish chances. If I wuz

called upon to mourn over a dead mule, I should stand in front ov him and do my weeping.

There is no man so poor but what he can afford to keep one dog, and I hev seen them so poor that they could afford to keep three.

I say to 2 thirds of the rich people in this world, make the most on your money, for it makes the most ov you.

I never argy agin a success. When I see a rattlesnaix's head sticking out of a whole, I bear off to the left and say to miself that hole belongs to that snaix.

I thank the Lord that thare is one thing in this world that money kant buy, and that iz the wag ov a dog's tail.

THE END

www.ingramcontent.com/pod-product-compliance
Lightning Source LLC
Chambersburg PA
CBHW032238010726
47494CB00002B/535